MICHELLE SMITH

Play On

Spencer Hill Press

Contact: Spencer Hill Press, PO Box 243, Marlborough, CT 06447
Please visit our website at www.spencerhillpress.com

First Edition: April 2015
Michelle Smith
Play On: a novel / by Michelle Smith – 1st ed.
p. cm.

Summary: The baseball star in a small town set on playing pro ball falls for the new girl and discovers the pain under her smile, which forces him to think about his own pain and what love really means.

Cover design by Jenny Zemanek
Interior layout by Jenny Perinovic
Author Photo by Laura Stockdale

ISBN 9781939392596 (paperback)
ISBN: 9781939392602 (e-book)

Printed in the United States of America

To those who listened.
Thank you.

chapter one

Forget Friday night lights—in Lewis Creek, South Carolina, it's baseball or bust three nights a week. Our world doesn't start revolving until March, when the fields are freshly mowed and the diamond's primed to perfection. Baseball is second only to breathing, and even that's debatable. So now that January's here, the only thing that matters is the chill in the air. It's a sign that official practices are right around the corner. And then? It's show time.

On Saturday nights, there's usually a pick-up truck parade heading toward either the river or Right Field Randy's house for a party (and no, right field is *not* what you want to be known for). Tonight, my old truck follows the others out to the school's ball field. After parking, I cut the engine and climb down from the green Chevy, grinning like an idiot. This place is heaven.

Brett Perry's Jeep swerves into the spot beside mine. Jay Torres, my right-hand man and catcher extraordinaire, hops down from the passenger side as Brett, all 6'5 of him, heads over. I lift my chin toward them and shove my hands into the pocket of my USC hoodie, bracing myself against the night's chill. Truck doors slam around us as I call out, "Surprised you pansies showed up."

Brett snorts. If anyone's going to show up to these meetings, it's us and his brother Eric, whose truck I tailed on the way here. The only thing to keep us from an open field would be our grandmas' funerals. Second only to breathing, remember?

"You're full of shit, Braxton." Jay gives me a high-five. "It's the most wonderful time of the damn year. Can you smell it?"

I take a deep breath as we head for the field, inhaling the scent of pine, dirt, and bonfire smoke in the distance. It's the best smell there is.

The full moon's our only light as we hop over the chain-link fence and onto the ball field. The frost-covered grass crunches beneath my boots. I'm home. A handful of other guys from the team have already made it to the pitcher's mound—my mound—where Coach Taylor waits for us. His blaze-orange cap is nearly as bright as the moon. All eight of us veterans made it out here tonight, which is a good sign for the season. You can tell who's in this for the love of the game and who's in it for the glory on nights when Coach sends out a mass text at 9:30 telling you to get your rear to the school. Glory's all well and good—and you'll get plenty of it around here—but heart rules on this field.

Frigid wind smacks me in the face, and I tug my beat-up Braves cap a little lower. Jay, Brett, and I join the semi-circle in front of Coach, who has the biggest shit-eating grin I've ever seen. I'm pretty sure this is one of his favorite nights of the year. Before I met him freshman year, I never imagined anyone could love this game more than I do. It took him maybe two minutes to prove me wrong, with the passion in his eyes when he shook my hand. He told me I was about to get my ass kicked, but it'd be the most worthwhile ass-kickin' I'd ever get. He was right. Between three seasons of boot-camp-worthy practices and his demand for dedication, I've gone from scrawny freshman to one of the top pitchers in Lewis Creek High's history.

I plan to keep it that way.

"Fellas," he drawls, rubbing his gloved hands together. "It's almost time to play some ball."

Kellen, our first baseman, and Eric whoop and holler at the end of the line. Jay elbows me, and my grin widens along with his. It's our last season playing ball in this town. I'll be damned if I'm not ready to get on the field. Being out here tonight is only a taste, a cruel tease, of what spring has to offer.

"I brought y'all out here for two reasons," Coach continues, "and I won't keep you long since your butts better be in church tomorrow mornin'. Reason number one: the obvious." He gestures to the field. "We're going to make this clear, right here and now. For the next four months, this is your home. These guys, and the ones who join us after tryouts, are your family. You with me?"

"Yes, sir," we say.

He nods once and crosses his arms. "Good. Next, I want to talk some business. Behavior. Grades." His gaze flickers to me. My stomach drops, but I keep a straight face. "Some of you had a rough fall semester on both those counts. Y'all are my veterans. You know my rules."

Darn right, we do. I watched him bench last year's shortstop because the guy flunked Biology. I'm the screw-up when it comes to grades. Fall semester kicked my ass; Statistics was no joke. This semester has me scared shitless because Chemistry is just as bad, but Coach doesn't have to know that. All he needs to know is that I'll do whatever it takes to be on this field five days a week. I swallow but hold his gaze until he looks to Eric, who's obviously on the "behavior" side of this speech. Being both Brett's younger brother and a pastor's kid, all the crap he pulls looks twenty times worse.

"For some of you, this is your last year with me," Coach says. "Let's make it count." He shoves his hands into the pockets of his coat and nods toward the parking lot. "Some dates to remember: tryouts for the open positions start on the twenty-eighth. I want all of you there, even if you think you're a shoo-in. Practice starts early February. You've got some time until you're officially on my field, so try not to get into any trouble between now and then. Y'all get on home."

Matt, our center fielder, and Right Field Randy murmur something about "waste of time" while they turn for the lot. I snort as Jay, Brett, and I follow them. They're only juniors, but they should know better. There's a reason Coach brings us out here every year, on the night Lewis Creek High opens the field for the season: to test our loyalty. Our dedication. When Coach tells us to jump, we don't just ask "how high"; we jump as high as we can until he tells us to stop. He's our leader. Hell, he's more of a father than most of our dads—for those of us who still have dads, anyway. I can't count how many times he's called me into his office just to ask how things are at home, especially since Dad died two years ago. He stood by my side at the funeral. He gave me a ride to school every day until I got my license because Momma had to run the shop by herself and couldn't take me. He even invited us over for Thanksgiving and Christmas dinners, although Momma "would never want to impose."

The man's a hardass, but he's got the best damn heart of any hardass I've ever met.

"Braxton," Coach calls out.

I whirl around. He jerks his head, signaling me over. I shiver, and not because it's twenty degrees out here. He knows how bad my GPA dipped last semester. He watches my report cards closer than my momma does. And to answer his earlier question, yeah, I know his rules all too well. But Coach wouldn't bench me. He wouldn't dare bench me.

I don't think he would bench me.

Jay claps a hand on my shoulder. "Just don't say anything stupid, Braxton," he mutters. "Treat him like you'd treat the sheriff: nod and 'yes, sir' the hell out of him."

Brett waves to me as Jay jogs up to meet him. *Yes, sir. No, sir. Got it, sir.* Easy enough. Taking a deep breath, I make my way toward Coach. If there's anyone who can put the fear of God in me, it's Coach Taylor. The man holds my entire season in the palm of his hand.

Coach rocks back on his heels, his hands behind his back. "That verbal commitment with Carolina seems to have gotten you too comfortable," he says as I approach, his voice carrying across the now-empty field. "Early recruitment doesn't mean you can slack off. You know the NCAA's policy about grades."

I nod. "Yes, sir," I say, stopping a couple feet away from him. "I need a 2.0 to practice once I get to Columbia in the fall and a 2.3 to compete once the season starts up." Easy enough to manage, as long as I keep my head focused and don't let last semester's crapstorm repeat itself.

His dark eyes bore into mine. "We're going into our fourth season together, Austin. You know my rules better than anyone. How about you tell me what those rules are."

My breath catches. "Y-yes, sir. We need a 2.0 to play for the school. We need a 3.0 to play for you."

He takes a step toward me. Folds his arms. Stares some more.

Crap. You know the saying "shaking in my boots"? It comes from stares like his.

"You're below my cut-off line," he says quietly. "You wanna tell me what happened last semester?"

Off-season practice five days a week. Working like crazy at the shop. School. More practice. Plus there was that "sleep" thing thrown in once in a while.

I swallow. "It won't happen again," I tell him. "That's all that matters. You've got my word."

Holding my gaze, he nods once. "Keep that eligibility in mind, Austin. I want you on my field this year. I'm sure your mother wants you out here, too."

Damn straight, she does. My agreement with University of South Carolina is the only shot I have at affording a decent school. And by "affording," I mean I've got no chance without that full ride. The only reason my grades are good enough is because most teachers wouldn't dare keep me off the field. But there are always the few who actually, you know, go by the rules. And that's how I got into this mess.

The wind whips around us as we head toward our trucks, the only two left in the lot. Other than Momma, Coach is one of the few around here who gives a crap about something besides my arm. Of course, my arm is what's going to get me out of this Podunk town in eight months. And baseball's the only thing that makes living here worth a damn.

Just don't tell my momma I said that. She would cry, yell, and sentence me to spreadsheet duty at the shop, which is hell in itself.

Coach waits for me to climb into my truck before tossing up a wave and backing out of his spot. I flop back against the seat and crank the engine, closing my eyes as it roars to life. I can do this. I have to. I just have to be, like, proactive. Douse the flames before they spread. Actually read the book and take notes. No big deal.

My phone buzzes in my pocket. I dig it out, the screen lit up with a text from Jay.

Jay: *Going to Joyners. U in?*

OMW, I type back and shift the truck into gear. The only remedy for some nights is good barbecue, good friends, and Coke. Whiskey's even better, but I have a feeling that drinking and driving might get me into even more trouble. That's the last thing I need.

Joyner's BBQ is way on the other side of town, so by the time I pull into the jam-packed lot twenty minutes later, Jay, Brett, and Eric are already inside the brightly lit dive, sitting at our usual table beside the window. My phone buzzes again as I jog across the lot. Groaning, I skid to a stop at the door and pull it from my pocket.

Momma: *Church tomorrow.*

It's barely past ten, for Christ's sake. I type out a quick reply—*Joyners, then home.* I hit Send and stuff the phone into my pocket while yanking the door open.

A girl shrieks. A bag hits the ground. Shrieking Girl, whose breathing could probably be heard five miles up the road, looks like I just popped out of the bushes with a chainsaw.

You've gotta be shittin' me.

With a sigh, I kneel and pick up the white paper bag, which I hold out for her. Her hands tremble as she snatches it from me. I'm officially a grade-A jackass, because I scared the poor girl crapless.

"I'm so sorry," I tell her. "There's nothing in there that could be ruined, right? I'll pay for it."

She shrugs a shoulder, keeping her gaze on the sidewalk. This night just keeps getting better.

"You okay?" I ask.

She shrugs again. "Fine," she mutters. "It's just been a really bad day and my parents decided they wanted chicken and barbecue at ten o'clock at night. I mean, who *does* that? So they sent me in here while they wait in the warm car, and I don't even *like* barbecue so I have no idea why they came here, and all I want is Diet Coke and my bed and—" She takes a deep breath, and the greenest eyes I've ever seen finally meet mine. Holy wow. "I have no clue why I'm telling you all this."

Her lips quirk into this insanely adorable smirk, and I can't help but grin back. "For what it's worth," I say, "I've had an awful night, too. And it's the worst kind of awful because it started off awesome and ended with getting my ass handed to me. So, I get it. Even if I think you're nuts for not liking barbecue." Really, who the heck doesn't like barbecue?

She bites her bottom lip, like she's fighting her smile, and shuffles the bag into the crook of her elbow. She holds out her free hand. For me to shake, I guess? I eye her before taking it carefully. Pretty sure I've never shaken a girl's hand before, but there's a first time for everything.

"Here's to hoping for better nights," she says.

At least, I think that's what she says. It's hard to know for sure when all I can do is stare into those pretty eyes, which are nearly as wide as the moon. She's tiny, almost a foot shorter than me, with wavy hair spilling across her shoulders. And she's definitely new around here. Everyone our age has been born and bred in this place.

Her handshake slows. "Can I have my hand back now?"

Shaking my head, I let go immediately. Smooth. Really smooth. "Yeah," I say, clearing my throat. "Sorry 'bout that. You have a good night."

She moves past me and laughs a little, but it sounds like one of those nervous I-think-I-just-met-a-serial-killer laughs. "Good night, Barbecue Guy."

I whirl around, watching her walk to the BMW SUV parked right up front. Sure enough, a man and woman are sitting in the front seats. She yanks the door open and climbs inside.

"Barbecue Guy," I mumble as they pull away. Safe to say that's one I've never heard before. Now I kind of wish I'd told her my name. Barbecue Guy ranks down there with Right Field Randy.

The restaurant's loud and bustling as I head inside. A couple junior girls lingering at the front counter call my name. I shoot them a grin and wave. I guess everybody else wanted chicken and barbecue at ten o'clock, too. Take *that*, Shrieking Girl. My chair screeches against the floor as I pull it out and plop down at the guys' table. Leaning forward, I pull off my cap and run a hand over my hair. The three of them stare at me until I say, "What?"

"You look like shit, that's what," Jay says. "Seriously, like you just got dog shit shoved in your face."

"Come on, man." Eric gestures to his mountain of barbecue and fries. "Trying to eat here."

Actually, I feel like I got mowed down by a combine tractor, but that works. I snatch a fry from Eric's plate. "Dog shit covers it."

Eric and Brett share a worried look. They're a year apart, but they might as well be twins.

Eric clears his throat and bites into a fry. "The hell *did* Coach want? You're good for the season, right? He didn't even keep me behind, and I'm the one who got locked up last week. I was scared as hell that I was a goner this year." He snorts. "But we can't have the USC hotshot screwin' up, I guess."

He's got a good freakin' point. "Seriously, dude. You get thrown in a cell for drivin' drunk—which was really damn stupid, if I haven't told you enough—but the man lays into *me* for my grades." I rub my face. "I don't know, y'all. He reminded me how much of a dumbass I am, and that I can't afford to be a dumbass anymore if I want to keep the mound. That's what I got out of it."

Brett narrows his eyes. "You all right, man?" he asks.

Nope. I bang my head on the table. "I will be."

chapter two

Momma's dainty little flower shop is a freakin' shrine to my baseball career, with newspaper clippings practically wallpapering the place. It's sort of embarrassing, but I *am* pretty proud of the write-up the paper did on me last year.

ENTER SANDMAN: BRAXTON PUTS BATTERS TO SLEEP IN NO-HITTER STREAK

You really can't go wrong with that headline. It makes being in here every afternoon more bearable. I'm going to miss these glory days once I'm in Columbia. Of course, there should be plenty more of those to come.

Hopefully.

Braxton's Bouquets has been in business since before I was born. Once I was old enough to know the difference between a lily and a tulip, my parents put me to work. Whether you're getting married or burying someone, Momma can hook you up with an arrangement that puts any big-city florist to shame.

Footsteps trail down the shop's stairs, and Momma heads toward me and the counter with a clipboard in hand. She grins from ear-to-ear as she plops it onto the counter. As soon as I see the spreadsheet-style form in all its jumbled-number glory, I groan. It's hell, I'm telling you.

"I don't want to hear it," she says. "The order needs to be done. We're low on just about everything. All those funeral arrangements we did over the weekend nearly wiped us clean."

She's right; the display room is a lot emptier than normal. The rush we had this weekend didn't help. Six people died, but Mr. Thornhill's family and friends almost cleaned out the shop on their own. Even still, I hate doing the order. I'm terrible with numbers. I always screw something up.

"I'm convinced you love torturing me," I tell her.

"I've got another interview coming in soon," she continues, "so suck it up and make it look like you're nice to work with. Gotta get someone in here to help me, since you'll be abandoning me for a glove and ball soon." She points to my Chemistry book, which is on the counter. "And school. You can abandon me for school. No slacking this semester, Austin. Think about that eligibility."

Well, someone's obviously been talking to Coach. My eyebrows scrunch together. "Wait, this is what? The sixth interview this week? You've managed without me every other year. Do you really need someone that bad?" We're not exactly in the poor house, but I'm not even sure Momma can afford to pay someone else. We need that money to, you know, eat. I kind of like food.

"I'm not as young as I used to be." She smiles and ruffles my hair. I bat her hand away just as the bell above the door chimes. She whirls around with her signature smile in place as she calls out, "Welcome!" She only wasted it on Jay, who's walking toward us with a damn limp.

My eyes widen. I rush from behind the counter as Momma hurries toward him. "What the hell happened to you?" I ask.

Momma takes his arm and guides him to the counter, which he leans against with a wince. "I'm fine," he says, but his dark eyes tell me he's full of it. He's hurtin'. "Don't yell. It makes the flowers sad."

If he wasn't already limping, I'd shove him, but this is bad enough. The two of us have been paired up for years, ever since JV. Going a season without him behind the plate isn't an option. The guy's my mind-reader. "What the hell happened? And how long's this gonna last?"

"Watch your mouth," Momma says, pointing at me. I hold up my hands. The woman's small, but fierce. "Now what in the Lord's name happened?"

"I'm *fine*," Jay repeats. "Br—um, you-know-who was walking me to my car after class, and I tweaked my ankle tripping over a curb. Guess I wasn't paying attention."

He glances at my momma out the corner of his eye. The only thing on her face is concern, so he's safe. Not that she would give a flying crap about the truth, but there's no convincing Jay of that. It's a secret that the guy's probably going to take to his deathbed. Or at least to Arizona in the fall. It's not something you talk about around here.

"Someone's finally got you stumbling over your feet, huh?" Momma asks. "Who's the lucky girl?"

Jay's not breathing. He's definitely not breathing, and I really don't feel like using mouth-to-mouth on this dude. I clear my throat and ask, "Momma? What time does your interview start?"

She glances at her watch. Jay rejoins the land of the living with a *whoosh* of breath. "Any minute now," she says. "I'll be in the office, so send her on up when she gets here." She squeezes Jay's shoulder. "Rest that ankle. I don't want Austin throwing a hissy fit about having to pitch to a second-string catcher this year. You hear me?"

He gives her a tight smile. "Yes, ma'am." His gaze meets mine as Momma heads for the stairs, and once the door to her office opens, he groans and smacks his head on the counter. "This sucks," he moans against the wood before straightening, pushing his shaggy dark hair away from his forehead.

Jay's been my best friend since Little League. He always knows what to say when I whine about school or when I complain about Coach. (Usually it's "shut up and grow a pair.") But even though it's been four years since he came out to me, I still have no clue what to say at times like this.

I want to make things easier for him, but as long as we live in Small Town USA, where life revolves around Jesus, baseball, and how high you can lift your truck, it's just not gonna happen. I know it, and he knows it. Heaven forbid half of Lewis Creek's All-Star Duo turns out to be gay. Or even worse, that the guy he's nuts about is the pastor's son and our team's very own third baseman. It's a damn shame that most guys in our class use and ditch girls within a week and no one bats an eye, but he and Brett have had to sneak around for six months, like they've been doing something wrong. It's bullshit.

I lean back against the counter, crossing my arms. "Well, we'll be out of this place in less than eight months," is all I can think to say.

The smallest hint of relief crosses his face. "Thank the sweet baby Jesus. Eight months until freedom to kiss whoever I damn well please wherever I want." He eyes me. "Speaking of which, when're you going to get yourself a fresh girl? You've had one hell of a dry spell since Jamie left for college last year."

And that's my cue. Ignoring him, I grab the clipboard and head for the first display cooler. We definitely need more roses. The cooler could use a good cleaning before I leave tonight, too.

"All right, I know when you're brushing me off," Jay says. He limps over to me, his face scrunching with each step.

"Dang it, Jay, if you genuinely effed up your ankle, I'll break the other one," I tell him. "I'm *not* pitching to second-string. Not during my last season."

He shoves his hands into his coat pockets and grins. "Nah, Brett checked it out before we left the lot. I'll be good to go come practice time. Quit your whining."

I move on to the next cooler and make a note to order more lilies of the valley. Mrs. Clark, the pianist down at First Baptist, cleans us out every Friday so she can take them to her son's grave.

"Anyway, I'm not blowin' you off," I tell Jay, looking at the clipboard and making my way down the list. "I just need to actually focus until we graduate. Chemistry is going to be a bastard, and ball takes up my entire week. I don't have time to squeeze girls onto that list."

He nods slowly. "Right," he drawls. "You said that last January. Remember? It was right before you hooked up with the hottie-hot-hot and lost your head in her ass for four months."

"Five months," I mumble, scribbling "5 dozen red" beside *roses* on the order sheet. "I dated Jamie for five months. Now can we drop it?"

The door's bell jingles again, and my head pops up. Sweet Lord, have mercy.

Jay turns to see the brown-haired girl who's already got my full attention, but it's not just any girl—it's *the* girl. The girl I nearly knocked down last night. Barbecue-Hatin' Girl. My clipboard slips from my hands, but I snatch it just before it clatters to the floor. In the daylight, her pale skin is a clear sign that I was right: she's definitely not from around Lewis Creek. Practically every girl here has her own tanning bed.

She pulls her blue-and-red jacket more tightly around her as her gaze lands on me, and holy mother, it's an Atlanta Braves zip-up hoodie. So, in review: she's a gorgeous, pint-sized girl who has the best possible taste in baseball. Did God just say *poof* and bring one of my dreams to life?

Jay nudges me a little too hard, making me stumble into the card rack. It crashes to the floor, sending cards and balloon packages flying all over the place. Shit. Barbecue-Hatin' Girl rushes over and crouches down to help just as I kneel. She gathers up the cards, and when those eyes dart up to meet mine, her lips curve into this cute half-smirk, like she knows I'm watching her.

Busted.

I jump up, straightening my scrunched apron as she stands with her little grin still in place.

"If it isn't Barbecue Guy. You work here?"

I think that's what she says, but her words aren't much more than gibberish because, like last night, I can't stop staring.

She's seriously going to believe that I am, in fact, a serial killer.

Jay coughs loudly, startling me. He tosses his arm across my shoulders and leans in between the girl and me. "I think my friend's lost his people skills. I'm Jay." He pats my chest. "And this dashing fella is Austin 'Floral Prince of Lewis Creek' Braxton. Who might you be?"

I shoot him a glare. *Floral Prince?* He's getting his tail whooped for that. "Really, bro?"

The girl narrows her eyes as her gaze darts between the two of us. She holds the cards out to me, and I know I should take them. My brain is screaming, *Take the stupid cards, you stupid, stupid idiot*, but my arms won't listen. Jay grabs the cards and slaps them against my chest. *Thanks, buddy.*

"I'm Marisa," she says. "I called about the ad in the paper? Ms. Braxton asked me to be here at four o'clock."

Silence blankets the room as she stares at me. Why's she staring at *me*? I glance over at Jay, but he's looking at me like I've lost my damn mind.

"So," Marisa says slowly, "where would I find Ms. Braxton?"

Oh. That's why.

"Um—" I clear my throat, which feels like tree bark, and point to the stairs. "Upstairs. She's upstairs. In her office. Which is upstairs. You just go up the, you know, stairs."

Jay slaps his hand over my mouth. "I think she understands," he says. Marisa nods. "Good luck," he adds. "Make sure you smile a lot. Ms. B. loves that."

She laughs. "Nice meeting you, Jay. Good seeing you again, Floral Prince." She waves and heads up the stairs I'm so nuts about.

Once the door to the office closes, Jay finally drops his hand and chuckles. Moving between me and the stairs, he crosses his arms. He glances back over his shoulder and smirks at me. "And the all-star player became the played. This'll be one hell of a show."

"I hate your guts, you know that?"

He winks. "Yeah. And you'll miss the hell out of me when I'm gone."

chapter three

I'm not a total idiot—I didn't think Chemistry would be as easy as hitting off a batting tee. I've cracked open my book every night since the semester started, which is more than I can say for my other classes. But when you're two weeks into the semester, throwing a surprise test into the mix isn't the way for a teacher to get on my good side. Especially when everything on this piece of paper may as well be written in Russian. Not that he gives a flying crap what I think.

I bang my head on the table. I can kiss Carolina goodbye next year if I don't pass this class. Scholarship? Gone. There needs to be a way to strangle fall-semester-Austin for dropping Chemistry, all because he didn't want to take it with Mr. Matthews after getting busted in the man's pond. I didn't take into account that the universe hates me, and the universe always gets what it wants.

"Mr. Braxton?" My head pops up. I look around the room. Everyone else has already finished their tests and left for the day, leaving me alone with Mr. Matthews. He points to the clock. "Time's almost up. Sure you should be napping?"

Yeah. The universe is a bastard.

My leg bounces as I look back to my paper. Freakin' periodic table. Who even *needs* to know this crap? I guarantee ninety-nine percent of the people in this class won't be science majors. Chemistry is an invention of the devil himself. Why can't my Chem class still be identifying beakers and tongs instead of memorizing this stupid stuff?

Shaking my head, I grab my backpack and carry my test to the front. I can't even look at Mr. Matthews when I put it on his desk; I stare at my boots instead. I know what he'll say if I make eye contact: "Think about that eligibility, son." I get it enough from Momma and Coach. If I hear it one more time, my brain will explode.

Mr. Matthews clears his throat, so I glance up. His nose is all scrunched as he stares at the test in what looks like disbelief. "Mr. Braxton..." He trails off with a shake of his head. "You do realize there's no element called—" he squints. "—does this say 'badminton'?"

He could give me some credit. At least I remembered hydrogen and oxygen.

"You can do better than this." He finally meets my gaze. "You do realize that I'm not just going to push you out the door with an A, right?"

My jaw stiffens as I nod. "Yes, sir."

"You've got to keep the big picture in mind," he continues. "Think about your eli—"

There it is. I head for the door and, throwing my hand up in a backward wave, keep on into the hallway. See, I've thought about the eligibility. I've thought about my grade. It doesn't make understanding the useless crap any easier.

I shove through the double doors, and the cold mid-January air hits me hard. I pull on my cap and stride to my truck, one of the few left in the senior lot. One of the best things about being a senior is that we can bust out of here early on most days. Staring at the Chem test put me behind schedule.

Maybe I do need some help with this school stuff. The problem is that asking for help isn't only embarrassing as hell, it's just kind of wrong. Admitting that you're dumb as a pile of rocks? Not tempting. When you've got the golden arm of Lewis Creek, everyone assumes that a golden brain goes along with it or something. Tutoring doesn't exactly fit that mold.

I toss my bag into the truck bed, climb into my seat, and tear out of the parking lot. I *could* get by with being a few minutes late to work, but being on time keeps me on Momma's good side—and gives me more time to look at the new girl who's starting today. Either way, I'm winning.

When I pull up to the shop, a blue Mazda with a Maryland license plate is parked next to my usual spot. I cut the engine, hop down from my truck, and head for the shop. It's not nearly as busy as it has been lately. The holidays are always crazy, so it's probably a good thing she starts this week. Best not to overwhelm her on her first day.

Stepping into the shop is like walking into a sauna, compared to outside. The display room is quiet, with no one in sight—not even the ones who are actually supposed to be, you know, working. I yank off my hoodie and toss it onto the counter, next to the register. Down the hallway, the back room is dark. Weird. No one there either.

"Lost in your own shop?"

"Holy sh—" I whirl around, my heart racing. Marisa stares up at me with the same tiny smirk she had on her face the other day. If anyone else looked at me that way, I'd peg them as a cocky ass. On her, it's pretty hot.

"Not lost," I say, still catching my breath. "Just wondering if the new girl swiped my momma and high-tailed it out of town, and how long until I had to call the cops."

Just shut up, Braxton. Shut up now.

She puts her hands on her hips. "Now why would I try and kidnap your mom?"

As much as I love a drawl in a girl's voice, I could listen to Marisa's little Northern accent all day long. She cocks an eyebrow, clearly waiting for *me* to do some talking. When did I turn into such an idiot?

"Because you're desperate for her flower fortune?"

Yeah. Even I wince at that. Should've shut up while I was ahead.

She bursts out laughing. *Smooth, Braxton.* Her wide smile stays in place as she backs toward the counter. I grab my apron from the hook next to the register, tie it on, and hang my hoodie in its place, right next to Marisa's Braves zip-up.

"I'm sure your mom's fortune is pretty high up there, but I'll pass on the jail time, thanks. Besides, she could probably take me any day. She seems tough." Marisa nods toward the stairs. "She's up in the office working on some accounting stuff. Said to tell you to 'take care of me.'"

Leaning against the counter, I smirk. "Take care of you? Really, now?"

She holds her hands up, palms facing me. "Her words, not mine. Can't use them against me." She pauses and adds, "Okay, wait. That could be taken so many ways. Keep your brain out of the gutter."

I shrug. "No clue what you're talking about."

She smiles along with me, a smile so wide that her eyes crinkle at the sides. I'd be kind of happy looking at that smile and those eye-crinkles every day. I guess I'll be able to until the season starts up. Lucky me.

Wait. No. Not lucky. No girls allowed this year. That was my freakin' New Year's resolution and everything. You can't go back on a resolution.

Shut up. It's legit.

The thing is that I can't let myself go nuts over some girl again. I fell head over feet for Jamie last year, but she left early for Georgia State in June and dumped me with a text. I was a worthless sack of crap for months after that. There's this thing that happens when you date people. It's a blast, and it's intense, and it's crazy (usually the good crazy). But when the other person moves on and leaves you behind, they take a chunk of you with them. And it sucks. I can't handle that feeling again right now. I can't.

I clap my hands together and start for the first display cooler. Marisa's shoes squeak against the floor as she follows me. "All right, then," I say on an exhale, turning to her. She stares up at me, all bouncy ponytail and bright eyes. "We're supposed to be training. So, first things first. Flowers: how much do you know about them?"

She giggles, and dang it, she needs to stop. *Please* make it stop. All these little things she does that make my stomach do weird flip-flops are going to turn into big things, and big things are a lot harder to ignore.

"It's safe to say I know a bit about flowers," Marisa says. "Your mom gave me one heck of a quiz during my interview to make sure I knew my stuff. She even asked what my favorite flower was and how often I'm supposed to change vase water. I mean, really?"

I twirl my finger, signaling for her to continue. "And your answers were...?"

She tilts her head to the side. "Purple roses. Every two-to-three days. Do you think I'm an amateur?"

Even if I did, it wouldn't matter. I'd train her all day, every day as long as she kept smiling at me like she is now. But that smile falters as her gaze falls to the floor. She clears her throat and says, "Before we moved here, my mom was obsessed with gardening. She taught me everything I know."

Her voice dips. Before I can ask if she's all right, she shakes her head and looks back to me, her eyes not nearly as bright, but still as piercing as they were before.

I shrug and force a smile of my own. "Looks like we have something in common. My momma's a gardening freak, too." As if owning a flower shop didn't already give that away. Strike two, Braxton.

She steps to my side, her arm brushing against mine as she gestures to the cooler. "Anyway, continue, Floral Prince. Teach me your ways. I'm sure you know much more than I do."

I narrow my eyes. "You're makin' fun of me, aren't you? Is it the apron? Because I'll have you know, I'm rockin' this apron."

She grins. "I would *never* make fun of a prince," she says seriously and curtsies. The girl freakin' curtsies.

I cross my arms. "All right, feisty pants. I see what you did there."

Her jaw drops. "You did not just call me feisty pants. What are you, sixty? Who even says that?"

"I do, obviously. And what I was going to say is, you can't put whatever flowers you want in the cooler. This is where we keep the special order arrangements and loose flowers. Single roses and stuff like that."

Instead of replying, her lips curve up again. My heart hammers against my chest. No matter how tough he acts, every guy dreams of someone looking at him this way. Like every word out of his mouth is coated in gold, even if it's the cheesiest thing that person's ever heard.

No one's ever looked at me this way before, not even Jamie. It's killer. And it's kind of freaking me the hell out because I'd never even seen this girl until a week ago, and she's got me acting like an idiot.

"What—" I cough to cover the crack in my voice. "What's that look for?"

She shrugs and moves past me toward the cooler. In its reflection, I see her staring at the arrangements, her fingertips pressed lightly against the glass. "I like your voice," she says. "It's laid-back. Easy-going. Like you have all the time in the world." She faces me again. "And your accent's kind of to die for. But you can pretend I didn't say that."

I don't want to pretend you didn't say that. This stupid shirt's suddenly too thick. And I'm pretty sure my cheeks are on fire.

She wrinkles her nose as her own cheeks flush. "Sorry. That was really, um, cheesy. Crazy inappropriate. Seriously, please pretend that I didn't say that."

Still don't want to pretend you didn't say that. I scrunch my eyebrows, feigning confusion. "Like you didn't say what?"

Her mouth opens and snaps closed when realization hits her. Her smile returns. And I'm freakin' goo.

Baseball. School. Work. Baseball. School. Work. Rinse and repeat until graduation.

I scratch the back of my neck as I head for the counter. "Moving on. Have you ever worked on a register?"

More shoe squeaking behind me. Her Converses are worse than those stupid squeaker-shoes parents let their kids wear in the shop. "Nope," she says. "This is my first job."

So, technically, she *is* an amateur. I punch my code into the register. "Can you count? Because that's a good start."

She leans onto the counter, staring me straight in the eye. "You know, you're kind of a smartass."

My mouth twitches. "Is that gonna be a problem?"

She shakes her head. "No," she says, her gaze lingering on me as she straightens. "I think it'll be fun."

Baseball. School. Work.
Baseball. School. Work.
Damn it.

chapter four

Forty-two. There's a forty-two on the test in front of me.

The final bell rings. Chairs screech and bags rustle and shoes rush to the door, but my butt's glued to the wooden seat. My test sits on the lab table, bleeding with red Sharpie. Poor paper. I killed it. It never stood a chance. In my defense, this isn't the worst I've ever done. But it's still pretty darn bad.

A hand lands on my shoulder. "Austin?"

I flip my test facedown, hiding the Sharpie massacre. Bri Johnson, a brunette junior and captain of the soccer team, stands beside me, holding her notebook to her chest. Lord, please don't let her have seen that number. Bri's one of those super-smart girls who would give Einstein a run for his money. "What's up, Bri?"

She stares at me for a moment. "Everything okay? There's a lot of red on that page."

I shove the test into my backpack. "Just need to study more. No big deal."

She's not buying it—that's clear from the pity clouding her expression. Instead of calling out my BS, though, she just nods once. "Well, I'm bringing you a message. Hannah asked me to remind you that the Spring Sports issue of the school paper is coming up. She needs to interview you for its feature." She glances at my backpack, where my test is practically screaming for attention, and back to me. "You *are* playing this season, right?"

She saw the grade. She saw the stupid grade. Panic grips my gut and holds on for dear life. Time for damage control. I force a grin. "'Course I'm playing. Why wouldn't I?"

She purses her lips and looks pointedly at my bag. "Just making sure."

Damn it. Clearly I'm terrible at damage control. "I'm pretty busy," I say, "but tell Hannah to catch me at lunch or something." I tilt my head toward my bag. "And if you could keep this quiet, I'll give you free flowers for the rest of your life."

The corner of her mouth twitches. She shakes her head. "Don't worry about it. I'll let Hannah know."

As she heads for the door, I lift my gaze to Mr. Matthews, who's watching me from his desk. He raises his eyebrows, silently questioning me. I've got nothin' for him. I don't know what he wants me to say.

Blowing out a breath, I sling my backpack over my shoulder and pick up my gear bag. My boots clomp against the floor as I walk to Mr. Matthews's desk. I shrug. "What?"

His eyes widen. "Is that really the route you're taking? Because I'm sure your coach would be just *thrilled* to hear about that attitude."

All right, let's try again. "What is it, sir?"

He tilts his head to the side. "I was hoping you'd have something to say to me. Or ask me."

All I can do is stare at him. Again, not entirely sure what he wants me to say.

He heaves a sigh and leans forward. "Okay, I'll level with you. I have a list of student tutors, each looking for work. Say the word and you can pick any name. All are A-students and all are free."

I blink. Look down at his desk. I know I should say yes, but there's a little hang-up: getting a tutor is a worldwide declaration that Austin Braxton is a moron who can't do his own work. I can hear the whispers already: *"How'd he even get to senior year?" "Does he know anything besides baseball stats?" "God, he's stupid. He thought badminton was an element."*

Mr. Matthews sighs again, disappointment all over his face. "You've got a good thing going," he says. "Don't let pride screw that up. You've got plenty of options here. I'm leaving this on the table, so let me know if you change your mind."

And that's my cue. I tighten my grip on my gear bag and hightail it for the door. Yeah, this is awful. It's terrible. It's no good. But it's also only the first test of the semester. Report cards don't come out for another month. It's an easy fix. Sort of. Maybe. Either way, I've got this.

"Austin?" Mr. Matthews calls. I stop in the doorway and turn. He leans back in his chair, crossing one leg on top of the other. "Have fun telling Coach Taylor that you turned down the tutoring list."

Son of a bastard, he plays dirty. My shoulders drop. "Who's on the list?"

He lifts his gaze to the ceiling. "Let's see. Off the top of my head, we've got Bri, Matt Harris—"

I snort. His gaze snaps to me. I cover my mouth, holding back a full-blown laugh. Matt Harris is known for two things: being a half-decent center fielder and being an uber-decent douchebag. Letting him tutor me? When pigs freakin' fly.

"I'll think about it," I offer, which is code for "not a chance in hell."

After changing into my practice clothes in the locker room, I take the long route through the now-quiet hallway, walking toward the double doors. If Matthews threatened to tell Coach about the tutoring list, then he's probably already told him about my test. Which means I'm screwed.

I pause at the door, peeking out the narrow glass to the ball field. It's conditioning week, the week we use before tryouts to ease back into shape. Every guy in Lewis Creek dreams of being a varsity Bulldog, and most of them are on the field already, either lined up in front of the ball dispenser or tossing balls around. But as much as I crave the burn in my arm and the smack of the ball against Jay's glove, I'm hiding. Like a wuss.

Coach is leaning over the fence, staring right at where my truck is in the parking lot. So even if I tried to make a getaway, I'd be shit outta luck. He'd probably outrun me anyway. He's fast as hell for a guy in his thirties.

Running away isn't an option though. Austin Braxton is no coward. It's do-or-die time, even if I may die today.

I take a deep breath and shove open the door. It's cool. It's fine. Coach might even understand. It's all good.

Yells from the field echo across the parking lot, Jay's being the loudest of all. Coach spots me walking toward him. He slides his sunglasses onto the brim of his cap. Straightens and steels himself, crossing his arms. It's not all good.

I stop at the fence. He stands on the other side like a gatekeeper, one who refuses to open the gate. My heart races as I hold his gaze for the longest minute of my life. The smell of fresh-cut grass wafts through the air, and dang it, I'm so close I can practically taste it. He stares. Stares. Stares some more. My gaze falls to the dirt.

He wins. He always wins.

Coach clears his throat. "You've probably figured out that Mr. Matthews stopped by my office this morning. Forty-two." He whistles. "That's pretty God-awful, Braxton."

I swallow hard. Nod once. "Yes, sir."

The fence rattles as he lifts the lock on the gate. A *whoosh* of air escapes me. Thank sweet Jesus. "Once he left, I called your momma," he adds.

Shit. My head snaps up. "What the hell, Coach? Did you really have to do that?"

He yanks the gate open, slamming it against the fence. I flinch. "You wanna try that smartass mouth again? You know damn well that won't fly on my field."

Not my brightest move. My jaw stiffens, but I manage a "No, sir."

He shoves his finger into my chest. I stumble back a step. "You know I keep my promises, Braxton. I trusted you to have this under control. You can't be on my field if you can't be bothered to put forth an effort."

"We're two weeks into the semester, Coach. It's one test." I chance a glance up. His eyes are narrowed, the exact same way my dad's used to be whenever I back-talked him. Taking a deep breath, I shake the thought from my head. "Sorry," I mutter.

He blows out a breath and puts his hands on his hips. "No," he says, lowering his voice. "No, you're not failing yet, and we're going to keep it that way. Here's what you're going to do: you're going to find a tutor, or I'll find one for you. Is that clear?"

I nod.

"Report cards come out at the end of February. You've got 'til then to get this under control, or you'll be warming that bench. Will that be a problem?"

I shake my head. "No, sir."

I look out to the field. Jay's standing off to the side, watching Brett play catcher while Eric warms up his arm. For a junior, Eric's got one hell of a fastball. That dude's going to own the mound after I graduate. If I don't get my crap together, it'll be a lot sooner than that.

Not happening on my watch.

"You're better than this." Coach moves aside, letting me onto the field. "Suck up your pride. You want to be a man? A real one knows when he needs help." He jerks his head toward the infield. "Go on and get that arm warmed up. Jay's been whinin' for you."

He slaps my shoulder, sending me on. I hurry to the dugout and drop my bags onto the bench. Glove in hand, I jog toward the mound, where Eric fires another ball into Brett's glove.

"Junior!" I yell. Eric's head snaps up. I hold out my arms, grinning. "What're you doin' on my dirt? This mound is for the pros, kid."

He snorts and catches Brett's return. "You get it for most of the season. It's my dirt today." He gives me a quick half-grin, tossing the ball into the air.

I smack his back and gesture for Jay to come over. "Can't throw fastballs all day. You need to work on that change-up."

He winds up and sends a scorcher flying across the plate. "My mound, my rules."

"Change-ups are deadly," I remind him, walking backward toward the outfield. "A killer fastball will make 'em respect you. A killer change-up will make 'em piss their pants. Work on it."

He glances over his shoulder. "I do love a good pants pisser," he calls out.

———————

By the time we wind down for the day, the sun's nearly set and the field lights have kicked on. As I climb into my truck and crank the engine, I can feel Coach's gaze on me. I hit the gas and peel out of the lot, tires screeching as I turn onto the main road.

I can't even be mad because I get it. He's even harder on me than he is on the others. He wants me to get out of this town just as much as I do. It just sucks that I'm in this position to begin with.

I park in front of Joyner's BBQ, jump down from the truck, and jog inside. The cashier, a blond junior named Laura, grins and holds up a finger, signaling for me to give her a minute while she's on the phone. I pull out a chair at my usual table and collapse into it, sprawling my legs in front of me. It's almost six o'clock, so I need to get a move on.

Daily dinner with Momma is this weird sort of tradition. It started when I moved up to varsity and sacrificed my soul to the baseball gods. During the season, I try to make it a point to at least have dinner with her whenever I can. Since Dad died, we're pretty much all the other has. And I like spending time with her. Sue me.

"Austin!" Laura calls. "You're all set."

I hop up and hurry to the counter. "Momma call you guys?" I ask, handing her a twenty. "That was quick."

She shakes her head. "You order the exact same thing every single time. Two pints of barbecue, two large fries, and half a dozen fried chicken legs."

"Don't forget my biscuits."

"I would never forget your biscuits."

I laugh as she returns my change, which only makes her smile widen. "Am I really that predictable?"

"It's okay. You need your strength." She leans onto the counter, her bright blue eyes shining. "Speakin' of, are y'all gearing up for the season yet?"

I grin. "Yeah, we're gettin' there. You gonna be there?"

She gives me an "oh, please" look. "Seriously? I'll be hanging over the fence, front and center. You won't be able to miss me."

Someone behind me clears his throat. I glance over my shoulder. Matt, our center fielder, waves his hand, hurrying me along. "Other people gotta eat too, Braxton. Get a move on."

Got to love juniors who think they own the town. "Oh, my bad." I gesture to Laura. "Laura was just asking if we're ready for the season. Are you? I know I am because I was on the field today, but I didn't see you."

He narrows his eyes. "Conditioning week isn't required."

"Real players don't miss a chance to practice." Turning back to the counter, I ask, "Actually, can y'all throw in an extra pint of barbecue? We have someone else working with us now and she might want some. Take all the time you need."

Laura's face falls slightly, but her smile returns as she shrugs a shoulder. "No prob." She disappears into the kitchen and returns with the container, which she stuffs into the bag. "So I guess the rumors are true? About the pretty new girl at y'all's shop?"

Well, that took less than a week to get around town. "You could say that," I tell her, grabbing the bag. "How much do I owe you?"

She shakes her head. "No charge. Tell your momma I said hi."

"Will do. Night, Laura."

If looks could kill, I'd be dead and buried thanks to Matt. It'd be hilarious if he wasn't such a prick. I slap his shoulder on my way to the door.

With my bag packed to the brim, I climb back into my truck and speed through town to the shop. I probably should've called to make sure that Marisa was still there before I got extra food, but it's not like you can go wrong with extra food. I mean, it's *food*.

Her Mazda and Momma's car are the only ones left on our patch of Main Street. Bag in hand, I head for the shop. A blast of wind chills me straight to the bone as I tug on the door's handle, but they've already locked up. I knock on the glass, praying that one of them opens soon because, God almighty, it's freezing. A minute or two passes with no answer. My teeth chatter as I knock again. Marisa pops up from the counter, and I can hear her yelp all the way out here. She jogs across the display room and clicks the lock, the door jingling as she opens it for me.

"It's about time. Freezing my rear off out here." I step inside and jump up and down a couple times, trying to get my blood pumping. "You didn't waste time locking the door tonight, huh?"

"Try dressing in something other than a T-shirt and baseball pants, Floral Prince. Then you won't have to worry about that precious rear."

My rear is pretty precious, if I say so myself.

She unties her apron on the way to the counter. "It was swamped tonight. I was counting down the minutes until closing."

"A rush is good for ya. Makes time go by faster. And you can handle it. You're a natural at the whole service-with-a-smile thing."

"Well, it's easy if you've had a good teacher."

She stops just short of the counter, hangs her head, and sneaks a look at me over her shoulder. I don't have a clue what to say to that. She reaches for her jacket and I head for the back room, flipping on the light switch. The tiny space is just big enough for a few boxes of extra stock, a table we use for making arrangements, and a couple folding chairs. I set up the chairs beside Dad's old trunk, which doubles as our dinner table.

"Hey."

I whirl around, finding Marisa leaning against the doorframe. My mouth drops open a little. Her face is flushed, and good Lord, I've never seen a girl look more gorgeous with messy hair and bright red cheeks.

"Your mom's up in her office," she says, jerking her thumb over her shoulder. "She might be a while. She has to finish up some order stuff because she couldn't get to it earlier."

I have no idea why, but my tongue feels like it's glued to the roof of my mouth when I'm in the same room as this girl. And when I *do* open my mouth, something stupid usually tumbles out.

"Do you eat food?"

Like that.

She laughs so hard, she snorts. I'm pretty sure I've never made a girl snort before. She covers her mouth, her shoulders shaking as those eyes of hers crinkle, just like they do every time she smiles. And my stomach does its flip-flops, just like it does every time she smiles.

Nudging the brim of my cap, I point to the food on Dad's trunk. "Trying again: Do you want to eat with us? I bought extra."

She cocks her head to the side and smiles. "You got extra for me? Even knowing I don't like barbecue?"

I shrug, feeling my own face flush. "I still can't believe you don't like it. Have you ever tried South Carolina barbecue, for Christ's sake? But there's chicken, too. And fries. You can't say no to fries."

She nods to the trunk. "You guys really eat on that thing? It looks like you pulled it up from the *Titanic*'s wreckage. I thought it was a junker."

She's not entirely wrong about that. I plop down on one of the chairs, but remember that Momma still has to come down, so I move to the floor so she and Marisa can each have a seat. "If you eat with us, I'll tell you why." I grin and pat one of the chairs. "Come on. You know you want to. They can hear your stomach growlin' down in Georgia."

She glances at her watch. "My parents are pretty big on the family dinner thing. They like me home by seven."

"It's barely six," I remind her. "That's plenty of time. Think of it as an appetizer. Everyone needs appetizers."

She chews on her lower lip, like she's weighing her options. "I don't know if I should."

"What? Think I'm going to try to poison you?" Wow. I've officially crossed into desperation territory. I wouldn't blame her for running now.

"Please." She walks over and sits beside me on the floor. She crosses her legs. "You don't have a bad bone in your body."

I narrow my eyes, handing her a plastic utensil packet. "See, now I'm a little insulted. You clearly haven't seen me on the field."

"And what's that supposed to mean?"

"I've been told I throw a badass fastball."

She shakes her head, her hair falling across her face. "You're such a dork, Austin."

"An adorable dork, at least?"

She rolls her eyes and tries to hide a smile. She should stop that. Let the smiles flow, girl. I grab one of the containers of barbecue and pop it open. "You sure you don't wanna try it?" I ask, waving it under her nose. "It's pretty amazing. Joyner's is the best there is."

She looks at the container and back to me. With an overly dramatic sigh, she takes it. "You should feel really lucky. I've never liked this stuff. And in Maryland, our town had a barbecue place that was featured on TV. I'm a tough critic."

"But they're not Joyner's. There's a huge difference between South Carolina barbecue and whatever they serve in Maryland." I nod to the container. "Go ahead. You can do it. I have all the faith in you."

She scrunches her nose, but scoops out a bite with her fork. "If I die, I'll haunt you forever."

"Won't be necessary."

With her nose still all scrunched up, she puts the food in her mouth. She narrows her eyes at me. "I hate you," she says through a mouthful.

I stifle a laugh. "Why? Because it's awful?"

"Because it's amazing, and now I don't have an excuse to not eat thirty pounds' worth of sodium-laden pig."

Baseball lover, and now a barbecue convert. She's officially a Lewis Creek resident. "You say that like it's a bad thing."

"My heart would argue with you." She passes me the container. "So what's with the trunk, Floral Prince?"

Dang it. I was kind of hoping she'd forget that part of the bargain. I stare at the battered black trunk, which does look like it belongs on the ocean floor. It's been two years since Dad died, but talking about what happened never gets any easier—which is why we don't talk about it at all.

"We've been doing this for years," I tell her, taking out my own fork. "My parents worked their butts off around here for as long as I can remember. But when I was a kid, I didn't really give a crap—I was just starvin' come dinnertime and turned into a demon child. So we'd have our family dinner right here."

She nods, pulling a fry out of the bag. "'Kay. Still doesn't explain the trunk."

"It was my dad's. It's where all his high school ball stuff is stored. He was, like, a local legend before he blew out his shoulder. Momma brought it here after he died. She thinks it's a way of having him here with us or something." Not that I agree with her, but sometimes you shut up and let people have whatever helps them feel better. She barely ate for a week after he died. Wouldn't come out of her room for two. If keeping an old, beat-up trunk makes her happy, she can have at it.

Marisa chews, studying me for a moment before asking, "What happened?"

My stomach clenches, but I shove a bite into my mouth anyway. *Breathe, Braxton.* "Car accident. He drove off the town bridge when I was fifteen."

I hold her gaze, praying to all that's holy that she leaves it there. She doesn't need to know that Dad had no reason to be on the town bridge in the middle of the night. She doesn't need to know about the letter Momma found on the kitchen table, about the nine words scrawled on the page: *All my love, all my promises, all my swears.* Dad used those words for as long as I could remember. He promised he'd never let anything hurt us, swore that nothing would ever tear our family apart. And he was the one who'd demolished it.

There's really no reason to tell Marisa that my dad fucking killed himself when he had a wife and kid at home.

The silence is deafening, slicing through me like a knife. Her expression softens, like she can tell my heart's about to burst through my chest. There are only four people in this world who know that part of Dad's story: me, Momma, Jay, and Coach. Jay and I have been joined at the hip for years, so bringing him into the loop was inevitable. Coach knows because he's the one I called when Momma couldn't get out of bed two days after Dad died. Literally couldn't, thanks to the medication cocktail she was on. I panicked and Coach was the only person I could think of to call. He spotted the letter, which was still on the kitchen table like some twisted keepsake.

Dad truly was a local legend. A baseball hero for the school. And he was a good guy when he was around. No need to ruin his legacy, even if I still kind of hate his guts for what he pulled.

More like *really* hate his guts.

Marisa nudges me softly. When I look down, she smiles and whispers, "Hi." And even though she just hit the sorest of my sore spots, I say, "Hi."

"'Hi' begins a new conversation," she says. "Sounds like you need it."

More than anything on God's green earth.

She shoves a forkful of barbeque in her mouth. "It's a good thing I trust you," she says. "I don't eat after just anyone. I could catch the plague or something."

All my muscles unclench. My heart's still racing, but I think I'm out of heart-attack territory. "Shows how much you know. It's chock-full of poison. I spit mine out when you weren't lookin'." After one more bite, I set my food on the trunk and lean forward, resting my elbows on my bent knees. "All right, let's talk about you. What's your story?"

She shakes her head. "I'm not that interesting."

"BS. Tell you what: if you can't think of at least five things about yourself, then I'll let you get away with"—I use air quotes—"'not that interesting.'"

She blushes. Her lips quirk. And as she tucks a piece of hair behind her ear, it's cut-and-dry: she's downright one of the prettiest girls I've ever seen.

"Fine. Let's see. Born and raised in Baltimore," she begins, ticking it off on her finger. "Eighteen. Moved down here during Christmas vacation after Dad accepted the chief of surgery job at the hospital. Homeschooled science nerd who knows a lot about flowers. Going to University of South Carolina in August." She wiggles her fingers. "That's five. Anything else?"

My ears perk. USC, she says? "See? Now *that's* interesting." I scoot across the floor until I'm facing her. "And while I have no complaints about you going to USC, why go there when you lived in Baltimore for eighteen years?"

Her mouth opens, but footsteps thunder down the stairs out front. Worst timing ever. Hanging my head, I take a deep breath, bracing for the hurricane. The calm was nice while it lasted. Momma appears in the doorway and snaps, "I need to talk to you," before storming back into the display room. Marisa winces. "Yikes. Harsh. Everything okay?" Here we go. I push to my feet. "Nope. Be right back." I walk into the dark display room, where Momma's waiting beside the counter with her arms crossed.

"Coach Taylor called me," she says.

Rubbing my eyes, I groan. "Of course he did."

Her own eyes widen, filled with lightning that's bound to strike. I take a step back. She steps forward. "Highly recommending that you watch that mouth, Austin Michael."

She waits for me to speak, but she's going to be waiting a while. We've reached middle-name status. Not walking into that trap, thanks.

When I say nothing, she continues, "You need to give me something here. Do you need help? Tutoring?"

"Shh!" I glance over my shoulder. I don't want Marisa, self-proclaimed science nerd, finding out that I'm an idiot, too. My stupidity is need-to-know business. "I'm fine. I'll be fine. I'm two weeks into the semester and it's one class, for Christ's sake. Can't y'all give me more time than that before you give up on me?"

Tears spring to her eyes, and now I've graduated from idiot to a pile of pure shit because I just made my momma cry.

"How can you even say that?" she whispers sharply. "We want the absolute best for you. If you can't see that—" The phone upstairs rings. Instead of excusing herself, she rushes toward the staircase, leaving me alone in the dark.

Fantastic. Just freakin' fantastic.

I blow out a breath and turn back to the stockroom, only to find Marisa in its doorway. She smiles tightly. "Sorry. Wasn't sure if I was supposed to hear that or not."

I fall into step beside her as she walks toward the front door. "Too late now. Is it time for you to leave already?"

She nods. "Yeah, I should get going." She zips up her coat and looks at the door, which is already covered with a thin sheen of frost. "Which class is it? That you're having trouble with, I mean."

"Chemistry," I say on an exhale. "The work of Satan. Whatever you wanna call it."

She smirks. "You know, I've aced everything up through Organic Chem in my homeschool program. And I'm going to major in Chemistry at USC."

My eyes widen. "Oh," is all I can think to say. It doesn't take a genius to know what she's getting at, but asking her for help? Nope. Not going to happen. I mean, we work together. Plus, she'd realize just how dumb I really am, and that's not an option. Of course, neither is failing.

Damn it.

The bell jingles as Marisa pushes the door open, snapping me back to the moment. I grab the door, holding it for her as she walks out onto the sidewalk. My muscles tighten and my breath downright disappears once the cold air hits my bare arms.

"Marisa?" I say. The door rattles behind me as it closes. She turns, her lips slightly parted. If I thought the cold took my breath away, it's nothing compared to her face shining beneath the downtown lights.

I clear my throat. "Thanks for—" I gesture to the shop. "For not thinking I'm an idiot, I guess. I just have a tough time with that whole balance thing. School, work, and ball all at once is rough sometimes. I'm handling it, though." Sort of. Not really.

She smiles. "I'm not sure I could think you're an idiot, Austin. A little crazy. We've covered dorky. But never an idiot." She shivers and bounces from foot to foot. "Sorry. Kind of cold."

I take off my cap and tug it onto her head. Now *my* head's freezing, but the sight of her in my cap is enough to keep me from complaining. Girls in baseball caps? You can't beat that.

"There," I say. "Better?"

She holds my gaze with this strange look of amazement on her face as her smile grows. "Much. I'll get it back to you tomorrow."

"Don't worry about it."

That smile stays glued to her face as she backs toward her car. Before opening her door, she pauses. "You got your phone?"

"Um—" I dig into my pants pocket and pull out my phone. "For what?"

She gestures for me to hand it over, which I do. The screen lights up her face even more as she types quickly. "Here," she says, giving it back to me. "If you decide you need help, now you've got the number of a science pro. No excuses."

Stunned, I stare down at my phone. I grin once I see the new contact listing. The girl's number without even asking? *Jackpot.*

She slides into her car, cranks the engine, and backs out of her parking space. But instead of driving on, her window lowers.

"I'm going to USC because it's where my parents went to school," she calls across the road. "Thanks for the appetizers, Austin."

With that, she starts down the road. As I watch those taillights disappear, I can't stop my grin from growing.

chapter five

All right. Here's the scenario: You've worked one-on-one with this girl for two days. The girl's cool as hell, a blast to talk to, and easy to look at. (*Really* easy to look at.) She even gives you her number and says she'll see you tomorrow. And POOF! She's a no-show for nearly a week. It's tragic, really. According to Momma, it's not a tragedy, but a case of the stomach flu. That only makes me feel worse. What if sharing food with me *did* give her the plague?

I've kind of missed her. Okay, I've really missed her. I haven't decided what level of pathetic that is yet. Because seriously—two days.

On my way to the cafeteria for lunch on Monday, I stare down at my phone. Marisa's number is pulled up, ready to go. All it would take is a few clicks to send her a message. But for real, we've only worked together twice. How stalkerish is *too* stalkerish, especially if it's just an "I hope you're not dead" text?

I stop in the cafeteria's doorway. Stare at the screen some more. Suck it up and type out a quick text.

Its Austin. Havent seen u in days. Little worried. U ok?

Good and simple. Before I chicken out, I hit Send and stuff the phone into my pocket. The cafeteria's swamped, with all the school's seniors and half of its juniors. I spot Jay, Brett, and Right Field Randy at our table across the room, by the back windows. After grabbing a plate of cheese fries, which I scored for free thanks to a well-timed grin for the cashier (being the star pitcher does have its perks), I weave through the obstacle course of people on my way to the table and slide onto the bench across from Jay and the others.

"That all you're eatin'?" Eric asks, plopping down beside me. Kellen sits on his other side and tosses up a wave to the rest of us. "You'll never make it through this afternoon. We'll be scraping you off the field."

Team tryouts are this afternoon, but for us, it's basically just early practice. The new recruits take the brunt of Coach's drills. "How about you worry about you, and I'll worry about me," I say.

He rolls his eyes and turns to Kellen.

"Austin," a voice singsongs behind us. Hannah Wallace drops her huge purse onto the table and sits beside me. She grins at me with a smile perfected by years of braces as she swings her tan legs over the bench. "Hope you're ready for your interview, because it's time to get this show started."

Hannah's been the head of our school's paper since we were sophomores. She's the head of almost everything in this school, really. Every year, she practically tackles me when it's time for the Spring Sports write-up. Give the girl five years, and I guarantee she'll be camera-ready for ESPN.

"Ready as I'll ever be," I tell her.

Another girl, who's wearing a lot less hairspray and eyeliner, sits on Hannah's other side, quiet as a church mouse.

"Oh!" Hannah gestures to the girl. "Guys, this is Morgan. She just moved here from Alabama. She's taking journalism this semester and I let her tag along. Y'all be nice to her."

"What do you think we are: animals?" Jay says. "Any friend of yours is a friend of ours, pretty lady."

Hannah's mouth drops open. "See, this is why y'all are my favorites. You're seriously the sweetest guys ever. I could kiss you right now."

Jay leans across the table, his head tilted. He taps his cheek. "Put up or shut up."

Hannah pecks his cheek, making the other guys whistle. Her smile grows even wider as she pulls out a notebook covered with cupcakes and turns to me. "Down to business. Ready?"

I shove a fry into my mouth. "Hit me."

"First up: tryouts are this afternoon. Are you nervous?"

I slap my hand over my chest. "I'm telling you, I am just *terrified*. Really."

The guys snicker as she laughs and scribbles something in her notebook. I bite into another fry as the new girl, Morgan, leans over. "Just a sec," she says to Hannah. "You told me we were interviewing some superstar pitcher. But the team hasn't had tryouts? So he's not even on the team yet?"

Hannah stops scribbling. "Well, duh. Coach Taylor isn't an idiot. Of course Austin's on the team. He's what we call a 'sure thing.'" She looks back to me and mouths *totally clueless*. "Onward," she says aloud, her smile returning. "We have to wait until March for the first game, and to that I say boo. What can you tell the readers to tide us over until then?"

I lean forward, propping my elbows on the table. "Well, Hannah, I can tell you that we're the Lewis Creek Bulldogs, and the Bulldogs are ready to kick some ass. Wait, can you say ass in the paper?"

"I cannot say ass in the paper."

"Then we're ready to kick some rear. And once we hit the field, every team that steps onto our turf is going home with their tails between their legs."

The rest of the guys whoop and clap, the sound echoing throughout the cafeteria. Hannah's smile grows as she writes that down.

"Okay, okay, time out," Morgan says.

The table falls silent. I think I liked this girl better when she was a church mouse. Hannah looks annoyed as all get-out, but she takes a deep breath and shoots the girl a smile. "What is it?"

"I don't get it," Morgan replies matter-of-factly. "All this craziness over baseball. Don't most schools go nuts over, like, football or something? My old school was all about football."

"Not when their football team sucks," Kellen says, right as Jay replies, "It's *baseball*."

Hannah lets out a breathless laugh and glances at her watch. "Bless your heart. Honey, you're new here, but you'll figure this out soon enough: Lewis Creek *is* baseball. Look around you."

Morgan does. She looks at the banner stretched across the right wall, which boasts last year's state championship win. She looks at the massive collage beneath it, made up of hundreds of team pictures that date back to the fifties, including photos of both Dad's championship team and mine. She looks at the trophy case, with dozens of trophies on display.

She looks back at us guys, dumbfounded. "I still don't get it."

Jay is just as dumbfounded as he repeats, "It's *baseball*."

How can you even begin to describe the magic that is baseball? "It's the rush of a strike," I tell her.

"The roar of the crowd," Brett says.

"Hot dogs and peanuts and slushies," Randy chimes in.

"Smacking the hell out of a ball," Eric says.

"And let us not forget the glory that is a boy in baseball pants," Hannah says. "Amen, hallelujah, thank you Jesus."

Wait. What?

All eyes fall on Hannah, who shrugs and slaps her notebook closed. "All the girls think it. I just say it." She ruffles my hair as the lunch bell pierces the silence. "I didn't get nearly enough, but I'll catch you again tomorrow."

I'm still not entirely sure what just happened here.

Trays clatter behind us as people file out of the cafeteria. Randy says "see ya" before grabbing his stuff and heading out, with Eric and Kellen right behind him.

Jay grins at Brett as they stand. "Girl's got a point. Your ass does look great in baseball pants."

Brett's cheeks flush crimson. He glances around and looks back to Jay, giving him a sneaky smirk.

Not gonna lie. I kind of want someone to tell me my ass looks good, too.

＊──────＊

As I walk to the field that afternoon, I sneak one more glance at my phone before stuffing it into my gear bag. Still nothing from Marisa. So she's either passed out in front of her toilet, or my barbecue really did kill her and she'll be haunting me for the rest of my life. Awesome.

The minute my cleats touch the dirt, every muscle inside me relaxes. And when the smell of freshly mowed grass hits me, I know that, somehow, everything's going to be okay. No wrong can happen out here. *This* is my safe haven. We've got a little over a month until the first game of the year, and it can't come fast enough. Give me those lights. The roar of the crowd. The rush of the winning strike. On this field, everything else disappears. I just hope the sanctuary's not ripped away from me before I can even play the first game of the season.

The new guys are already out here stretching, gearing up for tryouts. Most of us from last year are shoo-ins for the team, but geez, the noobs are already showing us up. I need to get my mind off school and a certain girl who won't get out of my head. This is the perfect way to do it.

I drop my bag onto the dugout bench and dig for my practice glove. Another bag drops next to mine. Jay slaps my back before yanking off his sweatshirt. "It's about that time, Braxton," he says with a huge grin. "You ready for this?"

"You don't even know how ready. I've been waitin' for this day since May."

We fist-bump before jogging out to an empty section of the field, away from where Coach is barking out orders to the fresh meat, and start stretching. Some of those wide-eyed kids across the field look like they just walked into boot camp by mistake. Boot camp wouldn't be too far from the truth. Coach's drills are no joke.

"Think any of 'em are worth their weight?" Jay asks, finishing up his lunges. "Or will Coach just beg last year's seniors to come back for old time's sake?"

Snorting, I do a couple more fingertip prayer presses. "He wishes. But I doubt any of those guys would step foot in Lewis Creek again, even if Coach offered them a million bucks." I sure as heck wouldn't. Breaking out of this town is like busting out of prison: you run as hard and as fast as you can in the opposite direction, without looking back. Even glancing over your shoulder will make you trip over your own feet.

Jay grabs his glove and ball, and I pick up my own glove. Sliding the worn leather onto my hand, I breathe in the sweet smell of fastballs and sliders and strikeouts. A familiar knot lodges in my throat. I swallow hard, forcing it away. Dad gave me this glove in the fall of sophomore year, just a few months before he...well, you know.

I shake my head and ready myself for Jay's throw. He fires the ball into my glove, its *smack* against the leather music to my ears. I rotate my arm a few times before pitching it back, and all I can do is thank God that finally, *finally*, I'm back on this field. I'm freer than anywhere else in this crazy world when I'm out here.

Well, I'm thanking God until Jay has to jump up to catch my wild throw. *Shit.* He shakes his head and lofts it back. "No worries," he calls out. "Fire another one. Nothing fancy. Just hit the glove. We'll work up to fancy."

Taking a deep breath, I focus on the center of his mitt and throw. He darts to the side, just barely snagging the ball. His mouth falls into a frown, but he says nothing before throwing the ball back. My heart races as I catch it effortlessly. *Focus. Just pitch like you've done for ten damn years.* Eight pitches later, I've given Jay a second warm-up session entirely.

"I'm not into the aerobics shit, Braxton. Stop making me run all over the place." He jogs over and leans in, his forehead gleaming with sweat. "You better straighten up. Coach has his eye on you."

Resisting the urge to turn and look, I ask, "Evil eye?"

"Evil as Lucifer himself. What's the problem?"

I scoff and punch my glove, walking back to the bench. If I keep this up, I'll be getting real comfortable on that slab of wood. "Matthews's class," is all I say. The man drilled me again this afternoon.

Jay falls into step beside me, yanking his glove off. "I thought he gave you some kind of tutoring list."

Shaking my head, I plop down on the bench, take off my own glove, and toss it on top of my bag. Coach glares at us from the field, his arms crossed in front of his chest. We need to get back out there soon before we have to deal with his wrath, but embarrassing the hell out of myself even more isn't high on my list. At this rate, he'll replace me with a JV freshman.

"He did," I say. "I turned it down."

Jay gapes at me. "And why the hell did you do that?"

I stretch out my fingers again. I know good and well they aren't the problem with my throw. This is all mental blockage, which needs to be fixed ASAP. "The only people on that list are people I don't feel like spendin' a bunch of time with. I mean, Bri's not so bad, but *Matt's* on there. Why the hell would I spend even more time with that guy?"

Jay points to the field, where the blond douchebag is talking to Coach. "That Matt?" I nod. He snorts. "Can't blame you. But Coach is gonna kick your ass. Or bench it. Or both."

Groaning, I drop my head. He's right. I can't get away with this for much longer, but I'll be damned if I trust my GPA to Matt Freakin' Harris. Of course, I *do* have a certain someone's phone number, but I also might have just killed her with barbecue.

Coach whistles sharply, waving us over. Jay and I jump up, and he slaps my glove against my chest. "Get your head under control," he says. "Suck it up and fix your shit, even if it means letting Matt teach you how to make stink bombs or whatever. This is our last year, bro. I need my pitcher on point. Got it?"

I nod, breathing deeply. I'm not sure how I'm going to fix it, but I have a feeling I'll be eating crow sometime soon.

———

Buzzing. The most annoying buzz on God's green earth.

I try to open my eyes, but it ain't happenin'.

Buzzzzz.

Somehow, I force my eyes open. My room is dark. Why is my phone buzzing when my room is dark? I glance at the clock on my nightstand while grabbing my phone: 1:49 a.m. What. The. Heck. Wincing at the phone's bright screen, I hit the Messages icon, which has a bright red number one in the corner.

Marisa: *Just got ur message. Thanks.*

I rub my eyes. Am I dreaming, or did this girl just text me at two in the morning? Still squinting at the screen, I type back, *Welcome. U ok?*

A minute passes. Two. Three.

That's it. I'm going back to sleep.

I toss the phone back onto my nightstand and roll over. *Buzzzzz.* Groaning, I grab the stupid phone and collapse back against my headboard.

Marisa: *U always awake this late?*

No. Sleep is magical and should be required for twelve hours a day. You woke me up. *Yeah*, I reply, yawning loudly. *How u feelin?*

Another minute passes. She's either half-asleep or the longest replier in history.

Marisa: *Not great. Bad night.*

Maybe she wouldn't feel so bad if she was asleep at two in the morning. But that could be why she's still awake in the first place.

Me: *Need to talk?*

My phone buzzes almost immediately, with her name flashing across its screen. Guess that's a yes. This probably isn't the best time to tell her that I'm not really a phone person and my offer was for text-talking. "Hello?" I answer.

She sniffles and croaks out a shaky, "Hi."

I narrow my eyes, listening intently. She lets out this tiny hiccupy cry, making me jolt up. "What's going on? What happened?"

She sniffles again. "Nothing. That's the problem. I'm sorry. I thought—" She pauses. "I didn't think I could do any more crying tonight."

Well, now I'm wide awake. I rub my face. I don't have any idea what to say to her. I've got zero experience with girls crying in the middle of the night, but I can't just ignore her. "I'm sorry," I tell her, and it's the truth. "Is it... I mean, is there anything you want to talk about?"

There's rustling on her side of the line, like wind blowing. "Does your brain ever just hurt?" she asks. "Like too many things are in there, all smushed together?"

I nod along, even though she can't see me. "And it feels like it's gonna blow at any minute?"

"Exactly. And there's nothing you can do but wait, either for something to budge or for your brain to just—" She makes an explosion sound.

There's more rustling in the background. "Are you outside?"

"Yeah. On the porch, with my blanket. It's perfect out here."

That does sound pretty perfect. "That's the best cure for a loud head, you know. Bein' outside, alone."

"It's one of the things I'm starting to like about this place."

I can't resist. She walked right into that one. Yawning, I lie back against my pillow, sinking into the cool cushion. "Just one of the things? What's some of the other stuff?"

"Shut up," she says, but I can hear the smile in her voice.

"No, really," I press through another yawn. "You can't leave something like that danglin'."

"I can, and I will. I'm pleading the Fifth."

I wonder if she realizes that pleading the Fifth is basically an admission of complete and utter guilt.

"Were you really awake?" she asks. "You sound like you're half-asleep."

The yawning must have given me away. "You caught me. But I did just go to bed, like, two hours ago." I glance over at my desk, where my Chemistry book is buried beneath the lab worksheets I brought home to finish. Tryouts lasted until seven, and it took another four hours to do all my homework. I guess I can sleep when I'm dead.

"I'm sorry I woke you up," she says.

The tree branches outside my window cast shadows in my room as they sway, in sync with the wind rustling on Marisa's side of the line. It's almost like we're right beside each other. "Don't worry about it. It's just good hearing your voi—" I clear my throat. "It's good hearing from you."

She's silent for a moment before saying, "I should probably go inside now. Get *some* sleep."

My lips twitch. "You sound better."

"I feel better," she says. "Thanks to you."

My heart skips a beat. "Sometimes we just need someone to talk to, you know?"

"Yeah," she says. "I do. Goodnight, Austin. And thanks."

It's kind of crazy how awesome it feels to hear a soft voice telling me goodnight again, even if it is two in the morning. "G'night, Marisa."

chapter six

*Q***uestion:** What do three days of baseball tryouts plus three days of nonstop homework equal?

Answer: An exhausted, cranky, zombified Austin. People say sleep is for the weak. If that's true, I'm waving the white flag. Call me weak. Whatever. Just let me sleep.

It doesn't help that trying to study while a pretty girl is working right in front of you is nearly impossible. If I do fail Chemistry, I'm blaming my momma for hiring that pretty girl. Marisa kneels to perfect the arrangements in front of the shop's window. With her hidden behind stacks of Valentine's bouquets and teddy bears, all I can see is her reflection in the window. And I gotta say, those jeans fit that girl just right.

Dang it. Chemistry. Book. Focus. Shifting on my stool, I look down at my opened book on the counter and scan the page. Wait a second. I flip through the last couple of pages, but it's useless. I— I don't remember reading any of this crap. *How* do I not remember what I just read? I bang my head on the counter. And again. And again.

"You'll knock something loose in there."

When I look up, Marisa's leaning on the counter, with her hair spilling across her shoulders. A citrusy smell fills the air (after way too much stalkerish consideration, I *think* it's her shampoo), and she's probably saying something about science or whatever, but those lips—

"And I didn't wake up until the rats started eating my toes."

I shake my head. "Huh?"

She sighs. "You sure you're okay?" She walks around the counter to stand beside me. "I don't think you're capable of focusing on anything for more than twenty seconds."

"Um, wrong. Ball games last for two hours, and I can focus on those just fine." *The problem is that you're just way too pretty. Sorry.*

Actually no, not sorry.

"Or you have issues actually listening to a girl, rather than staring at her. Maybe we should just talk on the phone more often. You did great on Monday night." She gives me a half-smile. "Thanks again for that, by the way."

I shrug. "Don't mention it."

She tugs on the ends of her sleeves, pulling them over her hands. "Speaking of ball games," she says, "since tryouts are over, will you guys start playing soon? Assuming you make the team and all."

And she called *me* the smartass. I jerk my thumb to the wallpaper of newspaper clippings. "If there's one guarantee in this town, it's that I'm on the team."

"Wow," she drawls. "You aren't cocky at *all*."

Some things are worth being cocky about. Chemistry, no. Baseball, definitely. "Practice starts Monday," I tell her. "Then it's practice, practice, and more practice until our first game March 4th."

"So I'm basically never going to see you again," she says.

She's smiling, but judging from the tone of her voice, that thought's just as awful for her as it is for me. I glare at my book. "You're more than welcome to eat dinner with us any night of the week. But I won't have to do much practicing if I don't get this crap straight. I need to pull a miracle out of my ass."

She not-so-subtly clears her throat.

I look over at her. Even with me sitting on the stool, she's eye level with me. Her gaze darts from me to my book, and back to me. "You know, it's okay to let people help you," she says. "There's a future Chemistry major standing right in front of you, offering free tutoring for the second time. And you've had my number for how long?"

"I know, I know. You're the genius offspring of a genius doctor, and I'm sure you come from a long line of genius geniuses."

My eyes widen right along with hers. And the award for shittiest timing in history goes to Austin Braxton, King of the Douches.

"Okay," she says. "You're feeling down, so I'll let that slide. Don't push it." She kicks off the counter and walks into the back room.

Dang it. I jump up and follow her, finding her at the arrangement table with roses spread out in front of her. She doesn't even bother looking up at me.

"I can't ask you to tutor me," I tell her, leaning against the doorframe. "It'd be weird, wouldn't it? We work together, for one thing, and—" My shoulders slump as she looks up at me, waiting for me to continue. *I'm an idiot, and don't want you to see that.* My mouth closes.

Her face falls, almost like she heard me tack on that last line. "I don't think you have much of a choice anymore," she says carefully. "You shouldn't be worried about weird when you're close to failing. I thought baseball was everything to you. Why do you care what

I think of you when you have a chance of not making it to the field?"

She's got a point. What she thinks of me should be at the bottom of my list—the key word here being "should." But I do care. A lot. What guy wants someone to see, firsthand, that he can't even read a page without its words going over his head?

I blow out a breath and walk over to the table so I can help her. "Are you going to be my miracle?" I ask, picking up the scissors.

She eyes the scissors, her forehead creasing a little. "Sure." She hands me a rose. "By the time I'm done with you, you'll be identifying chemical structures in your sleep."

I snort. This girl has no clue what she's getting into. "Then you've got one hell of a job to do. I'm not even sure where to start."

"Start by coming to my house this weekend?" she asks. "After you get off work tomorrow night?"

I glance up and catch her staring. She blushes. Waits. And I think my knees just turned to jelly.

"Sounds good," I manage to say. Clearing my throat, I start snipping thorns off my rose. "Why aren't you working tomorrow?"

Her smile falters as she hands me another flower. "Doctor's appointment. I bet you won't even notice I'm gone."

That's where she's completely, totally, out-of-the-park wrong. "Well, if you find some way to push that stuff through my head, I'll make sure you have a front-row seat to every game of the season."

"Won't I be working during your games?"

"We close up early on game days, along with half the other places in town."

She hands me the last rose, her hand brushing against mine when I take it. Her cheeks flush again.

There's no way I can hold back my grin. That seems to happen every time I'm around this girl.

"For the record," I say, "it's going to be awful lonely without you here tomorrow." And I don't think I've ever been more serious.

———————

Marisa and her parents live way out on the other side of the county, close to the line between Lewis Creek and Summerville. Once I leave the shop on Friday night, a twenty-mile drive brings me to the middle of nowhere, in the middle of nowhere. As I pull into the Marlowes' driveway, my jaw drops. I'm sure Marisa's dad makes plenty of money, but good Lord. Their place is bigger than any farmhouse around.

After parking behind Marisa's car, I grab my book and notebook and hop out onto the cobblestone driveway. On their wide front porch, the rocking chairs sway in the breeze. Marisa said that it was perfect out here, and now I definitely believe it. My house isn't some run-down shack, but we go against every Southern rule by not having a huge porch.

I press the doorbell and wait. And wait. And wait some more. The wind chimes jingle behind me, echoing in the night. Right as I hit the bell again, the door finally swings open, and I'm looking up at a dad who's got to be nearly a foot taller than me.

Well, hell.

"Evenin', Dr. Marlowe," I say, making sure my voice doesn't squeak like a field mouse. I hold up my book. "I'm here to, uh, study. With Marisa."

He stares me down until I *feel* about as small as a field mouse. Finally, he nods once and steps to the side, allowing me in. The smell of tomato sauce and fresh bread hits me full-force, and my stomach growls, reminding me I never ate dinner tonight. I came straight here after closing up the shop. A staircase a mile high stretches before me, and sounds from a TV drift from the living room on the left. The best part, though, is the dozens of pictures that line the wall next to the stairs. Most of them are of Marisa, from baby pictures all the way up to this past Christmas, when they moved here.

Her dad clears his throat, and I spin on my heel, facing him. The dude had to have been a basketball player at some point, or the scariest tight end in history. I thought doctors were supposed to be, like, friendly or something. But he's also a dad to a hot eighteen-year-old girl, so there's that.

"So, you're Austin," he says, holding out his hand. "I've heard a lot about you."

I shake his hand, hoping he doesn't notice mine's as sweaty as a game sock. "Good to meet you, sir." I glance around us. "About Marisa—?"

He crosses his arms, that stare of his still trained on me. "Do you like guns, Austin?"

You've got to be kidding me. "Yes, sir. Shot my first duck when I was eight."

He nods appreciatively and jerks his thumb over his shoulder. "Nice, nice. You know, I was born and raised down here. I took down plenty of bucks over in Dillon County. I've got one hell of a gun collection upstairs if you want—"

"Steven, stop trying to scare him!" a woman shouts from the kitchen right as shoes squeak against the kitchen floor. *Thank God.* I'd know those annoying Converses anywhere.

"Austin!" Marisa rushes into the entryway, her eyes bright and her hair pulled into a messy knot. Her yellow kitchen apron is splattered with tomato sauce. I kind of want to ask her for food. "Head on upstairs," she says. "My room's the second on the left. Make yourself at home."

Dr. Marlowe clears his throat. "It's time for dinner, Marisa." His voice is a heck of a lot softer than it was a minute ago.

"I can wait," I say. I glance between the two of them, but they're in this stare-down of the century that makes me wish I *was* a field mouse. At least then I could run away because, holy crap, this is awkward.

"You need to eat," her dad says. "You know your meds—"

"I'll eat later," Marisa cuts in. She smiles at her dad, but it doesn't quite reach her eyes. "Or I can carry something upstairs for us. When's the last time I missed dinner?" She places her hand on my back, pushing me gently. "Go on up. I'll be there in five."

She disappears into the kitchen, leaving me alone with *him*. I was never this much of a pansy around Jamie's dad, but I had about six inches on that guy. Plus, he was this super-quiet man who let her mom talk over him all the time. Dr. Marlowe scares the bejesus out of me just by standing there.

And we won't even talk about the gun collection.

I back toward the stairs, nearly falling flat on my ass when I hit the bottom step. "I think I'll just head upstairs?"

He cocks an eyebrow. "Good talking to you. See you later."

And that's my cue to get the heck out of dodge. I hightail it up the stairs and turn into that blessed second room.

Now, I don't have a ton of experience with girls' rooms. The ones I *have* been in were either splattered with pink or covered with monogramed everything. (Do the girls forget their own initials? Not really sure on that one.) But none of them have been like this.

Basically, Marisa's room wins by a long shot. The girl even has her own bathroom *inside* her bedroom. The walls are covered with posters—everything from

Chipper Jones to book cover art. Her bookshelves are stacked with books on top of books, with a bunch also piled on her nightstand, along with spiral notebooks. My Braves hat, the one I gave her that night outside the shop, sits on top of the notebooks. Nice. I could get used to being here.

Wearing my work boots on her white carpet feels like an outright sin, but she had shoes on downstairs, so I shove my momma's nagging voice aside and make my way to the chair at her desk. With the navy-blue comforter and dozens of pillows on her bed, it's like she took my bed and planted it in here.

Footsteps pound up the stairs. I plop into her leather chair right as she appears in the doorway with a bowl and two cans of soda. She pushes the door closed with her foot.

"Hope you're hungry," she says, walking over. She sits in front of me, on the edge of her bed, and passes me the neon green bowl full of popcorn. "Sorry. No spaghetti allowed in the room."

I shrug. "Popcorn's better. Spaghetti's the worst food to eat in front of people."

She tilts her head to the side. "Why?"

"Really? Slurp in front of someone and tell me it's not awkward as hell."

She hands me a soda and takes a handful of popcorn. I look down at the bowl. My stomach growls again. "You didn't have to make me anything," I add. "Really. I could've waited for y'all to eat."

She shrugs and scoots back on the bed. "I'm not going to let you starve." She pats the spot beside her. "But if you could sit up here and bring the popcorn with you, my stomach would be eternally grateful. I *am* missing the dinner I helped cook."

Grinning, I get up and sit on the edge of her bed, setting the bowl in front of us. She stares at me for a moment before saying, "Book?"

Oh. The real reason I'm here. I lean over and grab my book from her desk.

"Now," she continues, wiping her hands on her jeans, "this is killing me, so I have to ask. Why'd you wait so long to take this class? Don't most people take Chem way before senior year?"

"See, what happened was—" Wincing, I scratch my head. This made so much more sense the night it happened, when I was drunk off my ass with the rest of the team. "I was going to take it in the fall, but I didn't want to have this one teacher who hated me. Of course, I ended up with him anyway because karma is a heartless joker."

Her eyebrows scrunch together with confusion. "And why does he hate you?"

"Because he caught me swimming in his pond."

She waits. Keeps waiting.

I roll my eyes. "Naked. I was naked, okay?"

Her mouth opens, but closes as she blinks quickly. "Oh. I— Oh. W-why were you naked, exactly?"

"In my defense, it was a dare. A lot of beer was involved. And maybe some moonshine."

"Moonshine is an actual thing?"

Brett and Eric come from a long, long line of mountain folks. Every year that they visit their grandparents up in North Carolina, they come back with a stash of moonshine. No idea how their dad hasn't busted them yet, but you don't question miracles.

"It's a very real and very fantastic thing," I tell her.

She nods slowly. If I didn't lose her with the skinny-dipping, then I totally lost her with the moonshine. I've never felt more backwoods than I do now.

"'Kay," she says, tapping my book. "Let's get down to business. What're we dealing with tonight?"

I grin. "Changing the subject that quick, huh?"

"It's either that or me imagining you naked all night."

"You say that like it's a bad thing."

She holds my gaze, her lips pressed together in a thin line until she bursts out laughing. She slaps a hand over her mouth, her shoulders shaking as her cheeks flush bright red, and all I can do is laugh with her. Even though I am kind of getting a complex over here.

I flip through the pages in my book and find the chapter we started this week. "Here. My test on Monday is about all this. I've read this chapter, like, five times, and it's all blurring together."

Still laughing lightly, she leans over. "Really? This is just mass and stuff. Super-easy."

"Now I feel like even more of a dumbass." The words are out before I can stop them. As soon as her face falls, I wish I could take them back, even if I did mean them.

"I'm sorry," she says. "Really, really sorry. I didn't mean it that way." She squeezes my shoulder and smiles. "In all seriousness, you'll be fine, Austin. I don't know why you're convinced you're some sort of idiot because you're not. Isn't baseball the sport for smart people? You've got statistics, percentages, averages—all kinds of stuff."

I snort.

She nudges me. "I don't want to hear you calling yourself names anymore. No more 'dumbass' or 'idiot' or 'stupid.' If I hear it, I'll make you—" she waves her hand around. "—I don't know, copy the elements from the periodic table fifty times. Got it?"

"Yes, ma'am."

She nods once and passes me the popcorn bowl. "All right. Now. Let's make you smarter."

I take the bowl, unable to look away from her face. She holds my gaze, smiling this sweet smile that makes everything else in the room disappear. Maybe letting her tutor me wasn't the brightest decision after all. Or maybe it was the best damn decision I've ever made.

chapter seven

After church on Sunday, I drop Momma off at home and head across town to The Strike Zone. Practice starts tomorrow, but extra time at the batting cages never hurt anybody.

When I pull into the parking lot, Jay, Brett, and Eric are all crowded around Eric's Chevy, still dressed in their church clothes. As soon as I park, Eric hops off his tailgate and starts toward the building. He acted like a loner at church all morning, too. Instead of sitting in his usual spot between Brett and their little sister on the front pew, he planted himself in the back of the sanctuary.

I step down from my truck and lift my chin to Jay and Brett. "Who pissed in Eric's cereal?"

Brett tugs on a Braves cap and stuffs his hands into the pockets of his khakis. "He found out his girl was cheatin' on him," he says as we cross the lot. "With Right Field Randy, of all people."

"No kiddin'?" That's low. Lower than low. Randy's the kind of greasy, tobacco-chewing guy that gives other rednecks a bad name.

Brett nods. "Sucks, too, 'cause he's been doin' good these past couple of weeks. Finally staying out of trouble."

Damn. Eric needs someone to keep his rear out of trouble, especially if he plans to be a starter next year. Coach won't put up with that mess.

I look at Jay, who's been walking between us without saying a word. That's a first. I slap his shoulder. "What's with the silent treatment, Torres? Someone piss in your breakfast, too?"

He claps his hands together. "I hate to break it to ya, but Coach emailed out a roster change. I've got to tell you that you are not, in fact, on the varsity team this year. You're getting sent down to JV."

"And I've got to tell you that you are, in fact, full of shit." I stop short at the door. "You are full of shit, right?"

He laughs, but it's the fakest smile I've ever seen. Something's up. Brett holds the door open as we walk inside the building, which is empty except for the worker and Eric. This place is usually crawling with kids on Sunday afternoon. Major score for beating the post-church rush.

Eric's waiting for us at the front, leaning against the sign-in counter. Brett tugs on the brim of his cap some more, shielding his face as we approach the register. Jay scoffs, even though he tries to hide it with a cough. Whenever they walk into a room together, Brett acts like he's on some covert-ops mission, even though he's one of the most recognizable guys in town. It'd be nice to shake the guy and yell that no one gives a crap, but around here, people do care. They care a lot.

We grab our bats and helmets and split up, with Brett and Eric going to the cages lining the opposite side of the room. What's their deal? We always share a cage. Narrowing my eyes, I start to ask Jay, but he's already tugging his helmet on and stepping into Cage 1. The door slams behind him as he slides his token into the machine. The pitching machine kicks on, and

Jay swings, smacking the first ball. It's a miracle it's got any threading left.

I lean on the cage, lacing my fingers through the wire. "You all right, bro?"

"I'm ready to come out," he says.

I take a step back. "Come on out, then. I'll go first."

He hits the next ball and glances over his shoulder. "You that dumb? *Out*-out, Braxton." He points his bat across the room, where Brett's stepping into his cage.

My eyes widen as Jay squares up for the next pitch. I look around, making sure the room's still empty. If the wrong person heard that, all hell would break loose. I'm pretty sure that me and Jay's older brother are the only people who know. I don't even think Eric knows, and he's Brett's shadow.

"Dude," I whisper sharply. "Do you know what the hell you just said?"

He swings again. "You sound like Brett."

"Um, yeah. And we sound like we've got some sense."

He whirls around, his chest heaving, his face flushed and streaked with sweat. His bat drops to the floor. "And I thought you were on my side."

"I am, man. I just—" If I really have his back, there shouldn't be a "but" or "just." But Brett's got his reasons, too: he's a Baptist pastor's kid in the backwoods of South Carolina, for Christ's sake. He doesn't have much choice here. That said, I'm not even going to pretend to understand what they're going through.

The last ball pops from the machine and slams against the cage, snapping me back to the moment. "Yeah," I finally say, opening the door for him. "I'm on your side, man."

I tug on my own helmet as we trade places. I'm not sure what I may have just inadvertently agreed to. I'm not sure I *want* to know.

The first ball flies toward me, and I swing with all my might, sending it soaring. It hits the net at the back of the cage and plops to the floor with a weak *thump*. Blood pulses in my ears as I stare down the dispenser, waiting for the next pitch.

"How're things going with Barbecue Girl?" Jay asks from the door.

My fingers tighten around the bat. As soon as the ball shoots out, I smack the hell out of it with a *crack* that echoes throughout the room. Not bad, but I can do better. I *need* to do better. My batting average tops every other pitcher's in the region, and I'm keeping it that way.

I shrug, waiting for the next ball. "They're goin'. We're friends. And her name's Marisa."

My palms are hot and sweaty against the handle's grip as I square up for the next pitch. Any second now. CRACK.

Perfection.

"She actually making any difference with that hell of a class?"

"Yeah." I hit the next ball with a grunt. "Studied with her Friday night and all day at work yesterday. She's good at what she does." Really good at what she does. And she makes it fun. Every study partner should be that hilarious. And smart. And gorgeous.

After the final pitch, I yank off my helmet and turn, catching Jay gaping at me. He chuckles, disbelief all over his face. "You really like her."

Yep. "I guess," I say breathlessly, running a hand over my hair. "Why do you look so surprised?"

He shakes his head as I come out of the cage. "Because you haven't made your move yet. Or you have and haven't told me about it, which is just as weird."

"We've only known each other for a few weeks."

He cocks an eyebrow. "Seriously? Dude, you landed Jamie in your truck in less than an hour."

And we both know how well that turned out. Jamie left town and forgot I existed. I twirl the bat. "Marisa's different."

"How? Does she actually call you on your shit?"

I grin. "Yeah. That." Besides, she doesn't strike me as a back-of-the-truck kind of girl. And I'd really prefer to not screw this up.

We drop our helmets and bats off at the front counter and turn to watch Eric and Brett finish up their rounds. "So," Jay says on an exhale. "What the hell do we do?" He crosses his arms. "How do we fix this lovey-dovey bullshit?"

I lean back against the counter, glancing over my shoulder to make sure the worker's not around. "You want my honest-to-God opinion? No BS?"

He nods for me to go on.

"I think you need to give the guy some more time. Brett's one of the best people I know. He gives everything all he's got. If he decides to open up about this? I think it'd be worth waiting for."

Jay sighs and nods again. "Fair enough. And I think you need to have some balls when it comes to the genius girl."

I elbow him. "Screw you. It's called being respectful. I actually like her. Like, really like her."

"You'll be all right," he says, looking up at me. "You're good people, Braxton."

I slap him on the back. "So're you."

He gives me a half-grin, the same one he gave me when I told him I didn't give a shit whether he liked girls, or guys, or both. The same one he gave me when I told him that we are who we are, and that's all we can be.

He's an ass sometimes. He's also the best buddy a guy can have.

At 2 a.m. on the dot, my phone buzzes. Instead of being annoyed and pissed at the world for being woken up, I shoot straight up and snatch the phone. My body must've been ready for her. For her texts, I mean.

Dang it.

Marisa: *You awake?*

Now I am. I squint at the bright screen as I type. *Yeah. Dont you ever sleep girl?*

Marisa: *Insomnia is NOT my friend. Im wasting time by watching youtube videos. I just watched the chipper jones retirement ceremony. SO MANY FEELINGS.*

That's one thing that would beat sleeping. *Its like u want me to drive over there at 2am*

Time ticks by, minute by minute. She's either fallen asleep, or I've crossed the creeper line. I put the phone back on its charger, but the second I relax against my pillows, the phone buzzes again. I snatch it up.

Marisa: *Maybe.*

Well, hell.

Don't tempt me. I can make it happen. I can have my shoes on and be out the door in less than sixty seconds. Just say the word. Say the word.

Please say the word?

Marisa: *Don't you have a test AND practice tmrw? You cant be driving across town this late.*

Correction: I totally can. For her, I'd miss an entire night of sleep. But she does have a point. Practice kicking into full swing means that sleep is going to be nearly non-existent for the next few months. *Youre no fun*, I type back.

Marisa: *Night, Austin. Good luck on your test. =)*

Total buzzkill. In the best possible way.

chapter eight

Let it be known that I am a CHEMISTRY GENIUS. Okay, not really, but I did just knock my test out of the park. I think.

Once again, everyone's already cleared out of the classroom by the time I finish my test. At least this time I'm not ready to slam my head against a wall. With a wide smile, I grab my bags and take my test to Mr. Matthews's desk, placing it front and center. He holds my gaze while picking it up.

"You seem a lot more confident," he says.

My smile grows. "I got a tutor."

Nodding, he peers at my test. "No blank answers. That's a good start toward passing."

A guy can hope.

He grabs a red marker from his penholder. My eyes widen. "You know, I think I'll grade it now so we can see where you stand. Practice starts today, right?"

Does he *want* me to pass out cold on his floor?

Before I can muster a response, he takes the marker to the page. Yeah, I can't watch. I whirl around and stare at the back wall, which is covered with a blown-up version of the periodic table. Shame that wasn't up when I took my last test.

"Austin," he says a moment later. Cringing, I turn back around. He holds the paper out for me, facedown.

My hand trembles ever-so-slightly as I take it from him.

Seventy-two. Not genius-level, but it's a C. I'll take it.

"Significantly better." He recaps the marker and leans forward. "I'd say your tutor's earned a thank-you. Keep that up along with your homework and participation grades, and you won't have a thing to worry about come March."

My shoulders drop as I blow out a breath. I've got a ways to go, but this is one heck of a start. "Thank you, sir."

I hurry into the hallway and duck into the restroom so I can change for practice. The locker room's better, but on Coach's field, if you're not early, you're late. Every minute counts. After locking the stall door, I kick off my boots and jeans and stuff them into my gear bag. As I tug on my practice pants, my phone buzzes from inside my bag. And again. And again. And again.

What the actual hell.

I dig into the bag and grab my phone from my jeans pocket. Four texts light up its screen.

There's one from Brett, reminding me that practice starts today. *No shit.*

One from Eric, telling me they're on the field. *I'm coming.*

Another from Jay, asking where the hell I'm at. *Calm yourself.*

And finally there's Marisa, asking how my test went. She gets a reply. She's prettier than the other three.

Test went good, I type back. *OMW to practice. Hows work?* I place the phone on the floor, even though the germs on a guys' bathroom floor likely rival any hotel bed sheet. I yank off my shirt and replace it with a fresh T-shirt. The phone buzzes, echoing against the tile. I plop down on the floor and lace up my cleats before reading her reply.

Marisa: *Works good. Miss you though. Have fun!*

She misses me. It's right there, in black and white, that she misses me. Can't blow this. I stand and type back, *Dinner at the shop tonight?*

The bathroom door slams open. I jump. My phone flies straight for the toilet. I snatch it mid-air, just in time. The phone's taken a few plunges, but dear God, anything but the school's toilet water. I think that's the end of bathroom texting hour.

According to the roster that Coach posted Friday, there are sixteen guys on the team this year. By the time I reach the field, half those guys are lined up along the foul line that stretches from first base to home plate. Coach paces in front of them, his clipboard in hand.

"Braxton," Coach calls out. "Nice of you to join us. How 'bout some hustle?"

I'm hustling, I'm hustling. My phone buzzes in my hand as I high-tail it to the dugout and drop my bag onto the bench. I glance over my shoulder, making sure I'm not being watched, before scrolling to Marisa's message.

Marisa: *I'll be here =)*

Score.

"Braxton!" Coach barks.

Crap. I shove the phone into my bag and jog to the infield, falling into line beside Brett. He snickers. Coach is wearing his sunglasses, but I'm ninety-nine percent sure he's giving me the death glare. I clasp my hands behind my back, steeling my gaze straight ahead. At least I wasn't the last one out here.

Others file onto the field, one at a time, until Matt completes the line-up down near home plate. Though the wind's sharp as a knife, the sun beats down on us without a cloud in the sky. But once Coach stops pacing and stands still before us, silence thick as fog blankets the field.

Coach slides his sunglasses onto the brim of his cap. Scans the line. Studies us. Up until today, any time on this field was child's play. Now, it's more than a game. From here on out, it's business. We're winners. Champions.

"There are sixteen of you this year," Coach says, his voice booming. The man's voice gets louder every season. "We've got as many newcomers from JV as there are veterans, split right down the middle." He crosses his arms. "Let's lay down some ground rules. Are you listening?"

"Yes, sir," we all say.

He ducks his head, walking down the line. "Practice is non-negotiable," he begins. "If you want to play, you will be here every afternoon." His head snaps up once he reaches first base. "What's your hand up for? Did I stutter?"

Leaning forward to see past Brett, I chance a glance at the end of the line. Chris Lincoln, a sophomore and our new left-fielder, lowers his hand and asks, "What if we have jobs, sir?"

Rookie move.

Coach simply stares. "I'm your boss now. This team is your job. That clear it up?" Chris nods, and Coach keeps on, walking back in my direction. I straighten quickly. "I ran this by my veterans in January, but I'm going to make it loud and clear again today: I don't play around with grades. I get a copy of every single report card. The school requires a 2.0 to play baseball—I require a 3.0. If you dip below that line, I won't hesitate to bench you." He stops. Looks at me. "Am I a man of my word, Braxton?"

Thanks a lot. I clear my throat and reply, "Yes, sir."

His gaze lingers on me a beat longer. "Next up is behavior," he calls. "To the people in this school, in this town, you are gods. You will be put on pedestals. You will get away with things that your classmates would be expelled for. That said, if I hear of you acting like anything less than gentlemen, you won't step on my field. Understood?"

Another resounding, "Yes, sir."

He glances at his clipboard. "I want you to look to your right. To your left."

I do.

"This field is your home," Coach continues, his voice much lower. "These men are your brothers. You will play together, you'll win together, and you'll lose together. All of this?" He takes a step back and gestures to the field. "This is yours for the taking, down to the last inch. What matters is how much you want it."

The chilled wind slams against my skin, but my racing pulse is enough to keep me warm. This field is everything. And more than anything, I want it. I want it all.

"Let me ask y'all something," he says. "Do you want it?"

"Yes, sir," we answer.

He folds his arms. Stares at us, long and hard. And once again, his gaze settles on me. "I'm not sure you do. Let me ask you again: do you want this field?"

My heart hammers as I yell, "Yes, sir," along with the others.

He nods once. "That's better. Now go take it."

⊢――――◂

When I walk into Joyner's after practice, the place is packed to the brim for the dinnertime rush. At least a dozen people are ahead of me in line. My stomach growls, angry at having to wait after running my rear off during practice.

"Austin!"

I whirl around. Hannah is sitting at a corner booth, along with Bri and another junior, Becca. They're all dolled up with curls and those little sundresses the girls around here wear, even when it's February and the wind slices right through you. Sipping from her glass, Hannah waves me over.

But that means losing my place in line. My stomach rumbles again. Dang it.

With a sigh, I start toward their booth. Hannah raises an eyebrow as I approach. "I've got a problem with you," she says.

I squat and rest my arms on the table so I'm eye level with her. "What'd I do?"

She sets her glass down and leans forward, resting her chin in her hand. "We were putting together the place settings for the Valentine's dance, and I didn't see your name, or Jay's, *or* Brett's." She punches my shoulder playfully. "Why are y'all skippin' my dance?"

Well, at least I didn't actually *do* anything. "I don't have a date."

Her jaw drops. "Who the heck told you no? Ugh." She scans the restaurant. "Give me twenty seconds and I'll have a date for you."

I grab her wrist as she starts to stand. "Hannah. Chill. I don't want to go." If I did want to go, it'd be with someone who doesn't go to our school. I mean, I *could* ask Marisa, but would that be too weird? And besides—

Hannah gasps, snatching my attention. "Are you trying to break my heart?"

"Austin!" Laura calls from the register. I glance over my shoulder. She drops a bulging paper bag onto the counter. "Your order's up."

I never even ordered. *Do not look at the angry line.*

"Well," Hannah says, "if you bail on prom in May, I'll kill you in your sleep. Tell Jay and Brett to let me know if they decide to go this weekend. I'll get them hooked up."

Yeah, I have a feeling the last place they'll want to be is that dance. They'll be locked up at Jay's all night, thanks to his parents going out of town for the weekend.

"You won't have to look hard," Becca chimes in, taking a sip of her tea. "I'll go with Brett in a heartbeat. Have you *seen* that guy's hands?"

Bri shoots me a look that pretty much screams *HELP*. Can't help her much there.

"Good Lord have mercy, yes," Hannah says. "If his hands are that big, just think—"

I jump up. There are some things a guy doesn't need to hear. "Have a good night, ladies."

"Bye," they call in unison as I head for the counter.

I take the paper bag, peeking inside to make sure it's all there. It is, including the extra "just in case she stays" barbecue I've been ordering for Marisa. I look to Laura, who's soloing the register. She catches my eye and hurries over. I reach for my wallet, but she waves me off.

"No charge." She jerks her thumb over her shoulder. "Direct order from Mr. Joyner himself. I'm not allowed to charge you for the rest of the season."

Ah, yeah. Most wonderful time of the year, indeed. I tuck the bag under my arm. "You're sure?"

Laura grins and winks. "Go Bulldogs."

chapter nine

I've never liked Valentine's Day. There's all this pressure to buy the perfect flowers for whatever girl you're dating (which I'm actually good at, but that's not the point), to buy the perfect gift, to set up the perfect date, blah blah blah. When you work in a floral shop, the holiday is 500,000 times more annoying. It's scientifically proven. Just trust me.

Basically, you've got people rushing in and out all dang day while yelling that you're not going fast enough, even though their sorry butts are the ones who waited until the last minute. It sucks for Momma and Marisa, who've been through the ringer all day. Coach even excused me from practice so I could come give them a hand at three.

I got out of class at two. But there's no reason to tell them that.

As soon as the last customer is out the door with his date's bouquet in hand at 5:59, I rush over and lock the door behind him. I watch him climb into his truck and drive off, probably on his way to pick up that date. The stool behind the counter scrapes against the floor. I turn right as Marisa plops onto it.

"Holy cow," she says through a yawn, redoing her ponytail. "I thought you were full of crap when you told me how crazy it'd be. I'm pretty sure I waited on half the population of this town."

That's not hard when your town's population is less than 5,000. I walk over to her, untying my apron along the way. "Can't say I didn't warn you."

She rubs her hands over her face. "I'm tired," she groans as I hang up my apron behind the counter. "And people can be psychotic. They're just *flowers*, for cryin' out loud. How can people get so mean over flowers? Flowers make you happy!"

I move next to her and lean against the counter. "A little hard work never killed anybody, you big baby."

She stares across the room, slack-jawed. "See, I can't even argue with you. I'm too sore. I'm seriously considering sleeping under this counter instead of driving home."

The collar of her red shirt slipped down at some point, exposing freckled skin. I swallow hard. Her shoulders are right there, just begging to be rubbed. She said she was sore, right? Girls always go for that stuff.

Of course, she'd probably go for a restraining order if I grabbed her shoulders without asking first.

Momma clears her throat from the stairs. "I'm making the dinner run. Any requests?"

Marisa drops her head onto the counter. "FOOD," she says, her voice muffled. "Lots and lots of food."

Momma shakes her head. "I'll be back in a bit. Y'all start cleaning up." She stops in the middle of the display room, scanning the near-empty shop. "Actually, it looks like the customers already did that for you since the last time I came down." She glances over at Marisa, who still has her head down, and then back to me. She raises an eyebrow.

What? I mouth.

She bites back a smile and opens the door, the bell jingling as she leaves.

With a sigh, Marisa raises her head, turning to me with droopy eyes. She glances down, her eyebrows furrowing as she grabs my hand from the counter. "Austin, your fingers look awful. They make Band-Aids for a reason, you know."

My heart hammers as her fingers wrap around mine. This is a million times better than a shoulder rub. I follow her gaze to my hand. It does look bad, but it's no worse than normal. I came by the shop last night to help put together a gazillion flower arrangements, which was hell on my skin. Coach will be pissed when he realizes I didn't wear gloves like I'm supposed to.

"It's not as bad as it looks," I tell her. "Just wait until tomorrow, when you'll be putting together all the corsages for the dance this weekend. *Those* are a pain in the ass."

She scoffs, but her eyes are shining. "You're really going to make me do all those by myself? You know there are, like, almost 200 orders, right?"

My lips curve slowly. I wish I could be here to help her. As much as I love being on that field, practice starting this week has been a double-edged sword. I'm not getting nearly enough Marisa time.

Good God, I'm pathetic.

"There's no way Momma will let you do them alone. She'll help. Trust me."

She lets go of my hand. I fight a frown. *Come back.* "That sounds good. Are you..." Looking down at my now-lonely hand, she clears her throat. "Will you be going to the dance?"

I shrug a shoulder. "Dances are a lot more fun when you've got a date to spoil all night, which I don't. Never thought to ask anyone." And if I did ask someone, it'd be the girl in front of me.

She sighs and leans onto the counter, putting her chin in her hands. "Well, congratulations. You'll hang on to your soul."

Or not. I bite back a smile. "Not a dancer, I'm guessing?"

She shakes her head. "Never been a fan. Formal dances are the invention of Satan."

"That's where you're wrong. You have dances confused with Chem. That's where Satan focused all his energy."

She pushes me, smirking. "I'm serious. A girl has to suffer through frilly decorations, spiked punch, and the guy trying to get in her pants afterward, and for what? A corsage, maybe some dinner, and two hours of dancing, which results in foot blisters." She hops off the stool and grabs the push-broom. "I'm so glad I'll never have to go to another one again. Homeschooling for the win."

'Kay. So now I'm really glad I never asked her.

"See, I'm insulted," I say, moving around the counter. "Guys don't always try to get in your pants. And dances aren't *that* bad." Maybe a little bad, but not complete torture.

She starts sweeping, huffing a little. "So says Lewis Creek's god of baseball. Of course dances are awesome for you." She holds the broom to her chest, throwing her hand up to her forehead like she's in *Gone with the Wind* or some crap. "Oh, Austin! I never knew there was a difference between fastballs and sliders, but whisper it in my ear while we dance all night in the bed of your truck."

I wiggle my eyebrows. "And by 'dance,' you mean what, exactly?" She swats the broom at me. I hold up my hands in surrender. "All right, all right! But I will say that, after a few beers, truck dancin' is a blast. You should try it."

She rolls her eyes and resumes sweeping, turning her back to me. Okay, then. Challenge accepted. I dig my phone out of my pants pocket and scroll through the music app until I find a halfway decent slow song.

You can never go wrong with some Luke Bryan. Girls eat that shit up.

As the opening notes of "Crash My Party" fill the room, Marisa stops. Her head pops up, and she whirls around, cocking an eyebrow. "Um, what do you think you're doing?"

Grinning, I place the phone on the counter and hold out my hand. "I'm on a mission to prove that not *all* dance dates are evil. I'll have you know, I'm a darn good date."

Her gaze flickers from my outstretched hand to my face. "Are you serious?"

"As a heart attack." With the way my heart's pounding, that's entirely possible. Even though it sounds cheesy as hell, I think I finally know what girls mean when they talk about having butterflies in their gut, or stomach, or whatever. But even that's not a good way to describe it. The butterflies feel like they're all over the place.

And now I'm thinking about butterflies. Lord, help me.

She narrows her eyes. "You've been drinking moonshine again, haven't you?"

Maybe the Luke Bryan song wasn't as foolproof as I'd thought. "Please?"

She opens her mouth like she's going to argue again, but instead she sighs and sets the broom against one of the coolers. "That's not fair," she says, crossing the distance between us. "No one in her right mind can resist that accent."

When she slips her hand into mine, I pull her against me in one swift movement. She sucks in a breath, looking up at me with wide eyes.

"What?" I ask, resting my hands just above her hips. "Too close?"

She smiles. Looping her arms around my neck, she says, "I think it's just right."

Works for me.

We sway to the music, slow and steady. Those darn shoes of hers squeak against the floor, and she hangs her head and laughs right along with me.

"I'd be a great date, you know." I pull her a little closer. "I'd wash my truck. Pick you up. Talk about guns with your dad. Even bring you flowers."

Pressing her lips together, she nods. "Flowers?"

"I know a guy."

Another song switches on, this one a little slower and a lot more appropriate for truck "dancing." She doesn't say anything, though. She keeps rocking side to side, keeps smiling, keeps looking up at me with those Lord-help-me gorgeous eyes.

"You know," she says, "this experiment isn't entirely accurate."

"And why's that?"

Her smile wavers. "You're not like most guys, Austin."

Her gaze drops to the floor. I'd pay anything under the sun to make that ache in her voice disappear. I think I was screwed from the get-go with this girl. Nobody's ever made me fall this far, this fast. Nobody's ever made me care so much so soon. And it's scary. Exciting, but scary.

Instead of telling her that, though, I say, "Good. Because you're not like most girls."

She lets out a breathless laugh. "No, I'm not. Most girls don't have the issues I do."

I stop dancing, and she finally looks me in the eye. "That's the biggest bunch of BS I've ever heard," I tell her. "Every girl has issues. Hell, so does every guy. Anyone who says they don't is lying through their teeth."

Her cheeks flush. She blinks quickly. My heart lurches because, God, I better not have made this girl cry. I take her hand and back away, holding my arm up. The corner of her mouth twitches as she spins, her cheeks returning to normal. And there are no tears. Dodged that one.

"Is that right?" she says, beginning to sway again. "So what's your issue?"

My feet are killing me, but I refuse to let her go. I'd dance around this shop 'til daylight if she wanted. "My biggest issue," I say, leaning down to her ear, "is that I'm trying to decide whether or not friends can kiss each other."

She winces. "You shouldn't want to kiss me."

Ouch. Did she have to wince? I mean, is the thought of kissing me actually painful? 'Cause that's brutal. Forcing the biggest smile I can, I ask, "And why's that?"

"You deserve so much better than me."

Huh. So people *do* drop that line. "I see. We're really going with, 'it's not you, it's me'?"

She giggles as we come to another standstill, but there's something under that giggle—something nervous, something unsure. I should probably regret even asking, but you only regret the chances you don't take. She's a chance worth taking.

She takes a step back, lacing her fingers together. "Here's the thing," she says. "I think that sometimes, people get so caught up in a moment that a kiss feels right. And even though both people really, *really* want it to happen, the time isn't right."

I gape at her. "Congratulations. You just put more thought into a kiss than anyone in the history of ever."

She shrugs. "Maybe people should think more about them. Then so many hearts wouldn't be broken."

That actually makes a lot of sense.

"I like you," she says with a tiny smile, and my heart slams against my chest. "I won't even try to lie about that. You're fun, and you're sweet, and you're, well, kind of hot." She rolls her eyes. "Oh my God, don't give me that look."

"What look?" I ask, smirking. "You just called me hot. How am I supposed to look?"

She shakes her head, but her smile grows even more. "You're also a good friend, and friends are safer. Right now, I need safe. I need a friend." She takes a deep breath. "So can we do the friend thing?"

Safe is good. Friends are good. It's better to be safe than sorry and all that. And getting slammed into the friend zone kind of sucks—okay, it really sucks—but I'd rather have her as a friend than not at all. "We can absolutely do the friend thing."

She exhales with a huge grin. The next song on my playlist starts up, and she holds her hand out for mine. "Friends can dance, right?"

"If so, then I'll be the best damn friend you've ever had." I grab her hand and pull her back to me. She bites her lower lip, looking up at me through those long lashes. I swear, the girl turns me to goo every time. And that's why I can't resist saying, "Happy Valentine's Day, Marisa."

That smile of hers returns as she rocks to the music. Her cheeks flush again, making her skin nearly as red as her shirt. "Happy Valentine's Day."

It's a little terrifying, how one person can knock you clean off your feet before you even saw her coming. It's also pretty freakin' awesome.

chapter ten

Momma and I went to church this morning, like we do every Sunday. I took her home and drove off to meet the guys at The Strike Zone, also like I do every Sunday. When I came home, I found Momma locked in her room. Through her closed door, she told me that she needed some time alone. So without another word, I grabbed my keys and walked right back out of the house. I wasn't touching that with a ten-foot pole.

See, today would've been my parents' anniversary.

I wish there was something I could do to help. I wish I could suck it up and talk to her about what happened because I'm sure she *does* need to talk. Dad was her best friend. He was mine, too, for a long time. But that doesn't mean I can forget what he did. He left us here alone.

The worst part of it all is that I didn't see it coming. Neither did Momma. It literally came out of nowhere. Maybe it'd be easier if something had led up to it or if something catastrophic had happened right before. Then maybe, *maybe* it would have made sense. But things were perfect. *He* was perfect. And then he was gone.

The sun's already disappeared for the day when I turn onto the main road leading through town.

George Strait croons through my truck's speakers as I stop at a red light and flop back against the headrest, squeezing my eyes closed. The green light brightens my windshield, and I hit the gas, speeding through the intersection. But the second I see *her* walking in my direction, I slam on the brakes.

Even with my headlights shining right on her, Marisa doesn't seem to notice that a truck just skidded to a stop in front of her. She continues down the sidewalk, with her head down and hood pulled up. What the hell is she doing out here? I honk the horn, and she jumps, finally looking at the truck. I release the brake and inch forward a little, pulling up right next to her. She crosses her arms as I hit the passenger window button.

"What's a pretty girl like you doing in a place like this all by yourself?" I call, leaning across the center console. All I get is a blank stare. 'Kay, so she's possessed. Awesome. "Seriously, you shouldn't be walkin' out here alone. You need a ride?"

She shakes her head. All she's wearing is her Braves jacket, so she's got to be freezing, unless she's got an industrial-strength wool sweater on under it.

"I feel like walking," she calls back. "No big deal. You go ahead."

"Where's your car?"

She jerks her thumb over her shoulder. "I left it at the grill."

And she's been walking ever since? We're a solid mile from the grill. A chill shoots through me. I crank the heat up a notch. "Come on. I'll drive you back there, or I can just give you a ride home if you want. Aren't your parents freaking out?"

"I don't want to go home right now. I'm fine. My parents are cool as long as I text them every half hour." She sighs. "We have an understanding tonight."

What, is she planning on staying out all night or something? I put the truck in park. "Do they know you left your car in a parking lot and you're *walking?*" Her silence is the only answer I need. "Marisa, I can't leave knowing you're out here alone. As in, my conscience will eat me alive for the rest of the night. It's thirty degrees outside. Please get in the truck."

And I won't even tell her that drunk assholes still wander the streets in small towns like this. If anything, they're worse here.

She levels me with a glare I didn't even know she was capable of. Yikes. "I don't want to go home," she repeats, pointing a finger at me as she inches toward the truck. "Got it? Promise you won't try and trick me."

I hold up my left hand, placing the right over my chest. "Swear it. If it makes you feel better, I don't want to go home right now, either. We can be homeless together for a few hours."

Her face tightens. I understand wanting alone time, but walking by herself in below-freezing weather isn't the way to get it. Finally, she sighs again and opens the door, climbing inside. She stares straight ahead, silent.

Okay, then. At least I won that battle.

I shift the truck into gear and continue down the road, unsure of where to go next. I know where I *wanted* to go a few minutes ago, but now I have unexpected cargo. I don't want her thinking about being the topic of some creeper Lifetime movie.

Momma watches them. Shut up.

We drive for a solid ten minutes before Marisa finally says, "Where're we going?"

"Where were you heading?" I ask with a quick glance over.

She shrugs, still staring out the windshield. "No idea. I just wanted to be alone for a while."

Everyone wants to be alone tonight. I stop at the caution light, which casts a yellow glow across her face. There are streaks of missing makeup on her cheeks, and with the black smudges beneath her eyes, it's clear where they came from. What I wish I knew was why, and how I can make it better. My fingers twitch with the urge to wipe the tear stains away, but I grip the steering wheel instead. *Friends. She wants to be friends. Rein it in.*

"Austin." She looks at me, one corner of her mouth turned up in the tiniest hint of a smile. "Are you going to stare at me all night, or take me somewhere?"

My heart leaps into my throat. I'd be perfectly happy with staring at her all night, if she's giving me her permission. "Are you okay?" I ask.

She inhales deeply, looking back to the windshield. "Honestly? I'm kind of a mess tonight."

Yeah, I can't resist anymore. Using my thumb, I wipe her cheek, clearing it of a tear that slipped from her eye. "You say you want some quiet time?" I ask. Head still down, she nods. "Then I know the perfect place. But you have to trust me."

She buckles her seatbelt, finally seeming a little more relaxed. "I do."

Those two words sound better than anything I've heard in a long time. Trust is something that's earned. I'll take trust any day.

I hit the gas and drive through the caution light, taking us past the county line. It only takes a few minutes for us to leave civilization behind, surrounded by nothing but trees and the open road ahead of us.

"You're not kidnapping me, are you?" she asks. "Taking me out to the woods to slice and dice me?"

Called it. I flash her a grin. "Told you that you'd have to trust me. But if you want peace and quiet, this is probably the best place in a twenty-mile radius to get it."

"I feel like we've already driven twenty miles."

I chuckle. "Not even close. Lean back, kick up your feet, and relax. You're not used to backwoods drivin', are you?"

With a smile, she rests her head against the window and closes her eyes. "No. This is a first for me."

It takes everything in me not to stare at her, but I'd rather not drive this truck into a tree. By the time the road turns into the familiar dirt path, the moon shines brightly ahead of us. I slow down. The sound of rocks crunching beneath my tires takes my nerves down a notch, same as always. There's not much that beats that.

"Austin?"

Except for her voice. Marisa looks around as I park by the pond's edge, beneath the massive oak tree. And immediately, I regret coming out here. This place holds a lot of memories, memories that have no business attacking me while she's in my truck.

"Wow," she breathes, leaning forward to look out the windshield. "The stars are amazing tonight. They're like little diamonds. There have to be millions of them."

For the first time tonight, her face is peaceful. Maybe coming here wasn't such a bad idea, after all. Sometimes the best remedy is a few minutes out in the middle of nowhere, away from everything. Being alone with an old dirt road is better than therapy. It's one of the few things I'll miss about this place in the fall. I have a feeling there aren't too many dirt roads in Columbia.

"Do you come out here a lot?" she asks. "Since it's so far out?"

And the lump's back in my throat. I *used* to come a lot. Jamie and I would drive here when we wanted privacy for certain things, but I'm not about to tell Marisa that. "Not really," is my answer, and at least it's mostly the truth. It has been a while. Crap on a freakin' cracker, I really shouldn't have come out here.

"Crap on a cracker?" Marisa says. "That's new." Wide-eyed, I turn to her slowly. She shrugs with a small smile. "And you can tell me that you used to bring your ex out here. It's okay."

"Sorry, *what*?"

She kicks her feet up on the dashboard. "Don't worry, I'm not psychic. A little psycho once in a while, but not psychic. I just don't think you realize you're saying stuff out loud sometimes."

I shake my head. There's no way. Jay would've called me out on that a long, *long* time ago. "I think you're full of it. I think you're hiding some psychic mumbo-jumbo up your sleeve."

"I'm tellin' you, you do it all the time."

My jaw drops. "You just dropped a 'g.'"

She narrows her eyes. "Huh? No, I didn't."

"You definitely just dropped a 'g.'"

"Maybe you should focus on the fact that you talk without even realizing it."

I can't even be embarrassed because that was one of the most adorable things I've ever heard come out of her mouth. I toss my arm across the back of her seat and lean toward her. "Are you turnin' into a Southern girl already, Marisa?"

Her mouth opens, and I can't hold back my grin as she fights her own smile and fails. "I hate to break it to you, Floral Prince, but a month in the South doesn't create a Southerner. Besides, it wouldn't work for me. The accent sounds so much cuter coming from you."

I'm pretty sure my cheeks just caught on fire. "I highly doubt that."

"See? *Highly*. I'm telling you, I'm kind of melting over here." She looks down at her hands, tugging on her sleeves as she adds, "I bet it makes all the other girls melt, too."

My heartbeat stutters to an almost-complete stop. I don't know what gave her that impression, but it sucks that she thinks I'm some kind of girl-hopping a-hole. "There aren't any other girls. You're the first girl in a long, long time."

She plays with the ends of her sleeves, fidgeting in her seat, but stays quiet.

"The other night, at the shop," I continue, "with the kiss? I asked because I wanted to. Because I like you. And I know plenty of other dudes who make out with one girl after another, but that's not me. I thought you knew that."

Her eyes fill with tears. *Whoa, whoa, whoa. Shit.* She sniffles loudly as she hides her face in her hands. "God, I'm such a mess," she whispers. She sniffles again and looks at me, all wet cheeks and gut-punching frown and tears that just won't stop falling. "I'm sorry. I screw everything up. Even nights like tonight, when I'm supposed to be grateful and happy and—" Shaking her head, she presses her lips together. "I can't do this."

I grab her hand, which is cold as ice. "What's goin' on? Talk to me."

More tears. Lord have mercy, if she doesn't stop crying, my heart might explode. She looks down at the hand I'm still holding because, to be honest, I really, really don't want to let it go. Not only that, but I have a feeling that she needs it.

"What's going on," she says, her voice thick, "is that I'm a crazy, psychotic, certifiable mess. I shouldn't have come out tonight, and I definitely shouldn't have dragged you into this."

My pulse races. The last time I saw someone cry like this, it was when we found out about Dad and my momma was inconsolable. "Did someone die?"

She coughs out a laugh and wipes her nose with her other sleeve. "You don't want to know, Austin. Trust me."

"I do want to know. Seein' you like this? It's kind of destroying me."

She turns back to me, still sniffling, though the tears seem to have stopped for now. She pulls her hand from mine, and before I can say anything, she holds up her arm.

"It's not exactly something I parade around," she says, barely above a whisper. "And it's a secret that no one down here knows about, and I'd really like to keep it that way."

"You can trust me with anything," I say without hesitation.

With a deep, shuddering breath, she closes her eyes, pulls up her sleeve, and holds her arm out for me to see. The word "love" is tattooed in cursive on her wrist, and while it's nice and simple enough, that's not what snatches my attention. At least a dozen scars cover that wrist, along with the section of her forearm that's exposed. Some are tiny, some are long and jagged. Those kinds of scars don't just come from anywhere. Did—did she actually try to *kill* herself?

I can't breathe.

I lean back against my door, staring at her as seconds, minutes, hours pass. I have no clue how long it is before I'm pretty sure someone drives a knife through my gut. She won't look at me. Instead, she pulls her sleeve down with a trembling hand, shoves open her door, and hops down from the truck. She walks to the pond and stops at the water's edge, wrapping her arms around herself.

I should follow her. I should make sure she's okay. I should say *something*. All that would be a lot easier if I could breathe.

Opening my door sends in a rush of freezing cold air, but it's exactly what I need. I step down and start for the water, stuffing my hands in my pockets. Marisa was right; the stars do look like diamonds. Momma used to tell me to make wishes on them, as if little balls of gas hold some sort of magical power. I think I have too many wishes for those things to handle, anyway. They'd explode under the pressure.

Like right now? More than anything, I'd wish to have the answer to a question I've been asking for two years: why the hell anyone would kill themselves. I don't get it. I won't pretend to get it.

Twigs and rocks crunch as I step to her side. I glance over at her, but she's gazing out at the water, arms still crossed. Pieces of hair have fallen out of her ponytail and blow around, crazy in the wind.

I don't have a clue what to say. Things seem perfect for her: perfect house, perfect parents, perfect brain, perfect personality. So why the hell would she try and—?

No. Nope. I can't do it. I can't even think it. My throat tightens as I kick at the grass. Dad seemed pretty damn perfect, too.

"Please don't tell anyone else," she says. I look up. She turns to me, arms wrapped around herself like a security blanket. "I'm okay now, I swear. But I don't want people looking at me like I'm some sort of freak, you know?"

I nod once. It's all I can do. My words stick to my throat.

"I won't blame you for thinking I am a freak," she says, the words tumbling out. "And I won't blame you for running, or if you never want to see me again, or if you want me to quit the shop."

Hold up. How'd we get to that? I step toward her, but she keeps on.

"I just thought that maybe you should know the truth because I like you. I like you a lot. And I don't even know if I mean that I *like* you, like you, but I like spending time with you, and if we're going to hang out or whatever, you deserve to know the truth. But if—"

I grab her shoulders, silencing her. "Stop if-ing," I tell her. "I want to see you again. I would never ask you to quit the shop. And I like you, too. A lot. So please, stop with the ifs. It's just—"

I search her face, which is equal parts hopeful and amazed and utterly confused. And I have a feeling that what I say next will make or break whatever friendship we've built up over the last few weeks. I've known her for one freakin' month, so I have no idea why I'm so invested, or why my heart feels like it's about to jump out of my chest, or why all I want to do is hug her and have it be enough to make her okay.

But I am. It does. I do. That's all that really matters.

"It's just," I continue, "that seeing that scared the hell out of me. It's hard to imagine you not being here. To think about never having met you. Because you're pretty awesome."

Finally—finally—she smiles. It's tiny, but it's there. "You have no idea how much I needed to hear that tonight."

She shivers, and I unzip my camo jacket and wrap it around her shoulders. Her smile stretches a little more as she slides her arms into the way-too-huge-for-her sleeves. I grasp her hands and pull her toward me and rub her arms, trying to warm her some more. Her eyes are full of secrets, full of trouble, full of pain, but there's a twinkle of light in there. A month ago, I was convinced I couldn't have room in my life for a girl. Now I wish to all that's holy that she would make room for me.

"Maybe you should take some time to think about this." She gestures to herself. "About me, I guess? About whether you're sure dealing with me is worth the moments like this one when I melt. Because sometimes, I do melt. This wasn't the first time, and it won't be the last."

I'm not sure about what the heck is in the future. What I am sure about is the girl standing in front of me, right here and right now, and the way she makes me want more. I want more seconds, more minutes, more and more hours with her.

So when I tell her, "You're so, so worth it," I mean every word.

She gazes up at me, her lips slightly parted. "Thank you," she whispers.

"For what?"

"For staying here. For looking at me. Most people—most stop looking."

Ah, hell. I wrap my arms around her, bringing her to me for a hug. She rests her head against my chest, and I swear I hear her sniffle, which tears me all to pieces. My hold on her tightens, and when her arms wrap around my waist, I'm convinced that I'll never stop looking, as long as it's okay with her.

Resting my chin on top of her head, I say, "Well, I promised to be one hell of a friend. Here you go."

She laughs, a genuine Marisa-laugh, as she backs away just enough to look up at me. "You're doing a good job." With a heavy sigh, she glances over at the pond. "We should go. This is gorgeous, but I'm not a fan of pneumonia. I never should've gotten out of the truck."

"Your parents aren't freakin' out right now, are they?"

She shakes her head. "I texted them on the way up here, telling them that I ran into a friend. It took a whole lot of begging for them to agree on my being alone tonight, but—" She bites her lip. "I'm sure they feel much better, knowing I'm with someone now."

"And are you? Okay with me, I mean?"

"Yeah. I am. Because you're one hell of a friend." She backs out of my hold and turns, heading for the truck. As I fall into step behind her, I can't help but think that her arm isn't the only thing that was wrong tonight. Maybe she'll tell me one day. After all, we've got plenty of time.

chapter eleven

You know the number one sign that you're, like, ten feet off the ground for someone? When you text her all day, every day, for two weeks, even though you see her most of those days. Even when you wake up at one in the morning because your phone buzzes with a new message. I never thought that I'd be That Guy. Hell, I'll just say it: I'm whipped. And it's even more pathetic than usual because she isn't my girlfriend. She doesn't even *want* to be my girlfriend. But she likes me. And I like her. So that's as good a start as any.

The sun's dipping behind the trees as practice winds down. All the other guys hit the parking lot while I walk around the diamond, picking up the bases, and Brett and Eric look for the balls that sailed over the back fence. One more week until those bleachers open up to the public. One more week until we get down to business. One more God-blessed week.

With the bases tucked under my arm, I head back to the dugout, where Coach stands at its opening. I nod to him as he steps to the side, making room for me to drop the bases into the dugout's storage closet.

"You looked good out there today," he says. "That arm's lookin' sharp. A lot better than the first day of tryouts. Had me a little worried."

Because that was before I'd found my own personal Chemistry genius. I close the closet's door and toss him the key. "Thank you, sir. Chem had me riled up, but I've got it under control."

He watches me grab my gear bag. "I got the copy of your report card. I'm proud of you. I wouldn't want anyone else on the mound next week. Make sure you keep it up." He looks out to the field, where Eric and Brett are walking our way with the ball bucket. "Eric's good," he says, "but you've got your head in the game. He's got a lot of growin' up to do before he's a solid starter, you know?"

"Yes, sir," I reply, and I do know. Eric's a good buddy, but he's a pro at being in the wrong place at the wrong time. You can't lead a team when you're either drunk or locked up in a jail cell every other weekend. There's a time and place for everything. A starter needs to know which battles are worth fighting.

"You doing all right?" he asks, his voice lower. "You and your momma got everything you need?"

"We do. We're good."

"Y'all ever need anything, just ask." He slaps my back, his hand lingering until I step onto the field. Now, time to grab dinner and head to the shop. I'm in for a long, long night of homework if I want to keep the grades that Coach is so proud of. I sling my gear bag over my shoulder and follow him toward the gate.

"Austin?"

I trip over my own feet. Coach grabs my elbow, keeping me upright while Marisa, clearly trying to hold back a laugh, waves to me from the other side of the fence. What the hell is she doing here? She should be working. Coach holds the fence's door open for her, grinning as she walks by.

"Not too long, Braxton," he says, sliding on his sunglasses. "You got homework to do, yeah?"

"Yes, sir." But if my tutor's out here, can't that count as homework? Tilting my head to the side, I shift my bag's strap and ask Marisa, "Not that I'm complaining, but what're you doing here?"

She runs a hand through her hair, which is a mess of waves. "Your mom let me off early."

"Slacker."

She laughs. "So," she says, looking at the ground, "I thought I'd come see you. See where the magic happens." She peers up at me through those lashes, a smile creeping across her face.

She got off early and came all the way here to see *me*? That can't be right. Or maybe I should just shut up and take a miracle when it's handed to me. "Really?" I ask.

She nods. I step to the side, allowing her to walk past me and onto the field. Brett and Eric emerge from the dugout, laughing about something until they spot us. They stop short, each holding his own gear bag. Brett cocks an eyebrow. Eric looks her up and down, nodding appreciatively.

"Nice," he drawls.

Brett smacks the back of his head and shoves him toward the fence. "Later, Braxton," he says. I stifle a laugh.

"Sorry 'bout Eric," I offer. "He's, well, Eric."

Marisa just shakes her head and starts toward home plate. I drop my bag at the fence, watching as she toes the dirt. She's meticulous about it, being careful not to get any on the actual plate.

"It's been so long since I've been on a field," she says, glancing over her shoulder. "I wanted to see the one you're always going on about. It's okay that I'm here, right?"

Crossing my arms, I walk toward her. "It's more than okay. You played? On a team, I mean?"

She nods, her gaze passing over the field. "JV softball during sophomore year. I was going to try out for varsity my junior year, but..." She trails off, holding up her arm. "You know how that went."

No, I don't. She never told me the entire story. "What position?" I ask instead.

Her smile returns as I step to her side. "Catcher."

Nice. "You know, I have a soft spot for catchers. They're the backbone of the team." Pitching a game without Jay would be like pitching without my glove.

"But pitchers control the field." She gestures to the diamond. "All this? It's like your kingdom."

Well, the girl does have a point. I look down at her. I recognize that expression on her face, the magic a player feels when he (or she) is standing at home plate. When you're standing on this field, you can hear the crowd in your ears. Feel the burn in your arm. Your pulse spikes and it's almost dizzying, the rush you get.

"Wait here," I tell her.

Her eyebrows scrunch, but I jog past her to the dugout, where Eric and Brett left the ball bucket. After grabbing one of the balls, I toss it to her. She catches it effortlessly. "Gloveless," I call from the dugout entrance. "You're a natural, Marlowe. How's your swing?"

Her face glows as she stares at the ball in her hand. "Not bad. My dad used to take me to the batting cages." She clears her throat. "We don't go anymore."

I take a detour to my bag, which is still beside the fence, and pull out my bat. If you want to gauge whether or not a girl is a true ball fan, see how comfortable she is with a bat. "Why not?"

She holds up her arm again. "I'm not the only one who carries these scars, Austin." She tosses the ball up and swipes it, mid-air. "He loves me. They both do. But I think they've forgotten that I'm still me, not some problem they've been assigned to fix." She shrugs a shoulder. "He throws himself into work. And with this new job, it's even more work. He tries, he really does, but we don't talk like we used to. Now it's all about meds or whether I'm eating so I can *take* my meds."

Bat in hand, I stop in front of her and nod in understanding. "The family dinners."

She smiles tightly. "Family dinners. Yay."

Definitely time for a distraction. I pass the bat to her, watching her face light up like a full moon on a summer night. "Now, it's a little heavy," I joke. "Think you can handle it?"

Her eyes widen. "I don't know," she says breathlessly. "I may need the help of a big, strong, baseball player. Because we both know that baseball is so superior to softball."

I shake my head. "That's not entirely true. Your balls are bigger."

We stare at each other. Stare. Stare some more. She's the first one who breaks, bursting out laughing. It's one of the best sounds I've heard in a long time.

"Here," I say, still laughing. I carefully place my hands on her hips, helping her square up over the plate. "In case, you know, you're too out of practice."

She bites back a smile. "Yeah. Because I've totally forgotten how to square up for a pitch."

"Two years is a long time." Resting my hands on her shoulders, I remind her, "And relax these. You're too stiff."

She hangs her head. "You're killin' me, Smalls."

I walked right into that one. She relaxes her shoulders. Slowly, my hands move down her arms until they rest on top of hers. They're so warm, fit so perfectly in mine that it almost hurts to let them go. But I do, because, you know, *friends*.

"There," I say on an exhale. "Ready?"

Her lips curve up. "Let me have it, Floral Prince."

My mouth drops open. "All right. No mercy, Marlowe."

I grab the ball and jog out to the mound. I gotta say, she's the prettiest batter I've ever been up against. Taking a deep breath, I wind up and let my fastball fly.

That girl smacks the hell out of the ball.

Holy... I turn, watching it sail all the way back to the fence. When I whirl back around, she grins, pointing the bat at me.

"And that's how it's done," she calls to me, setting the bat in the dirt. She wipes her hands on her jeans.

All I can do is gape. Some of the guys on our team could take a lesson from her. It's not like I thought she would be bad, but damn. I pull off my cap as I walk toward her. As soon as I tug it onto her head, she laughs.

"Are you going to have any of these left?"

"I have an endless supply." I nudge the brim of the cap, so I can see her eyes. "And you've earned that one."

She quirks her lips into this little half-smirk that makes me pure weak in the knees. Takes a step closer. Another. And another. I swallow hard. My hands ache to touch her, to pull her to me and kiss the daylights out of her.

But friends, though.

"You know," she says, "I've heard that the fastest way to a guy's heart is through a killer swing."

Self-control no longer exists. I place my hands on her hips, bringing her even closer. Her breath hitches, but she doesn't pull away. She gazes up at me like I'm the only thing that exists in the world at this moment. Which is fitting because, right now, she's all that matters. Her, and her eyes, and those lips—all of which are absolutely, positively perfect.

"You heard right," I finally say, brushing her hair over her shoulder. "But you've already done a damn good job at getting to my heart."

"That was really cheesy," she says through a grin.

"That's a step up from dorky." Closing my eyes, I lean down—

She jumps back with a yelp, and my eyes pop open. The field lights have clicked on, which I'm guessing scared the crap out of her, because she's suddenly looking like she did the night I nearly ran over her at Joyner's.

She takes a deep breath and then another as she offers me a small, apologetic smile. "Friends," she whispers.

Ouch. Again.

I force a smile. "Friends don't kiss."

She shakes her head. "Friends don't kiss."

After what she told me, what she showed me, I understand why she needs time. I get why she'd rather be safe than sorry. That said, it doesn't make this much easier.

I pick up the bat and hand it to her. "I'll grab the ball, Hammerin' Hank. You square up."

Her shoulders relax. "Keep comparing me to Hank Aaron, and I'll hit balls all night."

Next sign the girl's a true fan: she gets your Atlanta Braves references. If I'm going to have a girl friend instead of a girlfriend, I'll take this one, please. "I've got all night, girl."

chapter twelve

March 4th: the best damn day in South Carolina this year. At five o'clock on the dot, the lights lining the baseball field flash on. My adrenaline surges. It's almost show time. I swear, Opening Day is fifty times better than Christmas.

The speakers across the stadium crackle and screech as the announcers gear up inside the press box. I breathe in the cool, crisp air as I wind up and fire another warm-up pitch into Jay's glove. Coach stands behind him, watching me like a hawk. From our place in the outfield, I spot the crowd steadily pouring in from the parking lot out the corner of my eye. Resisting the urge to look up toward the bleachers, I keep my gaze on Jay, who's crouched in front of me.

Focus. Tunnel vision. For the next couple of hours, everything else needs to take a backseat.

Jay lofts the ball back, and Coach whistles sharply. My head snaps up. "You good to go?" Coach calls.

I nod once. "Yes, sir."

He jerks his thumb over his shoulder. "Y'all head over to the bench. Keep that arm warm." He turns toward the mound, where the umps are congregating.

I circle my arm as Jay and I follow him across the field, detouring to the dugout. The scent of cheapo hotdogs and nachos carries from the concession stand, while the low roar of the fans grows louder and louder. Finally, I allow myself a glance to the bleachers, which are already packed to the brim. That's a double-edged sword. The crowd's a blessing when we're winning and they're going nuts, but a curse when we're losing and their silence can burst a pitcher's eardrums. Despite their cheers, my chest clenches. This is the third Opening Day without Dad sitting right there, on the bottom bleacher. No matter how much time passes, that spot will never be the same without him.

Tunnel vision. Now isn't the time for memory lane.

Jay slaps my shoulders, kneading them as we step down into the dugout. "It's game time, Braxton. You ready?"

I maneuver through the guys, making my way past the bench. Sunflower seeds and peanut shells crunch beneath my cleats. "I was born ready," I say over my shoulder.

He chuckles. "The arm's lookin' sharp."

Can't disagree there. "It's better than ever."

"Can you smell the rain with your nose stuck so far in the air?"

I turn and shove him. He stumbles back, cackling. We plop down at the end of the bench, and he grabs my coat from the backrest.

"Breathe that in," he says, chucking the coat at me. "It's the start of our last season, bro. Damn near heartbreaking."

"Fellas," Brett drawls. "Let's do this thing." Paper cup of Gatorade in hand, he rounds the bench and settles next to Jay. Jay scoots over until his thigh brushes Brett's. Brett's fingers clench the cup, sloshing the green drink all over the dirt as his eyes dart around.

"Nobody's watchin', man," Jay murmurs. He tosses his arm across the back of the bench, behind Brett.

Clearing his throat, Brett throws the now-empty cup on the ground and relaxes against the backrest. "Last season. Ready or not, here it comes."

Shaking my head, I put the coat next to me, since we'll be up soon, anyway. "Y'all are actin' like it's over already. Don't go gettin' all misty-eyed on me now."

Brett shrugs, sprawling his legs out in front of him. "Look at it this way: I'm just skippin' to the final stage of grief. Acceptance, right?"

"Well, that's cute. Go boo-freakin-hoo somewhere else." I lean forward, resting my elbows on my knees. "Ain't nobody got time for all that."

"I can't do it anywhere else. You need a guy on third," he points out.

"I'll play third," Jay cuts in.

"You've never played third," I remind him.

He snorts. "Like it's hard."

Brett smacks the back of his head. "Screw you. You get a mask and body armor."

Jay gapes at him. "Yeah. 'Cause this guy"—he points at me—"fires ninety-four-mile-per-hour fastballs at me on the regular."

Coach waves us over to the baseline for the benediction and anthem. While Brett and Eric's little sister belts out the anthem like she's next up on *X-Factor*, I hold my cap against my chest, staring at the sky. Evening clouds are moving in, swirls of gray clashing against this crazy mix of pink and purple and blue. The crowd bursts into a symphony of cheers, bringing me back to the field. My breath catches as Brett smacks my back and the home plate ump yells, "Play ball!"

The guys and I hurry back to the dugout to gear up. I grab my glove from the bench and slide it on, breathing deeply. My pulse skyrockets, going into overdrive. The crowd roars and hollers as we line up at the dugout's opening.

The speakers crackle, and the announcer's voice booms throughout the stadium. "Welcome to a brand-new season of Lewis Creek baseball, ladies and gentlemen! Skip Harris here, along with Jerry Cox, ready to guide you through another W-filled spring."

"We're going into our sixteenth season as your view from the top," Jerry says, "and I tell you what, these boys just get better every year. Let's hear it for them as they take the field! Your first baseman: Kellen Winthrop."

Kellen darts onto the field, waving as the crowd bursts into applause again. One by one, the announcers alternate player introductions. And second by agonizing second, my heart beats faster and faster.

"Second baseman: Jackson Davis."

"Shortstop: Landon Stephens."

"Third baseman: Brett Perry."

"Right field: Randy Eldredge."

"Center field: Matt Harris."

"Left field: Chris Lincoln."

"And these final two need no introduction," Skip says with a laugh.

Freakin' finally.

There's no holding back my grin as Jay and I stand next to Coach at the dugout's opening, waiting for our cue. All-Star Duo, remember? Coach smirks and slaps my shoulder.

"Tunnel vision," he reminds me. "Take your place, son."

The opening notes of Metallica's "Enter Sandman" blast through the stadium's speakers, and the crowd damn near explodes. Jay shoves me forward.

"We're up, Sandman," he shouts above the roar. "Let's put some batters to sleep."

Damn straight.

I jog to the mound, tuning out the cheers (and jeers, thanks to the visiting Cardinals' fans). This is my safe haven. Hell, Marisa was right. It's my freakin' kingdom.

While kicking the dirt so it's just right beneath my cleats, I scan the jam-packed bleachers and grin. Red and white pom-poms shake wildly in the air. Brett and Eric's momma holds their youngest sister, Emma, who's already covered in cotton candy and yelling louder than everyone in the stands. A bunch of junior and senior girls hang over the fence, wearing Bulldogs decals on their cheeks and cheering at the tops of their lungs. Rednecks and old-timers and cheerleaders, all mingled together for the best night of the year.

I'm telling you: it's magic.

Inhaling deeply, I zero in on Jay, who's crouched behind the plate. He pulls his mask down and wiggles the fingers on his free hand, signaling he's ready when I am.

The Cardinals' lead-off hitter steps to the plate, sending the crowd into another uproar. I study his stance. Gauge the cockiness in his stare. Watch how he grips the bat. He's good.

I'm better.

When Jay signals for a curveball, I'm reminded why he's such an important part of the All-Star Duo—he reads my mind like no one else. Game on.

I fire the first pitch of the season into Jay's glove, making the batter swing like an A-Rod wannabe. He's an eager fella. After throwing the ball back, Jay signals fastball. Don't mind if I do.

Wind up. Release. The ball hits Jay's mitt with a resounding *smack.* I smirk. No chance to even swing. Time to make him chase it? Once again reading my mind, Jay signals slider. I nod once and fire it in there.

"Strike three!" the ump yells. "You're out!"

At times like this, I wish victory dances were allowed on the field. *You're out, sucker.* Jay lofts the ball back, and while the next guy steps to the plate, I glance back to the stands. This time, Brett's momma isn't wrangling Emma into her lap. Now, she's making room for the people sitting beside her.

She's making room for Momma and Marisa. It's got to be Marisa because she's the only person I've ever let wear my lucky Braves hat, and that girl sure enough wore it here. She looks up and catches my eye, beaming as she waves. I can't help but grin like a fool. I tip my cap before moving back into position. The last guy was just a warm-up. Now it's time to show her what this arm can really do.

The next batter is a beanpole, as tall as Brett and half his weight. He readies himself over the plate, glaring me down like I'm the damn devil incarnate. It's all right; two can play that game. I steady myself, watching for Jay's signal.

He says fastball. I say sure thing.

And the ump says, "Strike one!"

Smirking, I hold the batter's gaze while catching Jay's throw. Next up is a no-brainer: change-up. Jay agrees. With the ball in the back of my hand, I make sure my grip's just right. *Wind up. Pitch.*

SMACK.

The ball barrels toward me. Shit. I throw my glove in front of my face. The ball slams right into the middle. The crowd's on its feet, but all I hear is the blood slamming in my ears. Releasing a heavy breath, I force a smile to everyone pointing and cheering and clapping. A ball flying at your nose is never not scary as hell.

But another batter down. Two outs. And I still have my face. Works for me.

———

As we file into the dugout at the bottom of the seventh, I'm convinced my arm's about to fall off. It's no surprise, considering I haven't pitched seven straight innings in nearly a year, even during summer and fall ball. But dang if the thing doesn't throb like a son of a gun. Nevertheless, the score's tied at 2-2, and I'm up to bat. I *could* ask Coach to send in an alternate, but that isn't happening. *Don't fail me now, arm.*

Jay slaps my back as I tug on my helmet. "You got this, bro. Smack that ball to kingdom come, and we're knockin' back shots at the river within an hour."

Easy enough.

I grab my bat and head for the dugout's opening, where Coach waits. He gives me a quick nod. "You good?"

"Yes, sir."

He eyes me up and down. "Uniform's too clean," he says, guiding me out of the dugout. "Go get some dirt on it."

I smirk along with him. Roger that. I stride to the on-deck circle, allowing myself a quick glance to the stands. Marisa's hanging over the top of the fence with Hannah and Bri, cheering along with them. Screw the shots; I want *that* after the game. Jay's right, though. I've got to get the job done first.

After a couple practice swings, I start toward home plate, sending the crowd into a deafening uproar. It's freakin' glorious. There's no stopping my grin as I ready myself at the plate.

Until I catch sight of the pitcher. Oh, *hell* no. Staring straight at me with a smirk on his face, the scrawny punk's making a show of kicking the dirt on my mound. He's digging a *hole* in my dirt. You don't screw with a pitcher's mound, especially on his home turf. That's fightin' territory.

I narrow my eyes. He gives the mound one more kick before preparing for his pitch. All right, then. Let's fight. But he should know better than to challenge someone who knows the game better than he does.

I've been studying this guy all night. He's got a tell: he takes about two seconds longer to prep his fastball than any other pitch. He's been clinging to that precious fastball all night, and he's gearing up for another one. I square over the plate. *Windup.* He fires the ball right down the middle. I swing with all my might.

Crack.

The ball shoots toward the outfield, and I take off to first. My pulse slams as I round the bag and, with a quick peek to the outfield, take the chance. I pump my legs as hard as they'll go, drop to the dirt, and slide into second. The ball smacks against the second baseman's glove above me.

"Safe!" the ump calls.

Damn straight. Keeping a foot on the bag, I push to my feet. My white pants are smeared with dirt. Finally.

Brett strides to home plate as I hunch down, ready to take off. As our lead-off man, he's one hell of a powerhouse. *Tunnel vision. Watch. Wait.* The pitcher glances over his shoulder, keeping me in place. Once he turns, I inch off the bag. A little farther. A little farther.

Sucker.

The bat's *crack* echoes across the field. I'm already halfway to third when the ball soars over my head. A quick glance to Coach tells me to push toward home.

On it.

Push harder. Faster. The catcher's crowding the plate, his glove at the ready. I slide into home beneath him, dirt flying everywhere. The tag hits my chest right as the ump yells, "Safe!"

Game.

I jump to my feet. Brett trots toward the plate and high-fives me. And out of nowhere the guys are crowding around us, hootin' and hollerin' and slappin' places hands have no right slappin', but whatever.

We fall into our post-game lineup. The Cardinals do the same, and our teams make our ways toward one another. We shake hands down the line, muttering, "Good game," over and over like a chant.

Our team spills into the dugout, the cheers of the crowd still ringing in my ears. I grab a towel and wipe off the sweat and grime covering my face. When I toss it into the pile of other nasty towels behind the bench, I see *him* talking to Coach Taylor next to the dugout. *Him*, as in USC's Coach Barlow.

And now I'm sweating in places I didn't even know had glands. He shouldn't make me nervous. I've met him plenty of times and he'll be my coach in a few months, but I didn't realize he'd be here today. It's a good thing I didn't see him until now, or I would've been all out of sorts. Slinging my bag over my shoulder, I squeeze through the guys and make my way toward him. Coach Taylor spots me first and curves his finger, signaling me over.

Coach Barlow turns as I approach, a huge smile on his face. He nudges the brim of his cap and holds out his hand. "Here's my man," he exclaims. "Hell of a game out there, Braxton."

I shake his hand firmly. "Thank you, sir. Didn't know you'd be here."

He waves me off. "Our boys had an off day, so I thought I'd drop in and check on my new right-hander. I can't remember the last time I saw someone end a game just as strong as he started."

My cheeks flush. I manage a nod and another, "Thank you, sir."

He nods toward Coach Taylor. "This old man tells me you're workin' your backside off. That's what I like to hear. Keep it up, yeah?"

"Yes, sir."

He turns back to Coach Taylor, who jerks his head to the side. Guess I'm done here. Spinning on my heel,

I search the crowd. Marisa's still by the fence, talking to Hannah and Bri. She's smiling and laughing and looking like she fits right in, which doesn't shock me at all. The girl's pretty awesome.

I head her way, stopping just short of the group so I don't interrupt whatever it is they're goin' on about. But her smile grows when she sees me, shining brighter than all the field lights combined.

Bri stops talking when she notices Marisa's stopped listening. She glances over her shoulder, spotting me. "Hey, hotshot," she says. "Good game." Her gaze darts from me to Marisa as she grabs Hannah's hand. "We'll get going. Nice meeting you, Marisa!" There's no doubt that Hannah wants to play Twenty Questions, but she stumbles after Bri.

Marisa calls out a "bye" before jumping up and wrapping her arms around my neck, surprising the hell out of me. I stumble, but laugh and wrap my own arms around her waist, holding her close.

"You were *amazing!*" she squeals, pulling back. "Seriously, Austin. Seriously."

"Seriously?"

She pushes me, still smiling from ear to ear. "That hug was okay, right? I mean, I don't want to embarrass you in front of your friends."

"Okay? Girl, if that's what a win gets me, I need to pitch every game this season." I wrap my arm around her, pulling her in for a side-hug. Everything else disappears; there's no cheering, no whoops, no pats on the back. All that matters is the way she fits perfectly beside me, and the fact that I can't do a damn thing about it.

Being crazy about one of your friends is great, until it's not. Soon, it actually starts to hurt. But telling her that would only hurt *her*, and that's out of the question.

She squeezes me back, snapping me to reality. "Hey," she says. "You all right?"

I grin and say, "Hell yeah, I'm all right," and she rolls her eyes and laughs before giving me one last hug, because that's what friends do. And besides, I am all right.

I am.

As she pulls away, I glance over my shoulder, catching Hannah and Bri staring and pointing from the parking lot. Hannah grins and waves. Marisa returns it with a weak wave of her own.

"Yeah," she drawls, dropping her hand. "How should I feel about them? Bri seems nice, but I'm not sure if Hannah's *nice*-nice or Regina George-nice."

Not entirely sure who Regina George is, but Hannah's harmless. A little overly excited, maybe, but harmless. "Hannah's good people. And she's a great one-girl cheering squad."

Marisa nods slowly. "I think she makes her tea with glitter instead of sugar. Maybe that's her secret to being so, um, *her*."

I snort. That's the most accurate description of Hannah in history.

Someone's car lets out a long, annoying honk. I whip my head to the side. Jay and Brett pile into Brett's Jeep, waving at me.

"River!" Jay yells. "Ass in motion!"

Marisa laughs. I wish I could laugh, but now it's time for her to go, and I really don't want that to happen. I look her up and down, unable to hold back my smile, and as she backs away one tiny step at a time, she returns it with one of her own.

"I should get home, anyway," she says. "Parents. Dinner. You know the drill." She offers a small wave. "Have fun." And just like that, she's gone. Now I'm not even sure if I want to go to the river. But tradition trumps throwing myself a pity party, so instead of pouting, I head to my truck.

By the time I reach the river, the sun's gone and darkness is inching its way over town. For years, our team's claimed the wooded area for drinking, parties, and, well, more drinking. There's a clearing that's perfect for nights like tonight, when a dozen trucks are crowded along the riverbank.

I back my own tailgate up to the water's edge. After changing into gym shorts and a clean T-shirt in my driver's seat, I hop out of the truck. Everyone else beat me here. Brett and Eric have already broken out their old, cheapo lawn chairs and formed them in a circle next to the riverbank. Right Field Randy's got his truck's KC lights on, shining like a blinding spotlight on our patch of woods. Matt jumps into the bed of his truck and tugs his jumbo-sized cooler to the edge of the tailgate. He pulls out a few beers, tossing cans to Randy and Eric. He looks to me, but I hold up my hands.

"It's Monday," I remind him.

Jay appears at his side and slaps him on the shoulder. "You know good and well Braxton doesn't drink during the week." He snatches the can. "I, on the other hand, do."

Jay digs a bottle of water out of Matt's cooler and tosses it to me. I'm surprised Matt bothered to bring water, but I'm damn grateful. I twist off the top and chug half the bottle. Beer's one of God's greatest gifts to mankind, but the last thing I need is a hangover during tomorrow's practice.

Someone cranks up his truck's radio, sending Kenny Chesney blaring through its speakers. I head for the circle of chairs, where Kellen, Randy, Brett, Jay, and Matt are sitting. Matt lifts his chin to me.

"You've been keeping secrets, Braxton," he says as I sit in an empty chair beside Brett.

The chair's threading sinks beneath me, barely holding my weight. This thing's been through its share of river parties. I gulp more water. "What're you talking about?"

Randy takes a swig of beer. "The girl. We saw you hangin' all over that hot brunette. You bangin' her?"

Kellen smacks the back of his head. "Your momma would beat your ass for that. Braxton ought to, too."

And Braxton really, really wants to. My bottle crackles as I squeeze it instead of the grease ball in front of me. "I'll bang your damn head against my truck if you say somethin' like that again, you hear me?"

He settles back in his chair, sprawling his legs in front of him. "All right, so you got shot down. That's all you had to say."

I drop the bottle onto the ground and rub my forehead, squeezing my eyes closed. Can't kill him. Killing him would lead to jail, and jail's no good. Why does not being with a girl automatically equal getting shot down? There is a middle. Douchebag.

Kellen leans forward, resting his elbows on his legs. He gestures to me, Brett, and Jay. "It's y'all's last season. Any of you crying about it yet?"

"Nope," the three of us say at once.

Jay, who's sitting on the other side of Brett, stretches out his legs. "Don't know about these guys, but I'm flipping Lewis Creek the bird on my way out. Peace out, assholes."

That covers it. "Big fat ditto," I say.

Kellen chuckles and nods to Brett. "Perry?"

Brett holds up his can. "I'll drink to that."

"Ah, come on," Randy says. "It can't be that bad. You bastards run this town."

"I'll drink to that, too," Brett says, sipping his beer.

I laugh along with the rest of them. Randy's right— we do run this town. It's like Coach said on the first day of practice: in Lewis Creek, we're on pedestals. We're heroes. And that's all well and good, but hero status comes with a price. From tonight until the end of the season, we'll be tracked more closely than fourteen-point bucks. Come August, we'll have paid our dues to the baseball gods and then some. We deserve to break out of this place.

I glance over to Brett and Jay, who're whispering to each other. Brett laughs and settles back in his chair, grinning. Them, I'll miss like hell.

"Gentlemen! I need your attention."

What the hell? I turn to see Eric standing at the edge of the dock, a few yards down. The sophomore guys are lined up in front of him, and—wait. Are they...?

Yes. Yes, they are in their boxers. It's initiation time, fellas.

Eric tips back his beer, chugging it before chucking the can into the grass. "I'm here to officially initiate the new Bulldogs of Lewis Creek varsity baseball." He turns to the sophomores and holds out his arms, gesturing to the water behind him. "You're not a true varsity Bulldog until you've gone balls to the wall. Or in this case, balls to the water. Luckily, I'm here to guide you." He twirls his hand, like he's waiting for a response. "Y'all should be thanking me. Get with it."

All of us burst out laughing. Every single one of us has landed in that river at some point. It's a rite of passage. At least Eric's letting them keep their boxers. Jay, Brett, and I had to let it all hang. And that water's damn cold in March.

Eric steps to the side. When the others remain still, Eric waves them forward. "Don't be shy. You heard Coach; we're your brothers."

Maybe I'll miss Eric a little, too.

I cup my hands around my mouth. "It's family bonding, boys. Get in the water!"

The first guy, Chris, steps onto the dock. He breaks into a run and, with a flying jump, splashes into the river. We clap along with Eric, who signals for the next guy. One by one, they leap into the bone-chilling water. And one by one, they learn what it takes to be a Bulldog: trust, with a healthy dose of humiliation.

chapter thirteen

Marisa's waiting for me in the parking lot once practice wraps up on Friday night. I have no idea why she's at the field instead of the shop, which is where she was, you know, hired to be. Not that I'm complaining, but Momma doesn't even let me out early when I work. Doesn't make much sense.

The other guys scatter as we exit the field and spill out into the parking lot. Marisa waves to Jay, Brett, and Eric, who all pile into Brett's Jeep. Engines fire up and tires screech out of the lot as I head toward her.

"Hey," I say, tossing my gear bag into the bed of my truck. "Managed to escape early?"

She pulls the hair-tie out of her knot, letting her waves spill across her shoulders. "Your mom kicked me out," she says, ruffling her hair. "She said I was working too hard."

Yeah, that's really not like Momma. "What were you doing?"

"Sitting on the stool. Listening to the coolers come on. Shut off. Come on again. Repeat for about three hours. It's fascinating stuff."

I laugh along with her, even though I need to ask about this. But again, not complaining about extra Marisa time. I'll take it whenever I can.

"So you got off work early and then came all the way here instead of going home?" She glares, one of those "I hate you for pointing that out" looks. I hold up my hands. "Can't a guy ask a question?"

She runs a hand through her hair again. "I was thinking," she says, playing with the ends, "that maybe we could get an early start on this weekend's tutoring session. Study both tonight and tomorrow. You have your book, right?"

Folding my arms, I lean back against my truck. She blinks quickly, not quite meeting my gaze. My lips curve up. She's so busted. "Let me get this straight: it's Friday night. We have an entire night ahead of us. And you want to study? You're an awful liar, Marlowe."

She eyes me up and down. Crosses her own arms. Finally she sighs and says, "Fine. I have ulterior motives."

"If it involves moonshine and skinny-dipping, it's so on."

Her jaw drops. She blushes as she looks around, but there's no one out here but the two of us. "No," she drawls. "And what makes you think I'd go skinny-dipping with you?"

Wishful thinking never killed anybody.

"It's something the one customer I had today mentioned," she continues. "She said there's this thing they do down at the riverfront. Some kind of movie night? Asked if I was going."

When a town doesn't even have a movie theater, people get creative when it comes to entertainment. It's something I've only been to once, though.

"They have something down at Mariners' Wharf. It's kind of cool, I guess. Everyone brings blankets, picnic baskets, and watches whatever movie they're playing. It's usually ancient, but it's something." *Wait a second.* Shoving off my truck, I ask, "Are you asking me on a date, Marisa?"

Dear Lord in heaven above, I think she just asked me on a date.

That earns me another "I hate you and your guts" glare. "I like food," she says as I step toward her. "And I like movies. And I like you. So I'm asking if you, my best friend in this tiny town, would like to go see an ancient movie with me on a Friday night."

If anyone else was standing in front of me, asking me to go see what's probably a fifty-year-old movie on Friday night, you'd have to drag me kicking and screaming. But it's Marisa, so hell to the yes, I'll go.

I twirl my keys. "I'm game. You ridin' with me or driving your car?"

Her gaze darts between me and my truck. She bites her lip. Blinks. Looks back to the truck.

I grin again. This is legit fan-freakin-tastic. *Be cool, Braxton. Don't blow this.* "Don't be all shy. If you wanna ride with me, all you got to do is say so."

Please say so.

She points at me. "Austin, I am warning you—"

I hold out my arms. "What? Just admit it: you dig the truck."

She rolls her eyes. "All right, fine. I dig the truck, okay?"

I do love her honesty.

"See?" I say, opening the door for her. "That wasn't so hard. Hop on in."

She growls at me. The girl actually growls at me while climbing up. I thought that was reserved for animals, but whatever. I tilt my head to the side. Good God almighty, those jeans—

"Stop staring at my butt, Austin."

Damn.

I round the truck and get into my own seat. I fire up the engine while she types out something on her phone.

"My parents," she says when I glance over. "So they don't wonder where the heck I'm at."

Nodding, I pull out of the parking lot and onto the road leading to town. It's weird; she's eighteen and probably has a tighter leash on her than most freshmen. I understand, I guess, but that's got to suck. I mean, she's good now. She said so herself.

But in a few months, she'll be in Columbia, at USC. With me. *That's* gonna be awesome.

"They like you, you know," she says. "They think you're *so* polite and *so* responsible and *such* a great influence."

I narrow my eyes. "What makes me think you disagree?"

She shrugs a shoulder. "Not saying that. Just saying that you're more than polite and responsible."

Stopping at a red light, I relax back against my seat. "Oh, yeah? Like what? Feed my ego here."

"Your ego's big enough." She looks out her window, trying to be sneaky about her grin. Unfortunately for her, her reflection in the glass gives her away.

"It's not that big," I argue as the light turns green. "It's small. Barely there."

She laughs. "That's what she said," she singsongs.

I glance over. She just smiles and looks out the windshield. Now my ego really is barely there.

After grabbing burgers from Sammy's, we drive out to Mariners' Wharf. The wharf is a long dock that stretches across the riverfront. This half of the river is reserved for families and older folks. The other half, the wooded area, is for the rowdy crowd, which'll be out in full force in a few hours. I would say I'd miss it, but—

"Austin," Marisa says as I park on the road, among the dozens of other cars. "I'm so excited I cannot even. I've lost all ability to even." She grabs our bag of food from the floorboard and hops out onto the road, not even waiting for me to cut the engine.

That makes it worth missing.

"Wait for me, girl," I call to her, stepping onto the sidewalk. "We've got plenty of time."

She walks over to me, holding the bag to her chest while bouncing in place. You'd think we were going to a Braves game instead of watching a movie. I reach into my truck's toolbox and pull out the blue flannel blanket.

She raises an eyebrow. "You keep a blanket in your truck?"

What's that look for? I slam the toolbox closed. "It's for emergencies, of course."

She shakes her head, smiling. "Right. Of course." She grabs my hand, tugging me to her. Her eyes shine as she says, "Now let's go."

As long as she holds my hand, I'll go anywhere she takes me. We jog toward the riverfront, her shoes pounding against the pavement as she leads the way. The lawn is already covered with blankets. There's a low hum of people talking, but other than that, it's quiet. Peaceful. Lights are strung across the railing that runs alongside the pier, where the boats are docked for the night. It's weird, seeing this part of the water at night. When I come out here with the guys, we stick to the woods. Less of an audience down there. And when you add in drinks, music, and a bunch of rednecks with jacked-up trucks, it gets a lot louder.

We find a small patch of empty grass near the back edge of the lawn. As soon as I lay out the blanket, Marisa plops down and digs into our bag.

I sit beside her, bending my knees. "I don't think I've ever seen anyone so excited for a movie."

She hands me my burger and shrugs while opening the wrapper on hers. "Normal is something I've always dreamed of." She gestures to the screen, which isn't much more than a sheet hung on the side of Murray's Mattresses. "This? A movie, burgers, and a night by the river with one of the sweetest guys in town? This is normal."

Her gaze locks on something behind me. She nods subtly, signaling for me to look. I turn just as old Mr. Joyner, the owner of Joyner's BBQ, squats in the grass. He nods to Marisa and pats me on the shoulder.

"How ya doin', son?"

I shake his outstretched hand. Because a shoulder-pat is never enough, obviously. "Hey, Mr. Joyner. I'm good, thanks."

"That was a hell of a game you boys played last night."

I smile. "Thank you, sir. Had a blast winnin' it."

He laughs, the booming sound echoing around us. "You looked a lot like your old man out there. That change-up? Outstanding."

My jaw clenches. I nod once. Drop my burger onto the blanket. Appetite officially lost.

"He would've been proud of that game. Reminded me of the no-hitters he pitched back in his day. Shame about his shoulder, huh?"

He waits, expecting an answer. I muster a "Yes, sir. Real shame."

He shakes his head. "Y'all got that game against Beaufort coming up at the end of the month. Think this'll be the end of that losing streak? You know, back when I was pitchin' for the Bulldogs, a man's curveball was the game-changer. I've got a few ideas about yours—"

Music from the movie starts, sounding throughout the lawn. He mutters a swear and pushes himself up. "Better get back to Doris. You kids enjoy the show." With one last pat on my shoulder, he waves to Marisa before heading across the lawn.

My dad died over two years ago, but he's still all over this town. He taught me how to throw, how to catch, how to bat. He taught me how to shake hands after a loss and congratulate the other team after a win. He brought me to the game. I owe my future to him. But it's hard to be grateful when he won't be around to see that future. When your worst memory is thrown in your face every day, it's enough to drive you up a damn wall.

Marisa places her hand on top of mine. "It's not that bad, is it?"

I stare at our hands. I want to grab hers and squeeze it tight, but—friends. "Just another reason why I'm countin' the days until I leave for Columbia."

"Slow down," she says. "Stop living every moment waiting for the next. Enjoy each moment. Make memories."

That'd be easier if the worst memories weren't the loudest. I've had some good times in this town, but the God-awful moments always manage to shove their way to the front of the line.

I look up at her. She holds my gaze, her own full of hope and sweetness and something I can't really place. She inhales sharply and her hand disappears, making mine feel cold and lonely. She scoots closer. Closer. Closer, until her outstretched legs brush against mine. And finally, she rests her head on my shoulder.

Okay.

Hoping I'm not making a killer mistake, I drape my arm across her shoulders. She wraps her arm around my lower back.

These moments? They're pretty darn good. I'll take more of these.

The movie starts up on the screen. I have no clue what it is, other than it's some black-and-white movie that probably is, in fact, fifty years old. But that's not what matters. All that matters is the girl curled into my side. She said she wants to be friends, that she wants safety. I'll be her safety net for as long as she needs me.

"Can I ask you a question?" she whispers.

"What?" I whisper back.

Silence. I look down, catching her already watching me. I narrow my eyes. "What is it?" I ask. "Is it the arm? 'Cause I can move the arm."

She shakes her head. "No. Um...I was just wondering something." She chews on her bottom lip. Glances at mine. "What happens when friends kiss?"

Holy— My heart slams against my chest. "I—I think it makes them a little more than friends."

She nods once. Looks at the movie screen. Takes my breath right along with her.

I can be friends. I can do the friend thing, if that's what she wants. But damn it, I'm not even gonna lie. If that girl kisses me or even *wants* to kiss me—

"Austin?" she says.

I swallow hard. "Yeah?"

She turns back to me, the tiniest of smiles playing on her lips. "Can we be a little more than friends?"

Hell. Yes. We can.

Rein it in, Braxton.

I lean down, resting my forehead against hers while fighting the biggest grin I've ever had. "You're sure?" I ask. This is her call. She wanted to take it slow, and I'll take it slow as molasses if she wants. Or I'll kiss the daylights out of her. Either way, I'm good.

Her smile widens, the sweetest smile I've ever seen on that face. And her lips are on mine, soft and sweet and so. Damn. Perfect. Hugging her even tighter, I close my eyes, memorizing every curve of those lips. These moments? These are the ones worth remembering.

She pulls away slightly, just enough to look into my eyes. Her smile's still there, gorgeous as ever. "I like being more than friends."

Home freakin' run.

I run my hand through her hair and bring her back to me, pressing my lips to hers again. Seconds, please. And thirds. Fourths. Fifths. As many as she'll give me.

Maybe memories don't always have to be so bad.

chapter fourteen

On our way back from the cemetery on Sunday afternoon, Momma won't even look at me. It's the first time we've been to Dad's grave together since Christmas, and this visit went about as well as the last. After I pull my truck into the driveway, she stays put in the passenger seat, staring at our house through the windshield. Her disappointment is kind of a given. I just wish she'd say something, anything, because the silent treatment is the worst punishment ever created.

"Momma," I venture. "I'm sorry."

She scoffs. Shakes her head. Keeps her eyes trained on our house, the same house that Dad's dad, my papa, built with his bare hands. And I'm sure she's thinking about that, about how our house is full of so much heart and so many memories, and wondering how I can be so insensitive about my own dad's memory, especially on his birthday.

Her words from earlier. Not mine.

"I can't do it," I continue, loosening the collar on my button-down church shirt. "I know today's his birthday, and I'm sorry. I'm so sorry, and I tried, but I can't get out of the truck at his grave. I can't—" I sigh. *I can't mourn someone I half-hate.* But I'm not going to tell her that. "I just can't."

She nods slowly, as if she's thinking about my words, and unbuckles her seatbelt. "I know you're still having a rough time with this. But at the end of the day, he's still your daddy. One day, you'll regret holding on to the bitterness. It'll eat you alive."

It's not the first time she's told me that. It won't be the last. "I think I have a right to be pissed—"

She cuts me off with The Look. You know the one: the one that says to shut your mouth while you have the chance. She shifts in her seat, facing me. "You listen to me right now, Austin Michael, and you listen real, real good. You need people in your life. People you can count on, people who love you, people who *you* love. And when you find those people, you hold on to them for dear life. That's why I still hold on to your daddy, and that's why I make sure you get time with your friends. With Marisa."

Oh.

"The way your daddy left this earth was horrible," she says. "I don't understand why, and I know you don't either. But don't you dare, for one second, speak ill of him now that he's gone. Maybe you should think about the years he spent teaching you how to throw a ball. Think about every single one of those games he showed up to since you started T-ball. Think about how that man used to be your idol. Think about how you were *his* everything."

My throat tightens. I can't think about those things. I can't, because they'd reduce me to a pathetic, sobbing mess. And I clearly wasn't his everything, considering I wasn't enough for him to stick around.

"Do you hear me?" she asks.

Say something. Say anything. "I—"

"I said, do you hear me?"

I nod once. "Yes, ma'am."

She gets out of the truck without another word, not that there's anything left to say. I bang my head on the steering wheel. There's no way in hell I'm going into that house for a while. I'd rather take my chances in hell, actually. Satan would be more welcoming.

I pull my phone out of the pocket of my khakis and scroll through until I find Marisa's number.

Need to go somewhere. Wanna drive with me? Flopping back against my seat, I hit Send and wait.

Friday night was amazing. Marisa was amazing. Everything about the night was straight out of a dream or something. I never thought a kiss could be so flawless, so perfect, so damn addicting, but she went beyond proving me wrong.

My phone lights up. **Marisa**: *Dad says no bc we're going to church tonight.*

Dang it, it's not even four o'clock yet. This day will never end if I don't have something to do. *How about the batting cages? Even bring the guys if it makes him feel better. Be done by church time.* While I wait for her to answer, I send out a text to Jay, Brett, and Eric, telling them to get to The Strike Zone. I don't even need a reply from them; those three have never turned down an invite to the cages. And I'm going whether or not Marisa does. Smacking the hell out of a ball is better than therapy.

Right as I hit Send to them, her message comes in. *Sure. Meet u there.*

What? Uh-uh. *I'll pick u up*, I type back quickly.

Marisa: *Already in town with parents. They'll take me.* =)

Oh. Okay, then. I back out of my driveway and head across town, which is quiet thanks to it being Sunday. There are only three cars in the parking lot at The Strike Zone, one of them belonging to Marisa's parents. She hops out of their car right as I park.

"You can drive me to church, right?" she asks while I step out of the truck.

Uh, yeah. Duh. Her mom's window is down, so I call out, "I'll get her there, Mrs. Marlowe. No worries."

Her mom smiles, and Dr. Marlowe leans across her to say, "Not too late."

Backing away from their car, Marisa waves. "I'll be fine. Bye, guys."

As they pull out of the lot, Marisa walks over to me, all smiles in her bright green dress and jean jacket. "We were eating at Baker's Grill when you texted. You have good timing." She slides her hands into mine and leans up to kiss me. Yep. Still perfect. "Are your friends coming, or—?"

"They're coming. Just takin' their sweet time." I search the parking lot and look out to the road, but there's still no sign of them. "You want to wait out here, inside, or in the truck?"

She looks past me to my truck. "Definitely the truck."

Pursing my lips, I nod. "Well, well, well. Looks like we may have a country girl convert."

She holds up her hands. "I'm not saying that. I'm just saying that you were right: I do dig the truck." She climbs up into the passenger seat while I circle around to my side. "And you're sure your friends won't mind that I'm here?" she asks as I close my door.

Yeah, right. They might like her more than they like me. "Trust me. But maybe this'll help." I reach into the backseat, feeling around the floorboard until I grab my USC hoodie. "Here," I say, handing it to her. "Now you can be one of the guys. And it's garnet, just like our team colors. You'll fit right in."

She rolls her eyes, but shrugs off her jacket anyway. My heart jumps into my throat. For the first time since that night at the pond, her scars are out in the open. She doesn't notice me staring, thank God. She tugs on the hoodie, laughing when it practically swallows her whole.

"Dude," she says. "You're a giant."

"I'm not that tall. You're just that short."

She swats my arm and settles back against her seat, kicking her boots up on the dashboard. "I wish I'd known you were coming into town. I would've invited you to eat with me and my parents."

I shake my head. "Nah. I wouldn't have been able to come anyway. I had—" I clear my throat. "I had a thing today."

Looking down at my lap, I force away the thought of nearly making my momma cry, again, in the exact seat that Marisa's sitting in. I'll be the first to admit it: I'm a momma's boy. She was my best friend for a long, long time, and she's been my number one fan from day one. The last thing I want to do is make the woman upset. But it ties with the other last thing I want to do, which is getting out of my truck when we're at the cemetery. It's a vicious cycle.

"Do you want the whole truth and nothing but the truth?" Marisa asks.

I'm about to ask what she's talking about when I realize I'm flat-out staring at her wrists. Crap. I look up at her, but she doesn't seem bothered at all. I grab her hand, lacing my fingers through hers.

"I'm sorry. I didn't mean to—" Hanging my head, I groan. This day keeps getting better. "I'm sorry."

She pushes up her sleeve on the arm of the hand I'm holding—*the* arm. "It's okay. We're more than friends now, right? And more-than-friends should know these things."

I nod, urging her to go on. Ready or not, here comes the truth, I guess.

"The night you picked me up was the one-year anniversary of all this," she says, holding up her arm.

I don't think I can handle the truth.

"It's weird," she continues, "and you'll probably think I'm a freak, but that night is kind of like a birthday,

I guess? I wanted it to be a celebration. It didn't exactly pan out like a celebration, considering I cried my eyes out until you picked me up, but whatever. A girl can try."

Really don't think I can handle it. "You're losing me already," I admit, my voice cracking. *Keep it together, Braxton.* "I thought your birthday was in December."

She lets out a breathless laugh. "'Kay. From the beginning. I've had depression for as long as I can remember. It's something I've always just kind of dealt with, you know?"

Not at all, but I nod anyway.

Her gaze falls to our fingers, which are still entwined. "Last year, I spiraled downhill. Way downhill. At, like, supersonic speed." She presses her lips together, her cheeks flushing. I squeeze her hand gently, hoping it gives her some sort of relief. "I was in the bathroom," she continues softly, "exactly like some stupid clichéd movie scene. I was curled up in the bathtub, sobbing my eyes out, with the shower pounding on me. The water had gone Arctic-cold. I remember praying for God to make it hot again because I was too weak to turn it off. You see, there's this darkness that comes with rock bottom. It sucks you in like a black hole. It just—it swallowed me whole."

Her eyes meet mine again. My heart stutters at the pain there. I can't imagine. I don't want to imagine.

"It hurts," she whispers. "You have no idea how much it hurts when that happens." She sniffles. Shakes her head. "All I wanted was for the pain to go away, no matter what it took. The razor was there, and something inside me snapped. That's the only way I know how to describe it. My parents found me right on time, but it was—" She pauses. "It was bad. A mess."

Red clouds my vision. All I can see is Marisa covered in blood. Marisa's parents freaking the eff out. Marisa not breathing. And now I can't breathe. I. Can. Not. Breathe. God, please don't let her notice.

"Breathe, Austin." She gestures for me to take a deep breath, which I do.

This has nothing to do with me. This is her story, the weight on her shoulders, the scars she carries around. But damn it, my heart is downright clenching at the thought of her hurting.

"I'm going to sound like a dick for this," I say, "but how the heck is something like that even close to a birthday? It sounds more like a..." I can't even finish.

"A funeral?" She smiles, surprising the hell out of me. "You're not a dick. You sound like my mom. And that's why I didn't want to go home that night. We would've had our usual family dinner, except it would have been silent, with my parents trying their best to not slip up and say something that might trigger me. Being alone was infinitely better." She pauses, then adds, "Until you came along."

This strange look comes to her face, almost peaceful. Content. And I have no idea how someone can talk about the night she nearly died with a smile on her face.

"That night last year," she says, "I was kept in the world for a reason, I think. And while I was in a hospital bed, covered in bandages and being force-fed medicine and treated like a complete psycho, I felt more at peace than I ever have in my life because I was a survivor. That's the night I decided to really live my life, not just exist. Therefore, my birthday."

I hold her gaze, my heart racing and my hands shaking and my breaths refusing to come yet again. I want to cry. I want to hug her. I want to tell her that I don't ever want to hear about anything bad happening to her again. For a split second, I want to say that I don't have a damn clue why someone would intentionally hurt herself.

Or himself. Especially when they have people who love them more than anything.

But the difference between her and my dad is that she's here. She's alive and she's here and she's real, holding my hand and breathing the same air as me. And now I'm breathing again. My heartbeat steadies. The shaking subsides. I see a girl who knows pain, true pain, on the inside and out. She's tougher than I could ever dream of being. She saved herself.

"Austin?" she whispers. "Please say something."

My mouth opens, but no words come. I clear my throat and try again. "Is that why you moved?" I ask. "Why you moved here?"

Relief floods her face. "Yeah. Sort of. People are vicious. My softball girls, the ones I would've trusted with my life? When I got out of the hospital, they were the worst. The phone calls, the words scribbled on my locker, the pushing in the hallways. It was too much for me to handle. Mom started the homeschooling thing, but a few of them decided they weren't done. That's when they came to our house."

My eyes widen. "They went to your freakin' house? Are you kiddin' me?"

She shakes her head. "Nope. They TP-ed the place, smashed eggs on our cars." She barks out a laugh. "My favorite was when they spray-painted PSYCHO on the front door. That was fun." Her gaze grows distant as she looks out her window. Brett's Jeep roars into the parking lot, with Jay's car close behind. "My parents grew up down here. Dad's from Dillon and Mom's from Summerville. So when I decided on USC, they figured what the heck? Let's all move, sooner rather than later."

Brett pulls into the spot next to mine. He blares the horn and tosses up a wave just as Jay swerves into the spot in front of his. Marisa hangs her head, pulling her sleeve back down.

"So now I have no locks on my doors," she says on an exhale. "I have to take my meds in front of them every day. As long as I do that and stay on top of therapy, they're okay with giving me some space, letting me go little by little. But..." She shrugs. "Like I told you before, it's hard for them, too."

My mouth hangs open. "You make my problems sound like shit. And I mean that in the nicest way possible."

She places her hand on my cheek, running her thumb across my skin. Everything inside me melts faster than a snowball in hell. "We all have battles to fight, Austin. Mine are just in my head."

Jay knocks on her window. She yelps and jumps. He grins like an idiot and waves, making her laugh. It's better than the sweetest song I've ever heard. The moron outside jerks his thumb toward the building.

"One minute!" I yell.

He rolls his eyes, but jogs to catch up with Brett and Eric across the lot. Rubbing my thumb across Marisa's knuckles, I smile as her eyes meet mine.

"You didn't have to tell me all that. I was crazy about you anyway. Now I'm even crazier about you. Congratulations."

She blushes, looking down at our hands. "You're kind of awesome, you know that?" She looks back to me. "I'm really lucky."

I shake my head. "I'm the lucky one here."

My phone buzzes from the dashboard. She grabs it with a glance at the screen and tosses it to me. "I think that's our cue."

Jay: *either kiss her or get ur ass out here.*

I look up at the building, where Jay's waving his arms. Shaking my head, I shove the phone and keys into my pocket. Once I meet Marisa outside the truck, I burst out laughing. My hoodie nearly reaches the bottom of her dress.

"You're such a shrimp," I tell her. She narrows her eyes. "A pretty shrimp?" I take her hand, sliding my fingers through hers.

A few other cars have pulled into the lot since we got here, which means we'll probably have to wait for a cage, but it's worth it. Knowing where she came from, what she went through? She's the strongest girl I've ever met in my life.

"You know, anyone can hit off a ball dispenser," I say as we head toward the guys. "Not to mention I went easy on you that day at the field. Have you ever hit a live curveball?"

She swings our hands between us. "Please. That's child's play."

And it's official. There is such a thing as perfection personified. "What about a slider?"

"Piece of cake. You think my dad raised a princess?"

We stop in the middle of the lot. I look down into those bright green eyes, full of beautiful chaos and plenty of stories still untold. I'm a goner. All I want to do is stare into them all day and all night long.

"Braxton!" Jay yells. "*You* called *us*. We playin' or what?"

But I guess that's not entirely possible. I drop my head and groan. Marisa and I continue across the lot, being openly stared at by the family walking past us toward the building. Good ol' Small Town USA.

"You know," I tell her, "they're probably whispering behind our backs."

"Who?" she asks, looking around.

"Don't stare." I nod toward the family, smiling politely when the dad locks eyes with me and waves. "You see, there's this thing called the Baptist News Network," I continue quietly. "Twenty bucks says that the mom is on its phone tree. She saw us holding hands, so we're basically already engaged. Your picture might even be on the sports page tomorrow. '*Girlfriend to Lewis Creek's Pitcher, Austin Braxton.*'"

Eric opens the door for the family, muttering, "Finally," when we reach the sidewalk. He holds the door for Brett and Jay, but I grab it so he can go on in. The air conditioning blasts through the doorway, making me cough as Marisa stops beside me.

"You all right?" she asks. "You better not be getting sick. If you get sick, I'll buy myself a Hazmat suit. Swear it."

"I'm fine," I insist. "Just a sore throat. No big deal." It actually feels like sandpaper, but she doesn't have to know that. She makes no move to go inside, instead standing there with this little half-smile. "What?"

She tilts her head toward the parking lot. "Back there. You said girlfriend."

I did what? My eyebrows scrunch together. "I did?"

She nods. "You did."

I mean, there are definitely worse things I could've said. Maybe my brain was doing me a favor. My pulse quickens as I ask, "Girlfriend?"

She nods again, her smile growing. "Girlfriend."

And now I'm grinning like an idiot. She walks inside ahead of me. The guys are lined up along the counter, all three leaning against it with their arms crossed.

"That's the sweetest damn thing I've heard all day," Eric says. "Now can I smash some balls to get it out of my head?" He turns to the guy manning the register and slides him a twenty. "Five, please."

The dude's a charmer. Really.

After picking our bats and helmets, we head for the only open cage, at the back. Little kids scream behind us, their screeches echoing throughout the room. Future Bulldogs?

Eric tugs on his helmet and nods toward Marisa. "What about it, Braxton? You gonna properly introduce us or what?"

Without him checking her out this time? Gladly. I slide my arm around Marisa's waist. "Marisa, you already met Jay. The Jolly Green Giant is Brett"—I point to Brett, who raises his hand—"and the kid is his brother, Junior. Or, you know, Eric. Whatever."

Eric glares at me while stepping into the cage. "I'm gonna kick your ass one of these days."

I smirk. "Good luck explaining that to Coach."

Jay leans on his bat, looking to Marisa as the pitching machine kicks on. "Braxton said you used to be a catcher," he says.

She crosses her arms. Stands up a little straighter. "That's right."

Jay studies her for a moment and says, "Greatest catcher of all time—go."

"Really, dude?" I ask, right as Marisa replies, "Ivan Rodriguez. No contest."

Jay holds up a hand. "Just watching your back, Braxton. You know how some girls are—they'll claim to be fans, but they can't name a single player." He points his bat toward Marisa. "She's legit. She gets the best friend seal of approval."

Leaning back against the wall, Brett crosses his arms. "All right, I'll play. Best third baseman."

Marisa steps away from me. This is getting good, actually. "Current or all-time?"

Brett smirks. "All-time."

Seriously? Please. "Chipper Jones," she and I say at the same time.

"What?!" All our heads snap toward the cage. Eric drops his bat. The machine spits out a ball as he charges the fencing. "Bull-freakin-shit. What about A-Rod?"

The girl's done gone and pissed off a Yankees fan.

Marisa scoffs. "Please. He spent nearly half his career at shortstop. He doesn't count."

But she can obviously hold her own. Brett and I eye each other. He grins and wiggles his eyebrows. "Pass the popcorn," he whispers. Jay's gawking like we're watching some live-action reality show.

"Jones was a shortstop, too," Eric retorts. "And they tossed him in the outfield a few times. Forget about that?"

Marisa moves toward the cage. "Still more time at third than A-Rod. But fine, you want to go by batting average? Three-oh-three."

I didn't even know Chipper's career average. I've been shamefaced by my girlfriend.

Eric's jaw goes rigid. "Homeruns: over six hundred."

Marisa steps closer, her nose pressed against the fencing. "Remind me, who was suspended for the entire 2014 season for—gosh, what was it? Doping?"

That girl plays dirty. Eric's mouth drops open. The final pitch slams against the cage, but he doesn't even flinch.

We have a winner, folks.

"I think you just killed Eric," I tell her.

She backs away from the cage, a smug smile on her face, and I'm pretty sure I've never been more turned-on in my life. I grab her hand, pulling her to me. "You know," I say, "I'm startin' to think you have a thing for forty-year-old retired baseball players."

She bats her eyelashes. "And what if I do?"

I lean down and press my lips to hers. She smiles, hooking her arms around my neck. "Don't care," I murmur. "As long as you're kissin' me, dream about Chipper all you want."

The cage door slams closed. Eric steps out, running a hand over his sweaty hair. "I'm still alive, no thanks to you," he says. "And I'm gonna puke if y'all don't take that to the truck or somethin'."

Marisa gets this mischievous glint in her eyes as she holds his stare. "Chipper," she whispers.

Eric slaps his hands over his ears. "Not listening to your blasphemy."

She smiles up at me. "I think he likes me."

chapter fifteen

A jackhammer wakes me Monday morning. My eyes pop open. 'Kay, no jackhammer in my room. But good God almighty, my head aches like a bastard. I would sit up, but there've got to be straps tying me to the bed. Either that, or someone tossed a two-ton weight on me while I was sleeping.

The jackhammer goes off again. I rub my eyes, squinting at the light spilling into my room. My throat's on fire and my head's killing me, and this must be some punishment for something I did in a past life, because this has to be what dying feels like.

The door to my room opens. Momma pokes her head inside. "You awake? I've been knocking forever."

Oh. So she was the jackhammer. "Yeah," I tell her, and cringe. Gross. My mouth tastes awful. I sit up, the navy sheets clinging to me as I rub a hand over my face. The sharp chill of the room smacks my bare chest.

She steps into the room, crossing her arms. "What time did you get in?"

"No clue." I could probably remember if I thought hard enough. Too bad thinking hurts right now. "It was dark. I downed Nyquil. That's the last thing I remember."

She sighs and looks around my room, shaking her head when she sees my laundry basket. "You going to be all right while I'm at work?" she asks. "Do you need anything?"

Wincing, I flop back against the pillows with an *oof.* "Fine. You don't have to yell." There have to be goblins using pickaxes on my brain. It's the only logical explanation. I cough and cough and cough, nearly cracking a rib in the process. Closing my eyes, I sink into the pillow. My muscles relax immediately. Soft pillow. Cool pillow. Favorite pillow. This is nice.

"Well," Momma says, "sorry to yell again, but you've got a really pretty visitor."

My eyes pop open right as Marisa appears in the doorway, wearing both my Braves cap and Gamecocks hoodie. She's holding one of those grocery tote-bag things. Momma pats her on the shoulder and waves to me before disappearing into the hall.

"Hey," I say through a cough. "You need a Hazmat suit first."

She smirks, walking toward my bed. "I like living dangerously." She sits on the edge of the mattress. "That bad, huh?"

"How'd you know I was sick?"

She scrunches her eyebrows. "You texted me."

"When?"

She pulls her phone out of the pocket of my hoodie. "Right here," she says, hitting the screen a couple times. "From four o'clock this morning, and I quote: 'I'm dying. Goblins are in my head and the TV mucus glob is in my chest. Erase browser history please.'" She turns it so I can see the screen. Yep, there it is. I am, in fact, a moron.

"Effin' Nyquil," I mutter. "I guzzled it when I got home because my throat was hurtin'."

She laughs and stuffs the phone back into her pocket. "Pretty sure that's not how it works. There's dosage for a reason."

Freakin' doctors' kids.

She digs into the bag and tosses me a pill bottle. "I wasn't sure exactly what you meant by 'goblins,' but I took a guess. It sounded painful, so I brought Tylenol. Dad swears by it."

"You brought me medicine?"

"That's not all." She holds up the bag. "OJ, chicken noodle soup, and ginger ale. It's not, like, homemade soup or anything. Just the canned stuff. I totally would've made you homemade, but it was super-early."

My mouth drops open. "You're Mary Freakin' Poppins."

Tucking her hair behind her ear, she shrugs. "What can I say? I'm perfectly perfect."

You really are. Clearing my throat, I nod to the bag. "No whiskey in there? You know it flushes out everything from colds to pneumonia."

She rolls her eyes. "We're going with science here, not wishful thinking. Plus your mom would have my butt if I got you drunk."

I lean back against the pillows, sinking into them once again, and *this*—this is what heaven feels like.

"You have fun yesterday?" I ask.

"So much." The mattress shifts as she stands. She leans over, her hair falling across my face as she kisses my forehead. She pulls away slowly, her mouth hanging open. "Oh. Oh, God. Dude, you're scorching."

Somehow, I manage a smirk even though it hurts like hell. "We both know I'm hot, Rissa. You don't have to tell me."

She places her hand on my forehead. "Well, your ego's still in shape, so you're not dying."

I grab her wrist gently, lowering it to my side. "I am dying. Stay here with me. You can't deny me my dying wish."

"I have schoolwork to do," she says. "And you need sleep, Goblin Boy."

My smirk stretches into a full-blown grin. "Are you scared of me now? Can I at least blame my stupidness on the fever?"

"Only for so long." She kisses my forehead again. "Get some rest. Text me whenever you can."

"You came all the way over here just to bring me soup and orange juice?"

"You took care of me. My turn to take care of you. That's what more-than-friends do, right?" She inches toward the door, clutching the grocery tote. "I'll put these down in the kitchen. Is there anything you need before I leave? I can heat up the soup or get some water?"

Her words blur together as my eyes close. Dying hurts. "Can't you stay a little longer? Please? I'm not above begging."

She sighs. Her footsteps move back toward the bed, and soon the mattress dips as she sits again. Her hand slides into mine. "I'll stay as long as you need me," she says. "Or until you go unconscious. Whichever comes first."

My breathing steadies. Her skin feels so good against mine. So nice. So right. "I wanna hold your hand forever," I murmur.

Her breath hitches, and I think she says, "Sleep, Austin," but her voice, along with the rest of the world, fades to black.

chapter sixteen

All I'm gonna say is that Nyquil should be illegal. The goblins are still picking away at my brain when I pull into Marisa's driveway on Thursday night. Luckily, the other crap that held me hostage in bed all week is gone. (Trust me, being in bed all week isn't as awesome as it sounds.) I grab my Chem book, hop down from the truck, and walk up to her front door, ready to get my study date on.

The thing is, I'm finally starting to understand this Chemistry stuff. But this gives me even more of an excuse to come to her house. What she doesn't know won't hurt her.

I press the doorbell and wait. Wait. Wait some more, because apparently the Marlowes have this thing where they're blissfully ignorant of doorbells or something. The door finally opens, with Dr. Marlowe manning its entry.

I nod to him. "Evenin', Doctor."

He steps to the side. "Evening, Austin. Marisa's in her room. Head on up."

Life lesson: you never question miracles, and a dad telling you to "head on up" to his daughter's room? One of the most miraculous moments. "Thank you, sir."

He closes the door as I jog up the stairs. Sure enough, light spills from Marisa's room and into the hallway. I peek inside the room, where she's sitting cross-legged on the bed, writing in a notebook. I knock on her door, which is half-open, and smile when her head pops up.

"You look much better," she says, closing her notebook. "Plague is gone, right? No more goblins?"

"Plague is gone. Goblins are stickin' around, but at least I'm conscious. And Nyquil-free." *So I won't be asking to hold your hand forever. Don't worry.*

Her mouth curves up as she walks toward me. "I'll go grab some snacks." Squeezing my hand, she reaches up to kiss my cheek. "Make yourself comfy. I'll be right back."

As her footsteps trail downstairs, I do just that by kicking off my boots and plopping onto her bed. I take off my cap and put it on her nightstand, which knocks a stack of books off in the process. *Crap.* I bend over and pick up the mixture of school books, weird girl books with prom-queen-looking cover models, and notebooks. She's, like, a book hoarder. After everything else is safely (and not nearly as neatly) back in place, the purple notebook she was just writing in lies open on the floor.

I shouldn't read her personal stuff. That's the first rule in the history of rules: never read a girl's journal, or diary, or even her freakin' notebook. But the scrawled writing across the first page practically screams at me as I pick it up.

I'm slipping again. Nothing's helping. Nothing.
I don't know what to do.

My heart races as I glance to the doorway. What the hell does "slipping" mean? Not literally, I'm assuming, considering it's kind of hard to slip and write at the same time. But it's not like I can ask her what it means, because then she'll know I was reading her stuff, and then I'll be the one mysteriously "slipping" down the stairs with a pissed-off girlfriend at the top. And I value my pitching arm a little too much for that to be a possibility.

Footsteps pound up the stairs. I slam the notebook closed and place it on top of the pile. Marisa appears in the doorway, cute and happy and sweet as ever with that smile that drives me wild. And all I can think about is what I read on that stupid piece of paper. This is what I get for being a nosy ass.

"Hey," she says, crossing the room with our bowl of popcorn. "You okay? You look like you just saw a ghost."

My mouth opens, but no words come. *Come on, words. You can do it. Speeeeeak.*

I got nothin'.

She sits next to me on the bed, the springs squeaking beneath us. She cringes, and finally, a laugh bubbles up in my throat. It's ridiculous and creepy and borderline psychotic, but it's better than silence. She nudges me over until I'm in the middle of the bed, and when I look into her eyes, all I see are scribbled words and scars etched into her skin. And I hope to God they're not connected. I don't know what I'd do if they are. I'm not sure I could handle it.

"Are you okay?" I ask, the words coming out in a croaked whisper.

Her eyebrows scrunch together as she crosses her legs on the bed. "I'm great. Why?"

She says she's great. She wouldn't lie to me. Run with it. "You promise? You wouldn't lie to me, right?"

She tilts her head, seeming insulted that I even asked her. "Are *you* okay? You're kind of freaking me out."

No. I'm confused as hell. "Yeah," I reply. "Yeah, I just—" I shake my head, looking down at the comforter. "I'm good. Fine. Never mind."

She shifts, placing her arm around my back. "I wouldn't lie to you. I don't have any reason to. I've told you pretty much everything there is to know about me. You know that, right?"

She gazes at me with those big green eyes, all wide and doe-like. I stare into them again, trying to find any hint of a lie or even a bent truth, but there's nothing but innocence. So if she says she's fine, she is, right? Maybe that wasn't the last thing she was writing. Maybe it was a passing thought of hers.

Maybe I should just stop thinking altogether.

I cup her chin, bringing her to me for a kiss. Here, with my lips pressed against hers, everything's okay. Everything makes sense. And I trust her. If she says she's fine, she's fine. That's all there is to it.

She rests her forehead against mine and asks, "You all right now, worrywart?"

I pull away with a nod. "If you're okay, so am I."

"Good, because I can't have you being all crazy when I leave for Maryland next week." She squeezes my leg and points to my book. "Now show me what we're working on tonight."

I flip through the pages until I land on the chapter Mr. Matthews emailed me the study guide for. "I missed all this while I was out sick," I tell her. "Alkali metals. The study guide doesn't look that hard. I've already memorized which elements are designated as alkali—"

"Wow." I look up at her. Her smile falters, but returns quickly. "It's just that you're getting good. At this studying thing. Soon you won't even need my help anymore."

There's something strange in her voice. Something almost sad. Unsure. Wrapping my arm around her back, I pull her to me for a side-hug. "You have no idea how far you are from the truth."

chapter seventeen

$\mathcal{E}$*very* season, the road to the away game at Beaufort is paved with blood, sweat, and tears. Usually ours. Okay, always ours. We haven't won a game on their turf in the three years I've played varsity. Tradition isn't on our side tonight.

Our team bus squeals to a stop outside the Eagles' field. I yank my earbuds out and stuff them into my gear bag, along with my phone. Their guys are already out there warming up. Their bleachers aren't nearly as packed as ours, but they've got a decent crowd. Baseball doesn't rule supreme here, but that doesn't mean a thing when they're whoopin' our asses.

"We're not gonna get our asses whooped today," Eric mutters beside me. I glance over. He slides on his sunglasses. "It's a good day to break the streak, Braxton."

No pressure.

Matt leans over the seat and slaps my shoulder. "Dude's right. Don't wanna disappoint your fan club." He points out the window. A white van with *Channel 5 Action News!* plastered on its side is parked next to us.

Panic shoots through me. They wouldn't be here for me, right? Our own town doesn't send a news crew to the games. A few write-ups in the paper are my only claim to fame.

I shift in my seat so I can see Matt. "The hell's that got to do with me?"

"Beaufort ain't nothin' special," he says, settling against his seat. "Why else would they have a news van out here?"

I turn back around, facing the front. "You're a prick, Matt."

"And you're an overrated—"

"Shut the hell up," Eric says. "Why don't you go fu—"

"Gentlemen," Coach shouts from the front of the bus. He glares in our direction, his face tight. I swallow hard. "You've clearly noticed we have extra eyes on the field today. Very public and very prying eyes. Eyes that would eat up even a hint of fighting amongst teammates."

He crosses his arms, steeling himself. "That night I brought y'all to the field, before this season even started, I reminded you of one fact: you are a family. And while you're on my field, or in my locker room, or on my bus, you will act like you're on a damn episode of *Little House on the Prairie* instead of some reality BS. Do we understand each other?"

I lower my head and mutter, "Yes, sir" along with everyone else.

"And for God's sake," he adds. "Watch your damn mouths."

The doors squeak. Coach stomps off the bus, which I guess is our cue to follow. The team mood's gone from low to downright funeral-worthy. This game should be a blast.

Coach is standing off to the side as I step off the bus. He curves his finger, signaling me over. I tug on the brim of my cap, shielding my eyes from the setting sun as I walk up to him.

"That van isn't here for you," he says in a low voice. "I got a message from the Eagles' coach, telling me the local news is doing a showcase on their pitcher. He's heading to Florida State this fall."

My lungs deflate. For some stupid reason, Matt got to me. I should've known better.

Coach pats me on the back. "Don't let people like him under your skin. You're better than that. He isn't worth your sanity. You hear me?"

I nod. "Yes, sir."

"Tunnel vision," he reminds me. "Go take your place, and let's play some ball."

———

We're winning. I don't know how the heck it happened or what twisted sacrifice one of our guys offered to the baseball gods, but I'm not one to question the powers that be. When who I hope is the final batter steps to the plate, we're up 4-3. All I've got to do is keep it that way.

I glance over my left shoulder. Over my right. Runners are at the corners, holding steady at first and third. My arm's sore as all get-out, but if I can just send this guy packin', we're golden. Three more strikes to conquer the Beaufort curse. I can do this. I *have* to do this.

Wind up. Release. The ball soars into Jay's glove with a solid *smack*. Okay. Maybe this is actually possible. I send another ball flying past the batter, one that he never even saw coming. Jay lofts the ball back to me, and I roll my shoulders, gearing up for the final strike. Because it will be the final strike, damn it. And in Jay's words, we'll be one step closer to knockin' back beers at the river and livin' easy during Spring Break.

On home turf, now would be the time to scan the bleachers for Marisa's smiling face, for that last push of motivation. Here, even glancing to the bleachers would be a death wish. Dozens of fans drove out here from Lewis Creek, but I have a feeling I don't want to see their faces.

My knees buckle slightly as I stare down the batter. One more strike, and I'm golden. Jay signals curveball. I grip the ball just right. *Wind up. Release.*

I already know it's off.

Crack.

The ball soars over my head. I whirl around, praying that Matt snags it in centerfield. Going. Going. Matt slams into the fence, his glove outstretched as the ball sails right over it. Gone.

Game. And a piss-poor one at that.

Jay stands as the Beaufort players spill onto the field, tackling their guy once he crosses home plate. He pulls up his mask, shock clouding his face. I know exactly what he's thinking: *What the hell just happened?*

And I know the answer: Long live the Beaufort curse.

Yanking off my glove, I head into the lineup that's forming. I walk down the line. Shake their hands. I hate 'em. But they played better.

Their pitcher is at the end, a guy named Troy. He grabs my hand in a shake, a smirk on his face as he says, "I'm still wide awake, Sandman. Didn't live up to your hype. Not that I expected you to."

I freeze. His eyes lock on mine, daring me to say or do something, anything, that'll make for a good show. But what he doesn't realize is that I just don't have the damn energy. I snatch my hand from his and keep walking.

The bus is silent as we pile on. I flop back in my seat, with Eric doing the same beside me. No one speaks to me. No one even looks at me. Here's to hoping it stays that way. Coach stops in the aisle up front, waiting for us all to settle down. His gaze passes over me. I lower mine.

"Y'all started off strong," he says. "I'll give you that. But after that first inning, your offense was weak." *Yep.* "Pitching was off." *Yeah.* "Defense was terrible and completely uninspired." *Nailed it.*

"But more than that," he continues, "you walked onto that field with God-awful attitudes. That was shameful. Pathetic. You don't win games like that. You're champions, and champions walk onto fields with their heads held high. Champions act like a team. You play like a team, even when you want to rip each other's throats out. Don't make me start eliminating weak links. You hear me?"

"Yes, sir," we all mumble.

"What was that?" he asks.

"Yes, sir," we shout.

He pats the driver's shoulder and sits in his own seat. As the bus lurches out of the parking lot, I dig into my gear bag and pull out my phone. My forehead wrinkles as I scroll through my messages. Marisa said she'd text after work. It's past seven, so she should be long gone by now.

Hey, I type. *Home yet?*

The time ticks by on my phone's screen. Seven-seventeen. Seven-eighteen. Seven-nineteen. At seven-thirty, I try again. *You there?*

By eight, still nothing.

Eric's got his head tossed back against the seat, with his earbuds in and his cap over his face. I glance across the aisle. Brett and Jay are in the seat beside ours, with Brett passed out against his window. Jay's mouth is dropped open like a fish as he snores. I don't need to wake everybody up, but—

Screw it.

I hit Marisa's number. The phone rings half a dozen times before I finally get a quiet, "Yeah?"

I stare out the window, watching the fields fly by. "Hey," I say, keeping my voice down. "Everything all right?"

"Fine."

Something tugs at me inside. She doesn't exactly sound fine. "You sure? You sound..." I almost say upset, but instead go with, "tired."

There's a quick sniffle. My eyebrows scrunch as I wait for her to say something, anything. She's been crying. She's been crying and I'm not there, and I won't be there for another hour.

Finally, she says, "I'm okay. Promise." There's this weird emptiness in her voice, a dismissiveness. "I'm kind of out of it, but I'm okay. I'll call you later, all right?"

No, it's not. It doesn't sound all right at all. I lean forward. "You sure you're okay?"

"I'm okay now, and I'll be okay the next time you ask," she snaps. I wince. "I'll call you later, Austin."

The phone goes silent. My heart screams at me to call her back, to tell her I'm here, to beg her to talk to me. My head tells me to wait, to trust her, to have faith that everything will work out. The sad thing is, I've never really been good at telling which one is right.

———————

One in the morning. Two in the morning. Three in the morning comes and goes with no call. No text. Before I plug in my nearly dead phone, I scroll through my contacts and hit Marisa's number. It goes straight to voicemail. I don't know what's going on with her, but it's safe to say that it's freaking me the hell out.

I don't think she's okay. And I have no idea what to do.

chapter eighteen

On my way to school Friday morning, I call her cell again. No answer.

Before homeroom, I break down and call her house number. Her mom says she's "fine—sick, but fine," and that she'll call me sometime later. And I've decided that I really freakin' hate the word "fine."

On my way to the shop that afternoon, I should be happy that I nailed another Chemistry test. I should be excited as hell that it's officially Spring Break and I'm free from school for two weeks. But the only things coursing through me are worry and panic because I haven't talked to my girlfriend in nearly twenty-four hours. When I was with Jamie, going a day or two without speaking to each other was nothing. She had her friends, and I had mine. But with Marisa, things are infinitely different.

Also, Jamie didn't exactly have a history of slicing up her arm. But I'm trying *really* hard not to think about that right now. And I feel like an asshole for my brain even going there.

I swerve into my spot in front of the shop, my heart skipping a beat when Marisa's space is empty. She's supposed to be here. She's supposed to be here and we're supposed to talk this out, because that's the way I've been envisioning things in my head all day.

Of course that'd be too easy. I must have seriously screwed something up in a past life.

I jump out of my truck and jog up to the door, where Momma's cleaning the windows. Marisa's job.

"Where's Marisa?" I ask.

Momma looks about as tired as I am freaked. "No practice today?"

"No more practice 'til after Easter. Where is she?"

"That's right." She uses her sleeve to wipe the hair out of her face. "She called out this morning. Didn't sound well at all."

Somehow, my stomach drops and leaps into my chest at the same time. "Momma—"

"I'm sure your girlfriend's just fine," she says, squeezing my shoulder. "I know you want to rush in and save the day, but for all you know, the poor girl's sick as a dog."

"Then I can help her. She came over for me. I'll take her soup, or ginger ale, or something. Anything."

"Relax." She shoos me on toward the counter. "That's what her momma's there for. Give the girl some space. Her momma can handle things just fine until we close up. If she says she'll be okay, then she'll be okay."

That's three hours from now. I can handle three hours. I think.

Dang it. No, I can't. I'm gonna go insane. I plop onto the stool behind the counter.

The sky darkens outside as clouds roll in. Our weatherman said to expect one heck of a storm this afternoon. I usually crave a good thunderstorm, but today, I really hope he's wrong. Storms always bring the bad shit that life throws at you.

The bell above the door chimes. Mr. Joyner strolls into the shop, a frown on his face.

Speaking of the bad shit.

See, people in this town love our team. They'll do anything under the sun for us when we're on a winning streak. But when we lose? You'd think we just proclaimed our love for torturing kittens. It turns nice guys like ol' Mr. Joyner into hornets.

"Lordy, Lordy," Momma mutters under her breath. She plasters a smile to her face as he approaches the counter. "What can we do for you, Mr. Joyner?"

Stuffing his hands into his pockets, he nods toward me. "Thought I'd take a minute to talk to Austin here about last night's game."

I'd prefer if he didn't. Coach talked to us enough. And I'm really in no mood to watch him smack on his chewing tobacco.

Momma folds her arms. "If it's all the same, Austin has work to do. Some other time."

Shock flashes across Mr. Joyner's face, but it's gone as quickly as it came. He strokes his chin, looking between the two of us. That Lewis Creek High baseball state championship ring on his finger glimmers beneath the store's lights. I've got my own ring from last year, but there's no way in heck I'd wear it on a daily basis; that thing's a prized possession. I'm pretty sure Mr. Joyner never takes his off.

He drums his hands on the counter and points at me as he backs away. "Remember to keep your eyes on the prize," he tells me. "Eyes always on the prize."

The door slams behind him. Momma blows out a breath and squeezes my shoulder, her hand lingering there. "There are more important prizes than baseball," she says. "That's all you need to remember."

———

At six o'clock on the dot, I flip the door's sign to Closed. Not that I really need to, considering I haven't seen a soul other than Momma since Mr. Joyner went on his way. Rain splatters against the shop's windows like nobody's business as the wind whips, rattling the awning above the sidewalk.

"Go check on your girl," Momma calls down from the office. "Be careful out there."

My shoulders slump as I turn toward the stairs. "I'm sorry. I'm just—"

"Worried. That's okay. Go on. Make sure you let me know how she is, all right?"

"Will do." I yank the door open, cringing at the wind and water smacking my face as I make a beeline for my truck. After hopping in and cranking up the wipers, I speed through downtown.

I grab my phone from the passenger seat, hitting redial over and over, but Marisa's not answering, just like she wouldn't answer the other dozen times I've tried calling today. And now my panic mode has shifted to full-blown freaking out. Pressing the gas down as far as it'll go, all I can do is pray there's no bored cop on the back roads today. Avoiding hydroplaning would be nice, too.

A twenty-minute drive only takes me ten. I swerve into Marisa's driveway just as the sky opens even more. Thunder crackles with the roaring wind, and I'm soaked in the few seconds it takes to sprint to her porch. My clothes cling to my skin as I ring the doorbell. No answer. I ring it again and again and again. I even bang on the screen door for good measure.

The door finally swings open, and Mrs. Marlowe stares at me, not seeming surprised at all that I was maybe ten seconds away from kicking down the door. "Yes, Austin?" she asks.

"Marisa," I say on an exhale. "Can I see her?" She looks like she's about to argue, so I add, "Please, Mrs. Marlowe. I'm goin' crazy here. I haven't talked to her since yesterday, and even then she was all down in the dumps and upset, and when Momma told me she was sick I panicked and drove all the way out here because I'm scared shitless—sorry, crapless—and I need to see for myself that she's okay. Please let me see that she's okay."

And now she looks like she's about to cry, and I don't know if it's my fault or what. Things have a tendency to be my fault, so my money's on that. She glances over her shoulder toward the stairs and steps to the side. I nearly run into her as I rush through the doorway into the quiet house. The silence is way too loud.

"She's up in her room," Mrs. Marlowe says. "She's had one of her rough days. I've been checking on her off and on, and all I've gotten are one-word answers." She rubs her forehead. "But at least she's answering."

I swallow the lump in my throat. "So—so sick was code for—"

"Sick," she finishes quietly. "Go on up. I'll be outside if you need anything. I need some fresh air."

Without another word, I barrel up the stairs, my steps sounding like a herd of elephants. Stopping in front of her closed door, I knock gently. I'd rather break the door down to get to her, but I don't think that'd go over well.

"Marisa," I call out. "It's me. Can you open the door?"

I'm met with nothing but silence, except for the blood pounding in my ears and the rain hammering against the roof. The dread in my gut is a level I've never felt before. It's terrifying as hell.

Screw it.

I turn the knob, push, and get nothing. I narrow my eyes. There's no lock on her door. She's not allowed to have a lock on her door, so why? I try again and it won't freakin' open, damn it. She's got to have something pushed against it.

I bang on the door again. "Marisa! I'm beggin' you, girl, open the door."

There's shuffling, and the door opens just a crack. I shove it open all the way. Slowly, I step inside the dim room, illuminated only by the lamp on Marisa's nightstand. It's cold in here. Freezing, actually. Dressed in black pajama pants and my hoodie, Marisa paces in front of me, chewing on her nail with her eyes trained on the floor, where clothes and books are scattered everywhere.

"Marisa?"

She stops mid-stride, looking up at me with a gaze so broken, it breaks my heart right along with it. I inch forward, almost like I'm approaching a deer or rabbit or something, and I hate myself for comparing her to an animal, for Christ's sake.

I reach for her hand, but she jerks away. "You need to go," she snaps.

Her words are daggers. I don't know if I did something wrong, but if I did, she needs to tell me. Preferably now, before I crumble to bits. "Marisa, what's goin' on?"

Chewing on that nail again, she resumes pacing. "It's nothing," she says. "Nothing. I'm having a really bad day, and I want to be alone right now. Need. I need to be alone right now."

"Please don't shut me out." She stops again but says nothing, so I continue. "If there's something you need to talk about, tell me. If I did something, tell me. Whatever's wrong, please just *tell me*. Don't push me away."

Her eyes finally flicker back to mine. "I'm not trying to shut you out. I just don't want you to see me like this, okay? All I need is a night of decent sleep, and I'll be good as new tomorrow. I swear. Trust me on this."

"Are you sure you're okay?"

"I'm *fine*," she shouts. "Stop asking me. I'll be fine."

She is so far from fine. Holding my hands up, I take a step closer. "All right, I get it. I..." I almost say "I believe you," but that's not true.

Last time something like this happened, that night in my truck, my holding her hand helped. So I grab that same hand and tug it gently, pulling her to me for a hug. It takes a few seconds, but her arms circle around my waist, gripping me tightly like she's latching on for dear life. Closing my eyes, I breathe her in, citrus shampoo mixed with the cologne on my hoodie.

As my eyes open, my gaze falls upon the nightstand. And right there, the world melts away. The floor disappears and the walls collapse and there's nothing, nothing, but—

"Marisa, what is that?"

Her body tenses in my arms. "What's what?"

Pulling away, I stomp over to the nightstand and grab the tiny straight-blade razor from beneath the lamp. My hand trembles as I hold it up. "I said, what the *hell* is this?"

"It's n-nothing," she stammers. "I wasn't going to—"

"You have a fucking blade beside your bed," I shout. "So try again, Marisa, because 'I wasn't going to' isn't going to work."

"I wasn't!" Tears spill down her cheeks as she steps forward. "I almost slipped, Austin. Almost, but I didn't. See?" She yanks up her sleeves, revealing nothing but the marred skin already there. "Nothing. And I'll be fine, I swear. I just need sleep." Her voice cracks. "Just let me sleep it off. Please."

My own tears cloud my vision. My lip quivers as I set the blade back on the cluttered nightstand, next to my old lucky hat of all places. God almighty, I don't know what to do.

I don't know.

I don't.

"Even with my meds, I slip sometimes," she continues, wiping her nose with her sleeve.

She slips. So this—this is slipping.

"I thought I could work through it on my own this time because things have been so good lately," she rushes to add. "But I'm calling my doctor first thing Monday, okay? I swear, Austin. You've got to believe me."

There's an awful lot of swearing going on. Dad swore in his letter. That swear didn't mean a thing once he drove his truck off a bridge.

The letter. Marisa's notebook.

I can't breathe.

"How long's it been?" I manage to ask. "Since this... this 'slip' thing started?"

She presses her lips together, tears streaming down her cheeks. "Not long."

"How long?"

She seems to struggle as she answers, "A little over a week."

My mouth drops open. "Are you shittin' me? And you said *nothing*? I've been right here the whole damn time, Marisa!"

Her lip trembles, and now tears are sliding down my cheeks. Shaking my head, I storm past her to the door. But I can't leave. I can't look at her, either—not without completely breaking apart. Instead, I grip the doorframe and stare down at my feet.

Breathe. Breathe. Damn it, breathe.

The front door slams closed downstairs, and her parents' voices mingle together. I sigh with relief. They can fix this. They'll know what to do.

Marisa lets out a sob. I whirl around, finding her on her knees, her face in her hands. *No, no, no.* I rush forward and fall to my own knees, wrapping her in my arms and holding her to my chest as she cries. I want to protect her from whatever's going on in that head of hers. God, I want to make it go away more than anything. I wish I could save her. Fix her. *Something.*

But I'm helpless. And that's the worst feeling of all.

"I'm so sorry," she cries. "I'm so sorry I let you down. I always let everyone down. I don't know why I do these things, Austin, but I'm so sorry. Please don't leave me. Please."

"Marisa," I whisper, blinking away my tears, "you didn't let me down, baby. But I'm going to call your parents now. I've got to."

"No." She pulls away to look into my eyes, her own wide and frantic. "You can't. You can't. They'll send me away again. I can't go back to the hospital. Please. I told you, I just need the night. I didn't even cut. I *didn't.*"

More than anything on God's green earth, I want to trust her. I want to wrap her in a blanket and pretend tomorrow will be better. But I can't.

"I believe you. But what happens when I leave? What happens if I leave and you don't go to sleep, and you have those same thoughts again? What'll you do?"

"I'll call you," she whispers, but it comes out as a question with zero certainty. And that's the only answer I need.

I press a kiss to her forehead, my lips lingering there because, Lord, I don't want to let her go. But I can't fix this. I'm in way over my head here. Staring into her eyes, I yell, "Mrs. Marlowe!"

She looks at me like I'm both nothing and everything. Like I just committed the worst betrayal she's ever experienced. It destroys me. Hell, it fucking kills me.

"I'm so sorry," I whisper, my voice wavering.

My head whirls as two sets of footsteps thunder up the stairs. Within seconds, Marisa's dad is snatching her away from me, gathering her up in his arms like a baby. And after he hurries from the room with my girlfriend against his chest, I finally know exactly what "slipping" means.

Mrs. Marlowe inhales sharply. She moves to the closet, grabs a bag, and begins stuffing clothes inside methodically, like this is nothing new. Like Marisa's going to a freakin' sleepover.

"You should go," she says, not bothering to turn around.

I somehow manage to stand without falling back on my ass. Without Marisa in here, the room feels even darker. Empty. Dead. "Where're you taking her?"

"Hospital," she says. "Again."

"Why?"

"There's no telling what she'd do if we didn't take her. I think you know that." She zips up the bag and starts for the door, still not meeting my eyes. "We don't ask questions anymore, because there are no real answers. It's just life these days."

How is she so calm right now? "I'll ride with you," I tell her. "Hell, I'll drive myself."

She stops in the doorway, hanging her head with a sigh. Finally, she faces me. "This isn't something you want to see. Do yourself a favor and go home." She walks toward me, her lip quivering. "Do you know what's going to happen at the hospital, Austin? They'll give her meds that may knock her out for hours. There'll be a revolving door of doctors and nurses. She'll have to see a psychiatrist and likely a therapist before they even think of letting her walk out the door. If they let her out the door anytime soon, considering her history."

The room spins. My stomach churns. Everything's off its axis because this can't be happening. This can't be happening to me, to this girl who's knocked me to my knees in two months, to what we had—*have*—brewing between us.

Taking a step forward, I open my mouth to tell this woman how much I care. How badly I need to be there with Marisa tonight. To be there *for* her. But the only thought my brain can formulate is, "Mrs. Marlowe, I love her." Saying the words doesn't feel weird. It doesn't feel out of place. It feels right. I just wish I could have told Marisa first instead of her momma.

She doesn't roll her eyes. She doesn't laugh. She doesn't scoff. She smiles, one of those "you poor sap" kind of smiles. She sniffles as a tear slips down her cheek.

"I love my daughter," she whispers. "I love her more than life. But loving Marisa is asking for heartache. Trust me."

"She's worth it," is all I can say, and it's the honest-to-God truth.

Shaking her head, she says, "Go home, Austin." And she turns away, leaving me alone in the room of a girl whose spirit still lingers here. But it's not enough. It's not her.

I could've stopped this. If I'd just said *something* about that stupid piece of paper I found, things may not have made it this far. I could've fixed it.

Somehow, I make my way down the stairs. Out the front door. Through the puddles left by the earlier downpour. Into my truck. I didn't want storms today, but I got a damn hurricane.

My phone, which is still lying in the passenger seat, lights up with a warning that the battery's almost dead. Not surprising, since I spent half the day calling Marisa. I grab it and scroll through my contacts and hit Jay's number. Tonight needs fixin', and he can help make that happen.

"Yeah," he answers. There's a bunch of hollerin' in the background, followed by a splash.

"You down at the river?" I ask, cranking up my truck. "They kept the party goin' with that storm?"

"Yup. A little rain ain't gonna drown out the river."

When Jay starts talking like that, there's only one explanation. "You drunk already, dude?"

"Yup."

"Good. I'll be there in a few."

"Need me to save you a six-pack?"

I scoff. "I need you to save me a lot more than that."

"That bad? Oh, and hey, is Marisa comin'? Thought it was your night with your girl?"

"Yeah, well, things have a habit of changing in my life at the worst damn time." Shifting the truck into gear, I back out of the mile-long driveway. "See ya soon."

The thing is, we always think we have plenty of time. Then, before you know it, time's ripped out from under your feet, and there's nothing but you and the hum of a truck engine. Because your girlfriend was *that close* to offing herself.

Again.

chapter nineteen

Thanks to whatever saint invented beer and whiskey, I can barely see a damn thing. I like it that way. It's a lot better than dealing with reality, when reality sucks balls.

The roar of the rushing river fills my ears as I settle back against the tree, next to Jay. I don't have a clue how long he's been here; all I know is that he was a goner when I got here. He had some fight with Brett over his brother's wedding, which is coming up soon. Jay wants to go together. Brett thinks he's nuts. It's the same fight, different day. I know it's shitty for him, but at least Brett's not down at the county hospital right now, being poked and prodded and doped up with meds.

"How many's that?" I ask Jay, tossing my empty can at the trash bag and missing by a foot. Whoops.

"Last of that six-pack." He holds out the bottle of whiskey. "'Nother shot?"

My stomach bubbles. I cringe. "Nah. Can't take more whiskey. Not yet."

"More for me." He shrugs and takes another swig. "Our love lives suck, dude."

Screw it. I snatch the bottle from him and knock it back, the alcohol burning my throat. "Tell me 'bout it,"

I say, passing it back to him. "You try callin' Brett? Talk out...whatever?"

He shoves me. "Shush!" Glancing around, he must see that nobody gives a crap about us. The other guys are busy snaking their ways into their girls' pants tonight. With all the trucks lined up along the water, there ain't no tellin' how many of our teammates are getting lucky right about now.

"You know, I figured out our problem," Jay slurs. "What we gotta do is, we gotta stop lettin' our lives depend on other people. Lettin' another guy control your life is killer."

"Yeah. Except a guy ain't controlling my life."

He snorts. "That's right. I'm the only fag out here."

I wince and nudge him with my leg. "Don't talk about yourself like that, bro."

"Just tryin' to fit in with the rest of the people in this town. Don't act like you don't hear worse every damn day. And look at it this way: at least your girl's not embarrassed to be seen with you."

"Yeah. She just tried to kill herself instead." I grab the whiskey again and polish off the bottle before chucking it across the riverbank. "Have you noticed that? How people close to me like to kill themselves? Wonder why that is."

He gapes at me. "You're *really* goin' there? Seriously?"

I shrug. "I mean, let's talk this through. Logic and all that." I count off on my fingers. "My dad was so nose-deep in depression that it drove him off a bridge, and I never noticed. My girlfriend, who I've been around every damn day for weeks, snuck a razorblade into her room without me realizing she was gonna try killing herself again. I'm a fucking jinx, Torres. Might want to run while you can."

He grabs my chin, jerking my face until he looks straight into my eyes. "I ought to beat your head against the tree for that. You're not gonna sit here and blame yourself for this shit. Any of it." He lets go of me, leaving my skin tingling. "And if you think about it, she didn't really *try* to kill herself."

Yeah, well, I don't want to think about it. I came here to forget. I push myself to my feet, swaying. The blood's rushed from my head and alcohol swirls in its place. I dig my keys out of my pocket. "I gotta get my drunk ass home before I end up facedown in the river."

I think he tries to grab my hand, but yanks on my pants leg instead. "You ain't drivin', Braxton. You can barely stand."

"I won't drive," I tell him. "I'll just sleep in the truck."

He shakes his head and tries to stand, but falls back on his ass. "Look for Randy or Eric. They're DDs tonight. Don't make me call your momma."

He pops the top to another beer and chugs it back. Maybe it's even worse for him than I thought. I turn for my truck, trying to tell my legs to walk, but they're worse than pool noodles. Dang. How much *did* I drink? And why the hell did I park in effin' Egypt? Once I finally reach the trusty old Chevy, I yank the door open, but it slams closed.

Eric steps in front of me, holding out his hand. "Keys, bro."

There's two of him. Does he know that there's two of him? I rub my head. It's already hurtin' like a bastard. "Junior, I got this. I'm just gonna sleep." He pushes my shoulder, making me stumble back. "The hell was that for?"

He scoffs. "You're drunk off your ass, Braxton, and you never trust a drunk. Now give me the damn keys before you kill yourself."

My throat tightens. "Like father, like son, huh?" I manage to choke out.

Eric's face falls. He blinks quickly, shaking his head. "You're not gonna be like your dad tonight." He swipes the keys right from my hand. "Get in. You're going home."

There's no use arguing. He's lucky I haven't puked all over his boots. I slide into the passenger seat and slump down, my eyelids growing heavy. Marisa flashes through my head, clear as ever, even through the alcohol haze. I squeeze my eyes closed. I don't want to think about her. I don't want to think about how tonight was my fault. I should've seen something was wrong. I'm her damn boyfriend, and I couldn't even tell that she was thinking about offing herself.

The truck lurches, taking my stomach with it. I puke on the floorboard. Flopping back against the seat, I close my eyes again. I hope Marisa's sleeping. That's all she wanted to do. Right now, that's all I want. Maybe we can sleep together.

"Do I wanna know what happened?" Eric asks.

"Nope."

"You gonna be all right?"

Nope. "Sure."

He snickers. "You're a piss-poor liar, Braxton."

The truck slows and rumbles over my driveway before it stops. I force my eyes open. The house is dark, which means Momma must have given up on me and gone to bed. There's no telling what time it is, but I'm in for it tomorrow.

Just as I reach for the door handle, Eric says, "You're the most together person I know. If you're losin' it and my brother's losin' it, I don't know who the hell to count on anymore. Y'all are making me look normal."

It's hard to hold it together when everyone leaves you. Jamie loved me, left me, and forgot all about me. And apparently there's something about me that makes people want to kill themselves. I wasn't good enough for Dad. I'm not good enough for Marisa. I'm not good enough for anybody.

Love sucks. It's a damn joke, and a bad one.

"Best advice I can give ya?" I say. "Put a steel trap around your heart." I step out of the truck. "Drive this on home. Bring it back whenever."

Stumbling into my room is a cruel reminder of what I thought tonight would be. This was date night, because Marisa's supposed to leave for Maryland on Sunday. So the pile of pillows and blankets still sits next to my door. They never got to be loaded up in the truck bed and taken out to the pond. And I never got to tell Marisa how nuts she makes me. How her smile makes me understand every stupid love song cliché. How crazy I go when she's not around.

How I love her. No matter how much it freakin' sucks, I love that girl.

Damn it.

chapter twenty

The goblins are back. They don't have pickaxes this time. They have drills, screwdrivers, and hammers. Basically, they came with the whole damn toolbox.

The sun streaming through my bedroom window is like a laser. I yank the comforter over my head with a groan. What I'd give to sleep in for just one Saturday, especially today. I can't remember the last time I got the chance. My door swings open just as blessed sleep nearly takes me again. Wait for it. Wait for—

Momma snatches both the comforter and sheet off me in one swift motion. "Up. Now."

I groan again, rolling my face into the pillow. "Five more minutes."

Her footsteps cross my room. I hear my blinds being drawn. Yeah, no way I'm opening my eyes now. The sun's shining on me, taunting me. *Wake up, ya hungover dumbass.*

"Why do you hate me?" I mumble.

"Off your ass. Now."

That wakes me up. My body fights me on it, and it takes a few tries, but I manage to sit up. Momma stands at the foot of my bed with her arms crossed and the nastiest glare I've seen on her face in a long, long time. And there's a good chance I might still be drunk.

"You've had some phone calls," she says.

My eyebrows scrunch. "Huh? It's early mornin'. Who the heck called me?"

She rolls her eyes. "Lord have mercy, child, you can be dense as they come. Since when does the sun rise on your side of the house?" I glance over at the window as she says, "It's six-thirty at night. The sun's settin'."

I rub my face, pressing the heels of my hands into my eyes. "Messages from who?" I ask. "And what's a guy gotta do to get some water around here?"

She cocks an eyebrow. "Really? Not getting drunk off your rear is a good start toward sympathy. You're damn lucky I let you sleep it off because Lord knows if I'd done what I wanted to this morning, your cheek would be feelin' the burn for a week."

I wince. "Momma, last night was bad. Really freakin' bad."

"Not bad enough to halfway kill yourself." She releases a shaky breath. A tear slips down her cheek, but she wipes it quickly. "Do you have any idea what that does to me, Austin?"

My gaze drops to my comforter. I can't stand seeing the woman cry.

"Jay called," she says, and I look back to her. "Wanted to make sure you got home okay. He sounded about as bad as you look. Marisa called the shop a couple hours ago, and called the house phone right when I walked in the door."

My eyes widen. I reach for my phone, but it's not on the nightstand. There's no telling where it's at. My dumb ass passed out in the same clothes I wore yesterday. I bet I smell awesome. Two-day-old clothes, beer, whiskey, and puke. Nice.

Momma tosses my phone into my lap. "Found it in the driveway. You're lucky I didn't run over it. Probably should have."

I click the phone's Home button, but it's dead as a rock. "What'd she say?" I mumble, unable to meet Momma's eyes.

"She told me what happened. That she's under at least a twenty-four-hour hold at the hospital. That her dad had to pull strings for her to call you, but you didn't answer." She pauses and adds, "I didn't have the heart to tell her why."

My stomach twists and flips and turns. Trash can. Need a trash can. I leap off the bed and run across the room, just barely making it to the can beside my dresser before everything from last night spills out.

At least I'm not drunk anymore.

"You all right?" Momma asks.

I fall onto my ass and lean against the wall, cringing at my own stench. It's a brand-new level of pathetic. "No." My head throbs, like all the blood in my body is rushing through a single vein. I squeeze my eyes closed. "This crap hurts. It hurts like hell."

She sits on the edge of my bed, in front of me. "I'm going to let you in on a secret, Austin, but I'm gonna start with this: I can't imagine what last night was like for you, but if you ever—and I mean *ever*—get that drunk again, I will personally beat the living daylights out of you. I don't have to tell you that drowning your pain in alcohol will never end well."

No, she doesn't have to tell me how it ends. How it almost ended. All I got to say is, thank God for Eric. But sometimes you just want the pain to go away, no matter what it takes.

Wait. Where have I heard that before?

"You can't carry another person's burden," Momma continues. My gaze darts back to her. "You can help them. But trying to change them is useless. We all have our battles, and this is theirs. You can't—"

"Fix them," I finish quietly.

She nods. Blinks. Before I can say a word, tears spill onto her cheeks. She doesn't even try to wipe them away. She just sniffles and looks down at her hands. At her ring, which she still wears every day.

"You can't fix them," she whispers. "But you can damn sure be there when they need you." She points to my dresser. "Now get off your backside, change into some clothes that don't reek, and wait for your girlfriend to call. Because when she does? She'll sure as hell need you."

She stands and starts for my door.

"Momma?" I say. She turns. Waits.

My gaze drops to her hand. That ring. I have no idea how she managed after Dad died. Right now, after what happened to a girl I've only known a few months, my heart feels like it's been shredded into a million pieces. My gut is more like chopped liver. And all I can wonder, all I can think, is why?

But maybe Marisa's momma was right. Maybe there are no real answers. As much as it sucks, maybe we're not even meant to understand. It's not my battle.

"I'm sorry," I tell her. "About Dad." About hating him, about making her pay for that hate, about wasting two years of my life resenting someone I loved, who was sick.

More than anything, I'm sorry I didn't tell him I loved him more often.

———

Marisa doesn't call until Sunday, right after church. All she says is, "I'm home," and I'm on my way.

It only takes one ring of the bell for the Marlowes' front door to swing open. Marisa's dad stands in the doorway, his face pale, but the space under his eyes dark. He opens his mouth. Closes it. Steps to the side, allowing me through.

I step inside the house, which is quiet except for the low hum of the living room's TV. Her momma's nowhere to be seen. There's no food cooking, no laughing, no anything. My pulse skyrockets as I eye the stairs. I shouldn't be so nervous. I mean, this is Marisa, for Christ's sake. The peanut butter to my jelly. The mac to my cheese. The ball to my bat. And she called *me*, so she must not hate me. Maybe. Hopefully.

Dr. Marlowe moves to my side, clearing his throat. "She's upstairs." His voice is hoarse. "Packing. We're leaving for Maryland this afternoon." He keeps his eyes on the floor as he says, "Thank you."

"For what?"

He shoves his hands into the pockets of his khakis. "For coming back. You're the first friend of hers that's ever come back." He walks into the kitchen, his head low.

I'm nothing special. I don't even deserve a thank-you. I just love her.

I take the stairs slowly, gripping onto the railing for dear life. The second floor is dark, with all the doors closed. I stop in front of hers, my muscles tightening as my fist freezes at the wood.

It's a stupid door. Knock.

Taking a deep breath, I do. There's a *crash*, followed by a muffled, "Crap!" I laugh, but it comes out more like a donkey heehawing. The door opens, and I think my heart stops. No, it definitely stops, because it's Marisa. It's my Marisa. There's a smile on her lips and in her eyes, and her cheeks are flushed, and her hair's in that messy-but-perfect knot. She's wearing jeans that fit just right and a just-barely-too-big long-sleeve Braves shirt. It's her.

She steps aside and gestures for me to come in, which I do. The overhead light's on with the fan whirring, creating a draft that feels like heaven to my iron-hot face. I stop in the center of her room. She clears her throat, and I whirl around, speechless. On the drive over, I didn't think about what to say or what to do. All I wanted, needed, was to be here. With her.

"Can you please stop looking at me like that?" she says, fiddling with her fingers.

My dead heart jumps back to life with a vengeance. "Like what?"

She rocks back on her heels, chewing her lip. "Like you're terrified of me."

A tear slips down her cheek, and I'm done for. I rush forward and wrap my arms around her as tight as I can, kissing her hair over and over because I don't know what else to do without letting her go, and that ain't going to happen. She sniffles against my chest, which only makes me hold her tighter.

"I think my parents have even given up on me," she says, her voice muffled by my shirt.

"They're probably scared as hell," I murmur, resting my chin on top of her head.

"Were you scared?" she whispers.

Is she serious? "Marisa, I was freakin' terrified."

She pulls away just enough to look up at me, with tears pooled in those green eyes. "I'm okay now."

She seems to love that word, but I despise it. We must have really different definitions. Instead of saying that, though, I ask, "What happened?"

She shrugs. "My head's still a little fuzzy. My psychiatrist was on-call, so he met me there. My psychologist rushed over yesterday. I was monitored every minute at the hospital, like I was some rabid animal. The only reason they let me leave this morning was because Dad pulled some power card."

That's not what I meant. Something boils inside me. As much as it hurts to do so, I back out of her hold with a shake of my head. I turn so I don't have to keep looking at the confusion on her face, only to be met with an open suitcase on her bed.

"Y'all are really leaving?" I ask, clenching my hands into fists. After everything that happened this weekend, they're still shooting off to another state. Un-freakin-believable.

"Yeah," she drawls. "For two weeks. My grandparents would never forgive us if we bailed. I'll be back a few days before Jay's brother's wedding. I promised your mom I'd help make the billions of arrangements." She grabs my hand, tugging on it gently until I turn back to her. She narrows her eyes. "Austin? What's wrong?"

My words build, but I don't know how to get them out without spitting them at her, and that's not really an option. I take a deep breath, and another, and then another before saying, "What I meant is, what *happened* to you? On Friday. What caused that—that—"

She tilts her head to the side. "Oh, my God." She gapes at me and takes a step back. "Are you *mad?*"

My mouth opens, and closes because I don't have the slightest clue how to form my whirlwind of thoughts into coherent words. I'm not mad. I don't think I could ever be mad at her. But it's not sadness. It's not bitterness.

"I don't get it," I finally tell her. "You were fine a few days ago. You were smiling, laughing, and kiddin' around with me. You kissed me. You hugged me. You *told* me that you were okay then. So how can I believe you now?"

She sighs, moving past me toward the bed. I watch as she folds a shirt, a pair of pants, then another shirt, and places them all in the suitcase, like this is all just another day. Like she didn't have a damn razorblade sitting on her nightstand less than forty-eight hours ago.

"There's something you have to understand about depression," she says. "Things can be going great, and for me, they were awesome. You helped make them awesome."

She smiles. Even though I know it's supposed to make me feel better, I can't return it.

"Depression's like a thief," she continues, closing the suitcase and zipping it up. "It weasels its way into your body. Sometimes it's slow, and sometimes it just barges in like it owns the place. It robs you. Before you know what's happened, coal is in the place of your heart. Your soul? Empty. Nothing and no one can bring you out of it. No one but you—and sometimes that doesn't even work. It can last an hour, a week, or six months. There's no telling."

She holds my gaze for a moment before adding, "And sometimes, nothing brings you out of it. And it's that fear that can drive a person to take it into their own hands. Make it end."

I can't handle the thought of her being in pain and there being nothing I can do about it. But she lied to me. When I asked her straight-out if she was all right, she lied. So yes, part of me *is* mad.

"Why are you mad?" she asks, crossing the space between us. "Your subconscious demands to be heard, Austin."

"I'm mad because you lied to my face." I'm surprised by the bite in my voice, but she doesn't seem to be at all. "I was right here, in this room, a week before this happened. You looked into my eyes and said, 'I'm fine.'" My throat tightens, but I force the words through. "Thursday, after my game, you promised me that you were okay. That was another lie. And you know what? You were right last week. You said that I already knew the worst about you, so you had no reason to lie. Why would you lie when the truth counted the most?"

"Because I didn't want to put that on your shoulders," she replies without hesitation. "This is my problem. It's my load to carry. You can't fix me."

"And you can't keep lying to me! I'm not trying to fix you, but you have to understand that it's freakin' hard to wrap my head around this. When this slipping stuff happens? Tell someone. Anyone. I shouldn't have been the one to call your parents in here." I breathe heavily, holding her gaze, silently pleading with her to understand. *Please* understand.

But instead she winces, like my words slapped her. "You said you wanted to be my boyfriend. I want to be your girlfriend. But if we're going to be together, this is part of it." She gestures to herself. "This is the package. I'm a little screwed up sometimes. I'm kind of crazy. I am who I am, and that's all I can be. I've accepted it."

I swallow back the lump in my throat. I don't know what to say, what I'm supposed to say. This isn't something they cover in the boyfriend handbook. In Health class, they tell you everything under the sun about how to handle condoms and pregnancy and STDs, but they don't tell you shit about depression and being head-over-heels for a girl who's tried to kill herself.

"You want to bring up things we've talked about?" She steps toward me, forcing me to take a step back. Another step. And another, until I'm standing just outside her doorway. "How about that night at the pond when I told you that this happens. That I melt sometimes. And I asked you to think about it, to really think about whether or not you could handle it. So maybe you should take the next couple of weeks to decide whether you still think being with me is worth all this."

"That's not what I'm—"

"But I'll tell you one more thing," she continues. "If it takes you two weeks to decide whether or not I'm *worth* it? I'm not sure I want you to decide."

Tears slide down her cheeks, but her gaze doesn't waver at all. Neither does mine. My voice cracks as I tell her again, in complete and utter hand-to-God honesty, "You are so, so worth it. But—" I choke on the word. "But you can't lie to me, either, Marisa."

She smiles a shaky smile. Places her hand on my shoulder. Reaches up to kiss my cheek. Her voice wavers as she says, "I'll see you in two weeks."

And when the door closes, for some strange reason, it doesn't feel like a goodbye. It feels like a "see ya later."

I hope it's not just wishful thinking.

chapter twenty-one

After leaving Marisa's house, I head straight across town toward Jay's neighborhood. While I'm already out, I might as well make the most of it. If I still feel like someone's drilling into my brain with some kind of hangover screwdriver, there's no telling how crappy he feels. Not to mention I never called him back yesterday, even though he checked on me while going through his own mess. And a distraction would be good right now. Really, really good.

Except for his car, the driveway's empty when I pull up to his house. It's different here than at Marisa's. Sunday afternoon relaxation mode is in gear, with his neighbors swinging on porch swings and a group of moms walking down the road with strollers.

Jay answers the door after my first knock. Wearing nothing but boxers, a T-shirt, and a scowl, he's not exactly the welcome committee.

"Where's everyone?" I ask, walking inside behind him. I close the door as he plops onto their leather couch. The widescreen TV's at full blast, with a Tampa Bay spring training game on its screen. I collapse onto the opposite end of the couch, sprawling my legs in front of me.

"My parents are meeting Felix in Charleston." He kicks his feet up onto the coffee table, which is covered with Sprite cans. Someone's still fighting a hangover. "His tux came in. Tell me: how many Torreses does it take to try on a tux?" When I don't answer, he rolls his eyes. "Three, Braxton. Three. No wonder you needed a tutor."

Well, someone's a special damn snowflake today. "That's cute. That's real cute. So why didn't you go with 'em, funny guy?"

He shrugs. Instead of meeting my gaze, he just stares blankly at the TV. "Didn't feel like going. I think I'm still half-drunk from Friday night."

Closing my eyes, I flop my head against the back of the couch. "What happened?" I ask through a yawn. "Friday. All I got out of you was Brett, a fight, and the wedding."

I look over at him. Now he's got his own head back, staring up at the ceiling. The crowd on TV roars, the sound splitting through the room.

"I asked if he wanted to show up to the wedding with me," he says. "*With* me, with me. He freaked. I yelled. It was ugly." He leans forward, resting his elbows on his knees. His leg bounces. "We've been sneaking around for more than six months. I'm exhausted with sneaking around. But I shouldn't..." He shakes his head and glances at me over his shoulder. "Where've you been? You look as shitty as I feel."

I lean forward along with him. "I came here from Marisa's. Asked her what happened on Friday, what led up to—" I wave my hand around "—whatever the hell that was. She said it was just a thing that happens. Like it was no big deal."

He scoffs. "People always say something is nothing when it means a hell of a lot of something."

No kidding. I pick at my fingernails while the crowd on TV erupts into cheers again. "I love her," I tell him. "May sound crazy, but I love the girl."

He grabs the remote from the coffee table and flops back against the couch. "Love's a crazy thing, bro."

That scowl must be glued to his face or something. I nod toward his phone, which is on the armrest beside him. "Why don't you call him?"

He shrugs a shoulder. Turns the TV up a notch. "He's got church tonight. I'm not going to bug him."

I look at the grandfather clock in the corner. It's only three in the afternoon. "Not for another four hours."

"I'm not calling him," he snaps. "I screwed up, so just let me give him some time."

"How could you have screwed up that bad? By asking him to the wedding? That doesn't seem like something unforgiveable."

He tosses his head back, groaning. "You don't get it. It's not just the wedding. I've been on him for a long time, telling him I'm sick of sneaking past everyone but you and Felix in this ass-backward town."

Still not entirely getting it. "How's telling him how you feel such a bad thing?"

He heaves a sigh. "Because by doing that, I was telling him how *he* should feel," he says. "And that's a dick move. I was trying to make the decision for him." He grimaces. "It's not my decision to make. That's where I screwed up."

Now that makes sense. I settle back against the couch. "You know, I bet if you called—"

"Stop, Braxton," he mumbles, shaking his head. "Just stop."

Damn. Seeing him like this is brutal. I nod toward the TV. "The Rays are lookin' good."

He stares at me for a beat before looking at the screen. "Stop trying to make me feel better. They're playing like shit today."

At least I tried. My phone buzzes against my leg. I dig it out of my pocket.

Marisa: *Leaving now. See u soon.*

She'll see me soon. That's a good sign, right? It means this is a fixable mess, that she doesn't hate me. I think.

I type back, *Have a good trip,* and start to shove the phone back into my pocket. Instead, I scoot away from Jay a little more, making sure he's not looking at me. I scroll through my contacts until I find Eric's number and type out another message: *Get brett to the field tmrw night. Around 9.*

"You better not be talking to Brett," Jay says. "Try anything funny and I'll break that precious arm." He looks at me. "Some people just don't get a love story, Braxton. When you accept that, life's easier."

I'm sure it does make life easier. I'm sure it makes it a hell of a lot more boring, too.

———————

I'm not a matchmaker, or a therapist, or a mediator. Actually, I'm probably more of an idiot for doing this. I kind of really need my arm, but friends help each other. We have each other's backs. And I know Jay's miserable as hell, so I'm not about to let him sink into his couch for the next week and a half of Spring Break. That'd be a waste.

I talked Jay into coming to the field tonight by convincing him that my arm was aching because of this afternoon's rain, and that I needed to work out the kinks. Considering that he believed me, he's obviously still off his ass about Brett. Hopefully that'll change tonight. And hopefully I get to keep my arm.

Jay's my friend. He also really, *really* hates being lied to. And he doesn't break a promise.

My arm's twitching already.

At 8:58, I park my truck next to the school's field and cut the engine. Jay unbuckles his seatbelt and hops out into the parking lot, and I do the same. Without the field lights, it's dark out here, which is one reason I knew it'd be the right place. Jay's family is home, Brett's family is home, and Momma's already sleeping, so my house was out. They'll get the privacy they need here, the privacy that Brett still craves. Not to mention, the field is where everything makes sense.

Jay tosses his glove into the air as we walk toward the fence. When headlights light up the field and a loud, familiar engine rumbles to a stop behind us, we whirl around. And when Jay's face twists into something that'd make Freddie Krueger run and hide, I'm tempted to do the same.

"You son of a—" He rushes me and grabs me by the shirt. He swallows audibly, but his hand is shaking. "Who in the actual hell do you think you are?"

Carefully, I pry his hand off my shirt. *Down, fella.* "I think I'm a friend doing you a favor."

He narrows his eyes. "Yeah, well, screw you and your favors. I'm going home."

I hold up my keys, jingling them. "See, that's the funny thing. I drove you here, and I'm not leaving until you talk to him, so—"

"This isn't your problem, Braxton."

"No, it's not," I agree. "But I'm not gonna sit around and watch my two best friends screw themselves because you're too much of a chicken shit to put all this out on the table. You say you effed up? Fine. Apologize."

The doors to Brett's Jeep slam closed. Eric and Brett walk toward us, both with their hands shoved into their jeans pockets, both wearing Bulldogs hats. Brett's the only one wearing one hell of a poker face.

I swear to God, if this backfires, I'll feel like shit. Jay was right when he said this isn't my fight. But when you see something that you can maybe, possibly, help fix, it's almost impossible to resist giving it a shot. Plus, we only have a little over four months before we're scattering to different states. They'd never forgive themselves if they wasted their last summer together.

Brett lifts his chin to Jay. "Hey."

Jay crosses his arms. "Hey."

Eric says, "Y'all want to tell me what we're doin' out here?"

I point to Jay and Brett, who are still staring at each other. "These two have somethin' they need to hash out. We're not leaving until they do."

Jay begins to say something, but Brett crosses the distance between them and takes his elbow. He heads toward the field, with Jay walking right along with him. See? That wasn't so hard.

Eric steps to my side. "What's their deal?" he asks. "Is that why Brett's been actin' like a wuss all weekend?"

I shrug. "Not sure I'd call him a wuss for it, but sure. I guess."

He looks over at me, his eyes narrowed. "You know something I don't?"

All I do is nod. If Brett wants him to know, Brett can tell him. Not my place. I sit in the grass, which is already damp with dew. With a grunt, Eric plops down beside me. A cool gust of wind smacks me in the face. Brett's standing by the fence, his face hidden in the darkness as Jay talks and talks and talks, his hands gesturing all over the place. This may take a while.

I pull my phone out of my pocket, lighting it up to see if I've missed anything. Nothing. Frowning, I shove it back into my jeans. I texted Marisa this morning just for the heck of it (and also because I miss the girl already), but all I got was silence. I guess she was serious about this waiting period, or whatever she wants to call it.

"What's he doin'?" Eric murmurs.

I glance up. Brett takes a step toward Jay. Then another. And another. And then—

He kisses him. Right there, beside the baseball field, in front of me, in front of his brother, Brett kisses Jay. And they don't look like they're letting up any time soon.

"Holy—"

I look over at Eric, who's staring at them with his mouth wide open. "You didn't know," I say.

Alert: Captain Obvious has entered the premises. Of course he didn't know. If he knew, he wouldn't look like...well, he wouldn't look like *that*. Like a largemouth bass.

He lets out a short, breathless laugh. "Now I do."

"You all right?" I ask.

He nods. "Yeah, I'm fine." His forehead creases. "It's just...the only thing that bothers me is that *he* must have thought it would bother me." He shrugs. "I don't give a shit what he does. He's my brother, you know?"

Yeah, I do know. Sort of. These guys are the closest to brothers I've ever had, but I'd do anything to back them up.

Eric pushes himself to his feet and smacks the wet grass off his jeans. "Since we're here, you feel like helpin' a guy out with this change-up you're always goin' on about? Spring Break's no excuse to slack off."

He holds out his hand. I let him pull me to my feet. He may still have a lot of growing up to do, but I've got to say, the team'll be in good hands next year.

I slap him on the back. "Let's go, Junior."

chapter twenty-two

The Tri-County Spring Break Tournament our town hosts every year always draws a huge crowd. Four teams, two games, six hours, and a whole lot of fans. It's going to be a good afternoon.

I circle the parking lot half a dozen times before finally saying screw it. I drive to the back of the lot, where Brett and Jay are sitting on the bumper of Brett's Jeep, and make my own parking spot in the grass. After cutting the engine, I check my phone one more time to make sure Marisa hasn't called. She's been in Maryland for two weeks. I've talked to her zero times in these two weeks. It's safe to say I'm going insane.

I really, really hope the "see ya later" thing wasn't just wishful thinking.

Brett lifts his chin to me when I hop down from the truck. "'Bout time you showed up," he says. "Just because you ain't startin' doesn't mean you can slack off."

I sling my gear bag over my shoulder. "How much money did Coach give you to say that?" They're on opposite ends of the bumper, each with his arms crossed and a pro-level poker face. To anyone else, they'd be two teammates relaxing before the game. But this, them being out here together, is huge. And I'm damn proud of them.

Jay's the first to stand and grab his own bag from the pavement. "On that note, we should be on the field already. Coach'll have our asses."

The sun blazes as we start across the lot toward the field. The bleachers are filled to the brim, with people lined up all the way down the fence. Three of Barton High's players linger behind the bleachers, laughing about God knows what. The middle guy, their pitcher, spots us heading their way and holds up his hands, silencing the others. I've batted against the guy before, but I can't remember his name for the life of me. I do know he's got a God-awful slider.

"How's it goin', fellas?" he calls as we walk past. "Heard you're not startin' today, Hotshot. Resting that gold-plated arm?"

I stop where the pavement meets grass, and chuckle. He's baiting me. It's working. I turn, shifting my bag on my shoulder. "Not gonna risk blowin' out my arm in a game that doesn't mean anything."

He crosses his arms and grins. "Right, right. God forbid you pitch a game for the fun of it. It's all about the glory, isn't it?"

His slider isn't the only thing that's pathetic. His trash-talk sucks, too.

He nods toward Brett and Jay. "What about you two? Y'all playin'? Because I didn't realize they let prisspots on the ball field."

I narrow my eyes. "The hell did you just say?" I'm not even touching him, but I can feel Brett go stiff as a sheet of plywood beside me. Jay crosses the distance between them, coming face-to-face with Bastard Pitcher.

That's his name now. Bastard Pitcher.

"Braxton just asked you a question," Jay says in a voice that'd have me pissing my pants. "What the hell did you say?"

The crowd grows louder in the bleachers, but it's nothing more than a dull noise. The pitcher holds Jay's stare, smirking. "I saw y'all two across the lot when you got here. Wouldn't have been able to get a hose in between you if I'd tried. Not sure who you think you're foolin'." He looks over at Brett. "And ain't you Pastor Perry's kid? How's he feel about his boy bein' a fag?"

Oh, hell no. Brett disappears, high-tailing it to the field. Probably a good thing; I've seen the dude's right hook. I grab Jay's arm, yanking him back so he doesn't get locked up today, either. He rips out of my hold and follows Brett.

Bastard Pitcher cackles, his two buddies going right along with him. "You see it all in this town: a Mexican queer and his pastor-kid boyfriend. It's classic, really."

Me? I'm not playing today. I can spend a day in a cell if he keeps runnin' off at the mouth. "You wanna try saying that to their faces?" I ask. "Or are you just gonna hide behind the bleachers all day like a pansy-ass piece of shit?"

The fool snorts and starts toward the field with his lackeys in tow. "Nah, I'll see 'em once I'm on the mound later," he calls over his shoulder. "I'll let 'em know how I feel then. Trust me."

So much for it being a good day.

The dugout's quiet as I approach, way too quiet for game day. Jay and Brett's tension has spread across the team like wildfire, even if the other guys don't know why it's there to begin with. After checking in with Coach, who's still ticked that two of his starters showed up late and pissed, I sit next to Jay on the bench. It's no different than sitting beside a rock, stone-cold and silent.

I catch him glancing at Brett, who's taking warm-up swings in the on-deck circle. They're finally moving forward, then this shit happens.

"Y'all gonna be all right?" I ask him.

Jay shrugs. "No idea."

"*You* gonna be all right?"

"No idea."

As Brett steps up to the plate, Barton's pitcher, the smartass from the lot, grins and toes the dirt. My chest tightens. I head to the fence that separates the dugout from the field, standing beside Eric. I know that grin. I've had that grin. It's one a pitcher flashes when he's up to no good. He winds up and fires a fastball so fast I'm surprised Brett doesn't have whiplash.

His fastball's definitely better than his slider.

"Strike one!" the ump yells.

Jay's by my side in an instant, rattling the fence. "Come on, Perry!" he shouts. "Smack the hell out of it!"

Brett steadies his stance, prepared for the next pitch. *Wind up. Release.* Brett slices nothing but air. He's our lead-off man for a reason. He can do better than this. Mental blockage is a batter's worst enemy.

Wind up. Release. The ball cuts sharp inside. Brett dodges, but the pitch still catches him on the elbow. He drops the bat, his face clenched. I cringe. I've had that happen before. It hurts like nobody's business. The crowd boos as he takes his base, and I'm pretty sure Jay's about to combust next to me.

"He'll be all right," I say. "He's good."

There's fire in Jay's eyes as he glares at the field. "That shit was on purpose. Look at the pitcher."

I do.

The bastard winks.

Damn it to hell.

———————

This is pretty much the worst our team's ever played. By the top of the fourth, no one's managed more than a base hit. We're already back to the beginning of the batting order. It's embarrassing as hell. We were state champions last year, for Christ's sake.

Jay, Eric, and I line up along the fence with the rest of the team as Brett steps up to the plate again. Good ol' Super Douche looks primed and ready. He didn't try any funny business with Jay; he's got his eyes set on Brett, for whatever reason. Everyone else has noticed, so I don't know why his coach is keeping him in the game. He just better keep it clean this time.

The first pitch shoots straight by the nuts. I grab Jay's shoulder to keep him from charging out there, but he shakes me off and smacks the fence. Eric isn't much better. Brett aims his bat at the pitcher, who just shrugs when the ump yells out a warning for both of them.

"Watch him, Perry," Coach shouts. He moves just outside the dugout's opening, arms crossed. "He's dirty. Eyes open."

Brett raises his bat, ready and waiting. The pitcher studies him for a minute before going into his windup. *Release.* Brett turns, but the pitch nails him right smack in the shoulder.

And now he's charging the damn mound.

"Fucking hell," Eric says as I mutter, "Shit."

We follow Coach in a dash to the mound just as Barton's dugout clears and piles on the field. Brett lowers his shoulder and rams into the pitcher, sending them to the dirt. Both of them are yellin' and punchin' and scramblin' and I have no clue who's hurt what, but I grab Brett's elbow, trying to yank him off. The dude's turned into the freakin' Hulk. Coach grabs his other arm and helps me pull him off the pitcher, whose nose and mouth are both bloody messes.

Jay snatches Brett's arm from my grip, slinging it across his shoulder to help Coach guide him off the field. Brett cringes and swears, leaning his weight against Jay.

"I got you," Jay says. "I'm right here, babe. Breathe." Coach's eyes widen, right along with Eric's. Neither says anything as Jay helps Brett hobble to the bench. The other guys file back to their dugout as Barton's coach pulls the pitcher to his feet.

"Learn your lesson?" I ask. *Don't spit in his face. Don't do it.*

He sneers. "What's it matter to you? You a fag, too?"

That's it. I step forward and his coach moves between us, but I'm not going to hit the bastard. Brett did well enough on his own. "It doesn't matter if I am," I say. "But when you mess with one of us, you get all of us. Remember that."

His coach shoves him on toward the dugout, and I turn to ours, my pulse pounding like a jackhammer. The crowd's all standing, most of them with their phones up and at the ready. Vultures probably just recorded every second of what happened. But when my eyes land on a pretty brunette standing off to the side with her parents, the crowd disappears.

I swallow the lump in my throat. She waves. I want nothing more than to run up to her, hug her, kiss her, tell her that I've been going nuts without her, but now's not the time for that. I tip my cap to her and head for the dugout, where the trainer's inspecting Brett's shoulder. Randy passes me on his way to the plate. He better line-drive that sucker out of the park.

Jay and Eric hover behind Brett, Jay chewing his nail as he watches the trainer's every move. "How bad is it?" I ask as I come up beside him.

"It's probably dislocated," he says, not breaking his gaze for a second. "May need the ER."

Letting out a heavy breath, I lean over the back of the bench. "Bro, you did a number on that prick," I tell Brett. "Did a number on yourself, too. Worth it?"

He winces, but says, "Worth breakin' every bone in my body."

"Better not be every bone in that body," Coach says. "Even though I'm tempted to break 'em myself after what y'all just pulled, actin' like a bunch of damn kids." He slaps my glove against my chest. "Eric's out so he can take Brett to the hospital. I need a closing pitcher and a third baseman. You want to take over the mound?"

I cringe. "I haven't warmed up at all. I'll have to take third."

Coach sighs and waves over Lance, the sophomore left-handed pitcher. He sucks. But it's better to have someone who sucks than someone who hasn't warmed up. *Sorry, guys.*

Randy trots back to the dugout after striking out, shaking his head as he tosses his helmet onto the bench. Coach would usually chew his ass out for that, but I guess he figures we all need some leeway right about now. Sliding on my glove, I follow the rest of the guys onto the field. I scan the bleachers and the fence, hoping to get a glimpse of Marisa before finishing this hell of a game.

She's right there, at the fence, watching me. Waiting for me.

chapter twenty-three

*A*s the hosting team, all of us are supposed to stay by the field, being supportive of the other guys participating in the tournament once our game's up (or maybe I should say, once we lost miserably). But I'm pretty sure that rule's meant to be broken in times like these. There are extenuating circumstances here.

I find Marisa behind the bleachers at the edge of the parking lot. She fidgets with her hands as I walk toward her. Rocks back on her heels. Tugs the brim of her Braves cap over her face. Thank God she's nervous, too. Double-thank God she's still got my cap. That's a good sign.

"That was a heck of a fight," she says. "Is Brett okay?"

Coach will make sure we pay for that fight. I see a lot of laps in our team's future. "They think he dislocated his shoulder. Eric took him to the hospital. You should see the other guy." Stuffing my hands into the pockets of my uniform, I say, "You didn't call me."

She shakes her head. "I didn't call you."

I lift my shoulders. "Why?"

She tilts her head, signaling for me to come closer. She sits in the grass, facing the parking lot. As soon as I sit beside her, she reaches over and grabs my hand, like she's been waiting two weeks to do just that.

"I needed to be away, I think," she says. "Those spirals, those crashes, are draining. I needed to just *breathe*. Reconnect."

"With?"

"Myself. My family." She stretches out her legs and crosses them. "Do you know the last time my family and I did anything together? Like, together-together?"

Not a clue. I shake my head.

"Me neither. But while we were gone, my dad and I went to the Orioles' opening day and pigged out on hot dogs and nachos. My mom and I spent two days planting a flower garden with my grandma." She smiles a tiny half-smile. "It was kind of perfect." She nudges me. "I was serious when I told you to take that time to think, you know."

"And I was serious when I told you that you were worth it. There was nothing to think about." Glancing down at our hands, I rub my thumb across her knuckles. "Marisa, I'm in this. I want you. That's it. That's all there is to it."

"It won't be easy."

"I don't want easy. I want you."

She hangs her head and giggles, which turns into a laugh and, finally, a snort. Looking over at her, I grin, my shoulders shaking as I laugh along with her. It's so good to see her smile. I was scared I'd never get to see that smile again.

"I needed the time to think," she says softly. "That's why I didn't call." Her gaze moves to the parking lot, where people are already starting to call it a day. "There's something I thought about a lot while I was gone." She looks back to me. "I shouldn't have lied to you. The whole 'I'm okay' thing just kind of flows out. A way of making people not worry about me, because that's the last thing I want. I don't want to be a burden, you know? Putting up with me has to be a pain."

I wonder if that's how Dad felt. If he didn't want to bother us with his problems, or if he thought that he'd be some kind of burden. And I don't know if I'm on to something or way off base, but not talking about his problems might have had a lot to do with why he gave up.

My heart races as I hold Marisa's gaze. Confusion wrinkles her forehead. I never told her exactly how Dad died. I don't know if now's the right time—probably not, actually. But I do know that not having her here, having her give up, would gut me.

And now my heart's raced right into my throat.

"My dad—" I swallow. *Get back in my chest.* "His car accident. He drove off the bridge on purpose," I tell her. "And I don't know why. I don't know if he was depressed or if something else was going on. I'll never know, obviously."

Her eyes widen. Her mouth drops open. "Austin, I—"

"I hated him for a long time," I continue, looking at the grass. She keeps her hand on mine, squeezing it a little tighter. "Mostly because I didn't understand why, I guess? I hated him for leaving us. And he left us this letter." My voice cracks. I study the grass, counting the sharp blades. I get to twenty-three before I'm positive I won't lose it in front of anyone who happens to look our way. "There was this thing he used to say all the time: 'All my love, all my promises, all my swears.' It was his way of telling us that we meant everything to him. And I'll never know why the hell he made those his last words to us when he knew he was leaving."

Leaving. It sounds so temporary. It doesn't even brush the surface of someone being flat-out *gone*. Forever.

"Can I take a shot at it?" Marisa asks carefully. I shrug, signaling for her to go on. "It may have been his way of saying that, even in those final moments, even though he was in the darkest of dark places, he was thinking of you. That he loved you guys more than anything. That you still meant everything to him. He wanted you to remember that."

That sounds good. It sounds like a nice, sugar-coated explanation, one that Momma would've given me if I were, say, five. But it doesn't make sense. "If he loved us so much," I say, "wouldn't he have fought for that? Isn't that worth fighting for?"

Her face falls. And now I'm a total asshole, but years of pent-up confusion is bubbling in my stomach. I'm doing the best I can here.

"Do you win every fight you get into, Austin?" she finally says. "Do you win every game?"

My shoulders drop. She smiles, a sad smile. "For years, I've fought a war in my head, so I may be a little biased here," she continues. "It's hard to bring people into that war, even if they're willing allies who want to help. And when you fight alone, sometimes..." She pauses. "It's hard to win a battle you're fighting alone."

Thinking back to the days before Dad died, I can't remember a single time when he seemed anything less than happy. He always had a grin on his face. He never missed a game. He kissed Momma like the sun shined just for her. He patted me on the back after every loss, stayed up with me every night I wanted to talk stats and teams and colleges. Never once did he ask for help. Never once did I ever think he was less than perfect. If he was depressed, if he needed to talk, I wish he'd known Momma and I were *right there*, ready to listen.

I look back to Marisa, giving her a shaky smile. "I'm gonna say this, and then I think we need to change the subject before I start cryin' in front of half the town. We don't 'put up' with the people we care about, Marisa. We don't 'deal' with them. We're just there because we lo—" I clear my throat. "Because we care. I care. I've got your back, girl. So for the love of all that's holy, promise me you won't try fighting alone."

She swallows audibly, gripping my hand even tighter. It's unimaginable that two weeks ago, she looked at me with more disdain than I could have fathomed. It broke my damn heart. Now, she's looking at me with the same gaze as her first day working in the shop. She's looking at me like I'm everything and the only thing that matters, which is fine because right now, she's *my* everything.

"I'll promise if you make me a deal," she says. "When I say that I'm okay, I want you to look in my eyes, really look. And if you know I'm lying, tell me. Don't let me lie to you again."

I nod. "You've got a deal."

And she kisses me. I close my eyes, letting go of her hand to wrap my arm around her shoulders. As she pulls away, my lips tingle, already missing her. She stares at me for a while, like she's searching for something. She must find what she's looking for because she smiles.

"What?"

She shakes her head. "It's crazy. You'll think I'm downright certifiable."

She kisses me again, moving onto my lap and straddling me. Not entirely sure where that came from, but there are some things you just don't question. My pulse pounds as I hold her close. And when she pulls away this time, her smile's still in place, still as perfect, still as gorgeous.

As she rests her forehead against mine, I grab onto her hips loosely. "Thank you," she whispers. "For being here. For being terrified and for not running away for good."

It's my turn to smile. "Part of being your boyfriend is being a friend. It's kind of key. I'm not goin' anywhere."

"I know that now." Her lips ghost mine, sending shocks to every nerve in my body. "Should we get out of the grass? I'm sure we've got an audience by now. Baptist News Network and all that."

No damn way. Tightening my arms around her, I shake my head. "I'm not goin' anywhere, remember?"

I don't care if they're watching. Nothing else matters but the way my heart is about to crash through my chest and the fact that I'm going to combust if I go one more second without kissing this girl. So I do, because I'm not a fan of combustion.

Screw the Baptist News Network.

Someone behind us clears his throat. Marisa's lips disappear, and I turn, ready to lay into whoever's interrupting my reunion, dang it.

But it's her dad. And her momma. And my momma. Two of the three are smiling. One's doing the exact opposite, and his daughter's still sitting in my lap.

I grin. "Hey, Dr. Marlowe."

He flashes the most effective "you're so screwed" smirk I've ever seen. "Hey, Austin."

Please don't kill me.

Momma just shakes her head, still smiling. "I invited the Marlowes to our house for an early dinner."

Okay.

She lifts her eyebrows. "So," she drawls, "you might want to get out of the grass."

"Getting my daughter off your lap would be a good start, too," Dr. Marlowe adds.

Dear God, he's going to kill me.

Marisa chokes back a laugh, but stands. I should probably look away from her dad. Actually, I really should, but I'm pretty sure he's hypnotizing me with that stare.

Marisa grabs my hand and yanks me to my feet. "I'll ride with Austin," she says, tugging me toward the lot. "See you there!"

At least one of us has some sense. I stumble after her, waving to our parents.

The parking lot's nearly empty as we head to my truck. She swings our hands between us, not letting go for a second. I really, really like having her back already.

I open her door for her. "Tell me more about Maryland. Or was it all Orioles games and flowers?"

"Mostly Orioles games and flowers." She leans back against the truck, her lips twisting into a tiny smirk. "But there *was* a pretty interesting grocery store visit."

"Oh, yeah?"

She nods. "I ran into a couple of my old softball buddies."

Oh. That sucks. I lean against the truck, too, just to be next to her. "I'm guessing they said somethin'?"

Instead of faltering, her smirk grows into a grin. "They cornered me in the ice cream aisle. First of all, major foul for blocking my ice cream. That was their biggest mistake. But then they thought they were being cute by saying, 'Welcome home, runaway.' Who even says that?"

My eyebrows scrunch together. Their trash talk is about as bad as Bastard Pitcher's from today. "Really? That was their best line?"

I toss my keys, which she swipes mid-air. "Right?" she says. "I just said, 'Bless your hearts,' grabbed my ice cream, and walked away. I wanted to dump the ice cream on their heads, but, you know, maturity and all that."

I snort. "You do know 'bless your heart' is basically Southern girl code for 'screw you,' right?"

"Um, yeah. Which is exactly why I said it." She tosses the keys back to me. "Hanging out with Hannah and Bri at your games has its perks."

This girl would make Hannah proud. Heck, *I'm* proud. I move aside, giving her room to climb up. But instead of closing the door, all I can do is stare, unable to rip my gaze from her. For a while, I was terrified she would never even talk to me again. But now she's here, and she's smiling at me, and she's looking at me like I've lost my damn mind, which I kind of have. But I'm okay with that.

"I'm glad you're home," I tell her.

Her smile widens. "So am I."

chapter twenty-four

$\mathcal{I}$'ve never been much of a whiner. At least, I don't think I have, but if I have to hear one more thing about acids and bases, my brain will explode. I don't care if I have a test tomorrow, and I don't care if Marisa's voice is my absolute favorite sound in the world. One more word, and I'm talking brain guts splattered all over her room.

She's sitting on the foot of her bed, her legs crisscrossed with my Chemistry book in her lap. She pretty much deserves sainthood for all the help she's given me, but good God, I know this stuff now. I swear. Just make it stop.

I flop back against her pillows and groan.

She clears her throat pointedly. "Strong acids completely transfer their protons to water—"

I roll over and bury my face in one of the pillows. Huh. This smells really good, actually. All citrusy, just like her shampoo.

"—and weak acids only partially dissociate—"

I groan louder.

The book slams closed. "You know, I get the feeling you're not listening to me," she says. She kicks me in the ass. Literally. "This test is tomorrow. No time for sleeping breaks."

I roll onto my back. "I know everything there is to know about acids and bases," I tell her, propping up on my elbows. She glares. "Babe, your voice is beautiful and angelic and sounds like a heavenly chorus, but if I hear one more word out of that book tonight, I'll yell."

She cocks an eyebrow. "Really?" she asks sarcastically. "You know everything?"

I sit up all the way. "Everything. All of it. I know all the things in that there book."

"You're so full of crap that I can actually smell it."

"That's kind of disgusting."

She stares at me for a moment with her lips pursed, like she's trying to decide if I am, in fact, full of crap. Finally, she cracks a smile and says, "All right." She pulls my study guide sheet from the back of the book. "I'll quiz you. If you get all my questions right, we'll stop for the night."

Fair enough. "And then what?"

"Winner's choice."

The girl's a pro at motivational tactics. I lace my fingers behind my head and lean back against her pillows. Bring it on.

She holds the paper up, shielding her face. "Name three of the most common strong acids," she says.

Easy. "Hydrochloric acid, hydrobromic acid, sulfuric acid."

"Next, define a weak base."

Just as easy. "It's a chemical base that doesn't fully ionize in an aqueous solution. Boom."

She lowers the paper. "Really?"

"I can go all night, Marlowe."

"Did you forget who you're talking to?" She crawls up the bed until she's sitting beside me, then flops back against the pillows and stretches her legs alongside mine. She glances at me out the corner of her eye, her lips twisting into a smirk.

She's not playing fair. This is distracting, damn it.

"I can go all night, too," she says. "Plenty of questions on here. Neutral pH is—?"

I drape my arm across her shoulder. "Seven. You could at least try and make it hard."

She looks back to the paper, and her smirk grows into a grin. She sits up a little straighter. "'Kay. True or false: your tongue is a great indicator as to whether something is an acid or base."

My jaw drops. "What the hell?"

She bursts out laughing. "I swear, it's an actual question."

I snatch the study guide from her and scan the page. Yep. Number eight, talking about tongues and crap. Shaking my head, I hand it back to her. "True. But I know you picked that one to throw me."

"Well, that's a gimme since you saw the answer." She places the guide on her nightstand. "But you passed, you Chemistry genius." She slides her hand across the back of my neck and pulls me down for a kiss.

Her bedroom door's wide open. We're on her bed. And the only light is coming from the lamp on her nightstand. If anyone walked by—

Screw it.

Closing my eyes, I kiss her back, slow and soft and, Lord have mercy, it's hot in here. She slides down until she's flat on the bed, giving me room to move on top of her. She tangles her fingers in my hair, holding me to her, not that she really has to.

Footsteps stomp up the stairs. And I'm suddenly on the floor beside the bed.

Ow.

I rub the back of my head, wincing as I sit up. Dr. Marlowe stands in the doorway, his arms crossed as his glare settles on me. "How's it going in here?"

"Good," Marisa and I both say, though I'm shocked I'm even conscious.

Her dad flips the light switch, turning on the overhead light. I wince at the sudden brightness. "Interested in that gun collection now, Austin? Because it'd be my pleasure."

Marisa chucks a pillow across the room. "Bye, Dad." He slowly backs into the hallway with his eyes never leaving mine. And only now do I realize my heart's racing faster than a NASCAR driver.

Rubbing my head again, I look up at Marisa, who's leaning over the edge of her bed. "You *really* had to throw me off the bed? Really? That was a thing you had to do?"

She holds out her hand. "I'm sorry! I panicked. Are you okay?"

She helps tug me to my feet. I crawl back onto the bed, though that's probably not the best idea. He didn't see anything, but her dad's not stupid. I'm pretty sure he's cleaning one of those precious shotguns right about now. "This arm's insured, you know. Coach'll have your rear for that."

She shoves me, making me laugh. "So what was winner's choice?"

It's a little late for that now. "Well, I *wanted* to drive out to the pond, but now I'm scared of your dad. How painful would my death be if I tried?"

She looks at the door. When she turns back to me, there's a sneaky smile stretching across her face. "I think the real question is, would your death be worth it?"

I grin. Oh, it'd be worth it. So worth it. I'd die happy. Painfully, sure, but happy.

"So?" she asks slowly. "What do you say?"

I say that you only live once. Might as well take the shots while you can. I hop off her bed and hold my hand out for hers. "You in?"

Her eyes shine as she slips her hand into mine. We head downstairs, where light spills out from the living room. I gesture for her to go ahead. She not-so-gently pushes me forward.

"You ask," I whisper.

"You," she whispers back. "You're the guy. Man up."

I narrow my eyes. "Really? You're pullin' the girl card right now?"

She raises an eyebrow. She has a point. Dang it. Taking a deep breath, I continue on to the living room, pausing in the doorway. Her parents are side by side on the couch, watching TV. Her mom smiles at me, but her dad remains stone-faced. I guess "liking me" doesn't mean much when he was five seconds away from catching me on top of his daughter.

"Dr. and Mrs. Marlowe," I say, smiling. "I'm wondering if it'd be okay to drive Marisa out to the pond? It's about twenty miles out."

Her dad barks out a laugh, and her mom chuckles right along with him. I'm no pro, but I'd say that's not a good sign. Marisa squeezes my hand. A little help here would be nice, girl.

Okay. Time for super-manners. I clear my throat. "I promise, I have nothing but the purest of intentions with your daughter."

Marisa slaps her hand against her forehead. "Oh my God," she murmurs.

I shrug at her. What does she want me to say? And come on, it wasn't *that* bad.

Was it?

Her dad's laughter finally subsides. "Right," he drawls. "That pretty much means the exact opposite. Nice try, though."

"What if we're back by eleven?" Marisa chimes in. About time.

Her mom shifts on the couch. "Ten," she says right as Dr. Marlowe opens his mouth. He shoots her a glare, but she focuses on Marisa.

"Ten-thirty," Marisa says.

Her mom looks between the two of us, her gaze lingering on me for a moment before she nods. "Done. But you better be in this house by ten-thirty. It's a school night."

I'll have her back at ten-twenty-nine as long as they stop looking at me like that.

Marisa backs out of the room, pulling me along with her. "Bye!" she calls as I stumble behind her. Before I can say a word, she's sliding on her flip-flops and hurrying out the door. I run outside behind her.

"You didn't give me a chance to tell them thanks," I tell her.

Her flip-flops clap against the driveway. She glances over her shoulder while heading for my truck. "I was doing you a favor, Pure Intentions Boy."

Fine. Maybe it was pretty bad.

She kicks her feet up on the dashboard while I back out of the driveway. I hit the button for the windows, and the cool night air whips through the truck. Her hair flies around as she leans her seat back and closes her eyes, relaxing.

We may not have long, but some time alone is better than none. For the past couple of months, it's been a bunch of baseball, school, work, and, well, hospitals. As much as I love ball and as much as I've loved watching her switch into tutor-mode to save my sorry ass, we need something different. Something fun. Something crazy.

Once we hit the dirt road that leads to the pond, Marisa sits upright. I park beneath the old oak tree and look over at her. My heart skips a beat. She's gorgeous. And now more than ever, I'm sure that I really, really love this girl. But the words stay bottled up, because there's no way I can tell her that. Not yet. The last thing I need to do is risk screwing this up. She wants slow and steady, so I'll give her slow and steady. Even if my pulse is anything but that.

"Why'd you want to come out here tonight?" she asks.

Because I love you. "Because I'm crazy about you," I say. "And with everything that's happened lately, I wanted to tell you that I'm crazy about you. Alone. Away from parents and work and school crap."

She smiles. "Crazy is good. I like crazy." She looks out at the water through the windshield. "We've come a heck of a long way since the last time we were here."

My chest tightens. The past few months have been nuts, but I'm not entirely sure I'd have it any other way. Stuff happens for a reason, even the bad stuff. If there's any fraction of a silver lining, it's that all of this brought us closer. And she's here. She's still here. That's what matters.

I reach over and grab her hand, bringing it to my lips. She glances at me out the corner of her eye. Smirks.

"The water looks nice tonight," she says.

There's something else buried under those words. It's in her voice. I follow her gaze to the pond. And now I'm smirking. I take in her gym shorts and T-shirt.

"How pissed do you think your parents would be if you came home with wet clothes?" I ask. "As long as it's by ten-thirty?"

She turns to me. "Again, I think we know the real question here is, would your death be worth it?"

Those really are words to live by.

We hop out of the truck. She leads the way to the pond, kicking off her flip-flops along the way. I yank mine off and toss them over my shoulder. No tellin' where they went. Don't really care.

I catch up to her at the water's edge, where she's stopped. There's hesitation written all over her face. The air's pretty crisp, maybe a toasty sixty degrees, and the water's a lot colder, but that can be solved with body heat. I'm more than willing to help her out with that.

"You in?" I ask.

She chews on her lip. "How deep is it?"

I shrug. "Right here? About eight feet. It's shallower on the other side—"

She jumps right in, plunging into the water with a splash.

"—of the tree," I finish. Damn, that girl's amazing.

I jump in after her, swimming up to the surface. She treads water toward me, her hair clinging to her skin, her mouth hanging open.

"I thought Southern water was supposed to be warm," she says breathlessly.

Grinning, I grab her hands, leading her to the shallower part of the pond. Once my feet hit the bottom, I pull her against me. Her legs hook around my waist, and I wrap my arms around her, holding her tight. Water drips from her skin as she drops her forehead to mine.

"Better?" I whisper.

She smiles. "Much," she says. And when she presses her lips to mine, all I know is the water on my skin and the taste of her lips and that she is so, so perfect for me.

I pull away just enough to look into those pretty green eyes. Crickets chirp all around us, with millions and millions of stars shining down as the breeze blows softly. This place, with this girl, is a special kind of heaven. More and more, this town grows on me. Right before I'm about to leave.

"How many ponds do you think there are in Columbia?" I ask.

She laughs lightly. Shakes her head. "I don't know. But we'll find them all."

We'll find them. "Can't wait." I swallow, unable to tear my gaze away from her. "I really am crazy about you," I tell her, barely above a whisper.

Her lips twitch into a tiny half-smile. "If you're crazy, then I'm insane. You make my heart so, so happy, Austin."

Closing my eyes, I kiss her again, deeper this time. With her chest pressed against me, her legs squeezing my waist, her lips against mine like she's kissing me for a final breath—I'm freakin' done for. And damn it, if I do die tonight, at least I'll go out with a bang.

chapter twenty-five

Weddings out in the boondocks of South Carolina are kind of a big deal, especially when those weddings involve Felix Torres, the pitcher who once held Lewis Creek High's homerun record.

(Guess which pitcher broke that record. But I digress.)

Standing in front of the bathroom mirror, I adjust my blue bowtie and straighten my black sports coat. Momma knocks on the bathroom door and pushes it open. She closed the shop for today so she can celebrate with everyone else in town. Considering she and Marisa spent hours on the wedding's floral arrangements, she deserves a day off. With her hair all pulled up and her makeup actually done, she looks like a million bucks. Heck, a gazillion.

"You've already broken rule number one of male wedding guests," she says. "You're not supposed to be more handsome than the groom."

I snort and flip off the light, following her into the hallway. "Please."

She stops. Turns to face me. And proceeds to burst into tears. I run back to the bathroom, grab the toilet paper, and hand her the roll. She rips off a piece and dabs at her eyes, waving me off.

"I'm sorry. I'm sorry. Your dad would just be so proud of you, all cleaned up and turnin' things around. School's so much better; your game's better than ever." She squeezes my shoulder, and dang it, now I'm trying not to cry. "I'm proud of you."

"Momma—"

"I'm sorry." She takes a deep breath and smiles. "Happy day. It's a happy day, so we're going to be happy and talk about happy things. I'll see you at the church. You heading out to pick up Marisa?"

I nod. As she starts toward the stairs, I duck into my room and grab the single rose from my dresser. My lips twitch. Marisa's going to love it. Considering how long it took me to track down a shipment of these things, let's just hope so.

Momma's sliding into her car as I walk out to my truck. I feel bad for her on days like this that are full of couples and all that romantic stuff. It can't be easy to watch. She's a trooper, that's for sure.

When I pull into Marisa's driveway, she's already standing on her front porch. With her dad. I'm still not his favorite person. Bring a man's daughter home soaked, and suddenly you're the bad guy. But Marisa's stunning enough to look past the slightly terrifying giant. She strolls down the driveway as I step out of the truck. Grinning, I hold out my hand for hers. She takes it and twirls, making her purple sundress flare at the bottom.

"Looking good," she says. "But a bowtie? Really?"

I stand a little taller and straighten my jacket. "Please. All the cool guys wear bowties. It's a Southern wedding rule." I wave to her dad. "Hey, Dr. Marlowe."

Nothing but a steel glare. Luckily, the night at the pond was so, so worth that glare.

Marisa gestures to my truck, her heels clicking against the driveway as we walk around to her side. "You washed the truck."

I open her door for her. "I did wash the truck."

"And you talked to my dad."

Somewhat.

She looks up at me. "You'd be on your way to good date status if you'd brought flowers." She *tsks* and climbs into the truck.

I glance to her porch, where her dad's still standing. Still watching. Maybe now's not the best time to prove her wrong. I slam her door closed.

———

The church is packed when Marisa and I walk inside. Some little girl in a super-puffy white dress is running up the aisle, screeching at the top of her lungs, with a woman chasing her in foot-tall heels. *Ouch.* We head for the right side of the church, where half the team's crammed into one pew. Momma, who's sitting behind them, smiles as Marisa slides in beside her.

I squeeze in between Brett and Eric, making sure not to knock Brett's arm, which is still in a sling. "How much longer in confinement?" I ask him.

"At least another two weeks," he says, staring straight ahead. I follow his gaze to Jay, who's standing up front with his dad, brother, and their priest.

"How are y'all?"

"Haven't talked in a few days," he says. "He called to check on me Wednesday. Not a word since." He blows out a breath. "A lot of people started askin' questions after the game. A break's good. Low profile and all that."

A small hand grasps my shoulder. I whirl around, finding Marisa leaning forward. She nods to the rest of the guys on my pew. "Maybe I was wrong. You guys and your bowties are pretty darn handsome."

I grin. Curling my finger, I signal for her to lean in closer. "You know, you missed your memo. You're not supposed to look better than the bride, Marisa."

She rolls her eyes, but smiles and settles back in her seat.

"Good for you, man," Brett mutters. "Good for you."

I slap his knee and toss my arm across the back of the pew. "You can do it, too," I say just loud enough for him to hear. Jay's eyes flicker to us. Brett tenses.

"You said beatin' that pitcher was worth breakin' every bone in your body," I continue. "Are you actually going to show that guy and everyone else that their opinions mean shit?"

Marisa smacks the back of my head. "Church!" she whispers loudly.

I glance over my shoulder. "Woman—"

She cocks an eyebrow and shushes me.

Noted. I turn back around. Remembering what Jay told me that night at his house, I add, "That said, the ball's in your hand. This is your call. You do what makes you happy. If you're not ready, don't push it. He gets it. He loves you, man."

He inhales sharply. Jay looks away. I swear, if I end up being the one with the normal relationship out of all of us, I'm buying five thousand lottery tickets.

"I'm ready," he says, meeting my eyes. "I'm just scared, Braxton."

I can't even imagine what the hell's going through his head right now. I don't have some motivational speech or any words that could touch his fear. All I can say is the one thing I know for a fact.

"Whatever you decide to do, we've got your back."

———

Felix's (now) wife is probably one of the hottest women to ever come out of Lewis Creek, and one of the sweetest. Back when Felix played ball for the school, the two of them were the town's golden couple. Good for them for being a golden couple that actually, you know, worked. The person other people expect you to end up with usually turns out to be a dead end. I've seen plenty of couples kick the bucket once the heat of summer hits.

Marisa must catch me staring at the (correction: second) hottest person in Lewis Creek because she swats me on the head again, right here at our table in the reception hall. I grin. She rolls her eyes for what's probably the hundredth time today, but she can't fight that little smile no matter how hard she tries. Wrapping my arm around her shoulders, I pull her in for a side-hug.

"It's craziness, huh?" I ask. "Half of Lewis Creek's population, plus bright pink and purple decorations, plus strobe lights, plus punch that'll knock you off your rocker, equals Marisa Marlowe's worst dance nightmare come true."

"It's like Barbie puked in here. Felix is lucky I love Jay, so I love him by association." She scans the room. "Speaking of your partner in crime, where is he?"

I crane my neck, looking around the hall, but there's no sign of Jay anywhere. "Dunno," I mutter. "The rest of the bridal party's here." In fact, Felix and Lana are already seated and about to start the toasts. I don't want to go looking for the guy, but he can't miss this.

The door to the hall opens, spilling the late afternoon sunlight across the floor. Brett steps into the room. So does Jay. Brett looks like he just ate Momma's attempt at deer jerky. Jay looks like he's about to pass out cold any second. Marisa reaches into my lap and grabs my hand right as Jay grabs Brett's, lacing his fingers through his.

Son of a mother-effer. They did it.

They're two deer trapped in headlights, unmoving, but what I think they realize is that no one even notices. Until they do start walking to our table, and I spot old Mr. Morgan and his wife scowling at them. And Mrs. Carter's mouth drops open. And Mr. Lincoln flops back against his chair with his face all twisted up. All of that's just at the table beside us. I know I shouldn't expect much more from folks in Lewis Creek, but a guy can hope, right?

Jay and Brett take their seats at our table, with Jay sitting on the other side of Marisa. Brett's usually tan skin is white as Casper himself. I think I can actually see his heart pounding through his jacket. His gaze stays on the table, but Jay meets my eyes. He grins like a fool. So do I.

"Brett," I say quietly. His head pops up. "Good for you, man."

While the corner of his mouth twitches, he doesn't fully smile, which doesn't surprise me. A pastor's kid walking into a reception holding another guy's hand isn't exactly on par with what's considered normal around here. I glance at Marisa, though, and I'm reminded of just how stupid normal is. A little bit of crazy is a hell of a lot better.

"Yeah," she says with a smile. "Crazy really is better."

"I'm startin' to think you're actually reading my mind."

"I'm startin' to think you need to get yourself checked out because you talk an awful lot without realizin' it."

Leaning in, I rest my forehead against hers. "You just dropped not one, but *two* Gs."

She shrugs and gives me a quick kiss. "I spend all my time with a Southern guy who hates the letter G. It was bound to happen sooner or later." She glances at Jay and Brett out the corner of her eye. "They're officially my favorite people ever. I'm so happy for them."

Glass clinks at the front of the hall, and as Felix stands with a microphone, the music and motion come to a standstill. Beaming, he raises his glass toward our table. Toward Jay. And I'm pretty sure Jay's about to stop breathing. I'm definitely not doing mouth-to-mouth on him here. Right as I'm about to start looking for a doctor, Jay lets out an *oof*.

"Damn, girl," he mutters to Marisa. "You didn't have to kick me."

Suppressing a laugh, I squeeze her hand, which is resting in my lap. The girl's resourceful.

"I can't thank you all enough for joining us today," Felix begins. "To my parents, my family, and Lana's family: your assistance in bringing this day together was outstanding. It's been perfect."

He lowers his gaze, seeming to be in thought, before looking to the crowd once again. "Today's about love. About finding that one person your soul loves and can't thrive without. And it doesn't matter who that person is—man, woman, or what have you. What matters is how you feel with that person, and, well, how she makes you want to be better. For her."

The guy hit the nail on the head; the hand in mine right now is proof of that. The rose in my coat is practically screaming at me, but it needs to wait a *little* bit longer. Felix smiles down at Lana, who looks at him with a gaze so warm I don't know how he isn't melting.

"Lewis Creek has its downfalls," he continues, "but there's one thing that brought me back to this town after college: the love each of us shares for one another. So let's celebrate love tonight. Let's party and raise some hell until the cows come running."

He raises his wine glass and takes a gulp before slamming it down on the table. The room erupts into applause and cheers while Felix holds his hand out for Lana's. The music resumes, and as they head for the dance floor, Felix winks in our direction. Instead of bordering on passing out this time, Jay nods back with a slight smile. And if I didn't know any better, I'd say Brett's skin has moved up from Casper to eggshell-white. It's a start, anyway.

I turn and catch Marisa staring at me with a smile even warmer than Lana's. The difference between me and Felix is that I think I *am* melting. Reaching into my coat, I pull out the hollerin' flower and hold it out for her.

Her face softens as she takes the long-stemmed purple rose and twirls it between her fingers. "It's gorgeous," she says. "Flawless, actually. Where'd it come from, though? We don't have any purple ones at the shop. And I should know since I was there all day yesterday."

Taking a deep breath, I say, "Well, here's the thing. I ordered some, like, three weeks ago for the shop, but our usual supplier was out, so I had to track down *another* one, who told me it'd be two weeks, even with extra shipping. So I broke down and paid thirty bucks to have them overnighted to my house from a shop in Alabama."

"Austin?"

"Yeah?"

"Breathe, honey. You've got to breathe when you talk." She smiles down at the rose. "Easier question for you, I hope: why purple?"

That is easier. I shift in my seat, facing her. "I never really knew what being nuts about someone meant until I knew that I'd do anything to make you smile. To make you happy. To make sure you'd never feel any pain again. And now I know that I can't always take the pain away, but I hope I'll be the one you come to when it's there."

Her lower lip quivers as her eyes well up with tears. "But why purple?" she asks, that little voice of hers trembling.

Chuckling, I grab her hand. "Because it's your favorite. And because purple roses mean love at first sight or enchantment. What you did to me? That's the reason they came up with a rose to define it. It's not just friendship; it's being absolutely enchanted by the girl who knocked you clean off your feet the second you met her. And I can't believe I just used the word 'enchanted,' but—"

Tears spill onto her bright red cheeks. "Oh my God." She fans herself.

I grab a napkin and shove it into her hands. "What?"

Her shoulders rise and fall as she wipes at her eyes, the napkin coming away with black crap all over it. Is she—shit, is she hyperventilating?

Over her head, I see Jay's eyes widen. "The hell did you do?" he whispers.

I shrug. Holy crap, what did I do?

"Do I need to apologize or—?"

Marisa's gaze softens. Her hand slips into mine. And even though her lip's still quivering, I *think* she's trying to smile.

"Austin?" she says.

I'm almost too petrified to utter a word. "Y-yeah?"

"You, my dear little country boy, have officially proven that there is such a thing as a Southern gentleman." She squeezes my hand and leans forward to kiss my cheek. "Don't ever change."

A grin sneaks across my face. "Told you I'd be a good date."

She scrunches her nose playfully. "Yeah, you're not so bad."

And now, time to go for the kill. I wrap my arm around the back of her chair. "So would not-so-bad be a good enough reason for prom?"

Her eyes widen. Her lips part, but instead of saying anything, she shakes her head. My stomach sinks, but I somehow maintain a shaky smile. I know she hates the dance thing, and I know it's a longshot, but it's my last year. My last prom. And call me nuts, but I actually kind of sort of want to go. With her.

If she stops staring at me like I'm certifiable.

"There's still a while to decide," I add. "If you need to think about it or whatever."

She inhales deeply. "Depends," she finally says. "Will you try to get in my pants?"

"Irrelevant. You won't be wearing pants."

She shoves my shoulder. "You're so lucky my dad wasn't around to hear that."

The girl's got a point.

"But yes," she says. "Even though I maintain that dances are evil, if I'm going to suffer through a night of blisters and terrible decorations, there's no one else I'd rather suffer with."

Not exactly what I was going for, but I'll take it.

A streak of sunlight flashes across the wall. I turn right as Pastor Perry walks out the door, letting it slam closed behind him. Well, damn it. I look over at Brett and Jay. They're both silent, staring down at the table. Any color Brett had regained is gone.

Immediately, two sets of heels click against the floor, heading in our direction. Mrs. Torres and Mrs. Perry approach the table, coming to stand between Jay and Brett. With one hand on her hip and the other on Brett's shoulder, Mrs. Perry smiles at the rest of us.

"This is an awfully good-lookin' table," she says. "Do y'all mind if we borrow these guys for a minute?"

Brett gnaws on his bottom lip, his forehead creasing. "Momma," he begins, glancing up at her. "I'm sor—"

She cuts him off with a shake of her head. She bends over slightly, until she's looking straight into his eyes. "You've got absolutely nothing to be sorry for."

"But Dad."

Though the words are quiet, they still make their way across the table, weighing tons. Mrs. Perry holds his gaze for a moment before saying, "If you remember anything, you remember this: your daddy loves you more than anything on God's green earth. He'll be just fine. *You* will be fine." She looks over at Jay, and when she smiles at the guy who walked in holding her son's hand, I'm pretty sure she gives Brett the strength not to crack in front of hundreds of people.

Mrs. Torres holds her hand out for Jay's. Mrs. Perry holds hers out for Brett's. And as they lead the guys onto the dance floor, I hope to all that's holy that the scoffers and eye-rollers in this room see what I've known for years.

People can hold hands with whomever they want. And that's okay.

chapter twenty-six

On our way back to Marisa's house, she's quiet, staring out her window for the entire drive. It's late and we've had a long day, so I'm sure she's exhausted, but there's something else radiating off her. Not sadness or anything. I just can't put my finger on it.

I pull into her driveway and cut the engine. She finally moves, only to unbuckle her seatbelt. I grasp her hand as she does. "You all right?" I ask.

She nods and pulls her hand away. "Mostly. But let's walk and talk. I need air."

I step out of the truck along with her. She walks around, meeting me at my door. This time she takes my hand, lacing her fingers through mine. Instead of starting toward the brightly lit house, she leads me into the grass, which shimmers from the night's dew. She kicks off her shoes, and her hand slips from mine as she strolls across the lawn, staring up at the sky.

I wish there were more ways to tell her how downright gorgeous she is.

"I was thinking about Brett and Jay," she says, turning to face me. "About how they'll be split up next year." She smiles sadly. "And I was thinking about how much that must suck, to find someone you're crazy about and then tell them goodbye."

I hadn't even thought about that with those two. Soon they won't have a secret keeping them apart anymore; they'll have states. I'm not sure which is worse. Moving away from the place you've lived your entire life is hard enough. Add that in with moving away from the person you're head over heels for? That sounds like a kick to the gut. I don't know what I'd do if Marisa was going anywhere other than USC.

And I'm not stupid. I know we might not be together forever or anything, but I'll be damned if I don't eat up every day that we are.

I look out to the field across the street, where the wheat sways in the breeze. There's this peacefulness that comes with Lewis Creek, with its spring nights and open skies and fields that go on for miles. There's plenty of craziness here. There's a lot of good, too.

Marisa sits in the grass and crosses her legs. "Do you ever get scared about next year?"

Shoving my hands into the pockets of my khakis, I cross the distance between us. I've had a lot of thoughts about next year, eagerness to get the heck out of this town being at the top of the list. Between that and focusing on ball and school and the girl in front of me, I don't think I've had enough brain space to be scared.

I sit beside her and rest my elbows on my bent knees. Instead of answering, I ask, "Are you?"

She considers that for a minute. "A little." She leans back on her hands. "While we were in Maryland, I think Dad convinced me to change my major from straight Chemistry to Pre-Med."

My eyes widen. The idea of her dedicating four years to Chemistry was crazy enough. If she goes the doctor route, well, more power to her. "Wow," is all I can say.

She lets out a breathless laugh and shakes her head. "I know. It's nuts. Chemistry's my thing, so I wasn't worried about that at all. But Pre-Med brings in all the science. *All* of it." She looks over at me. "All my life, I've watched Dad help people. And this just feels right, you know? He might be on to something. The question is whether or not I can hack it."

We stare at each other. She's the first to crack, bursting into laughter. "'Kay, so that was a terrible word," she says. "But you know what I mean. And I'm trying to remind myself that things have a way of working out the way they're supposed to. Maybe not the way we plan, but the way they're meant to be."

If anyone can hack it, it's her. Just not, you know, literally. So when I tell her, "I think you can do whatever the hell you want to do," I'm not sure I've meant anything more. "Anything you want is yours to take."

She smiles and lies back in the grass, staring up at the sky. All I can stare at is her.

"Stars are kind of amazing when you think about them," she says. "They're always there. Even when it's cloudy or when the sun's shining, they're still out there, in the universe. Sparkling." She pats the grass. "Come down here with me."

She doesn't have to ask me twice. I lie back beside her, blades of grass prickling the back of my neck.

"You told me I can have whatever I want." She turns her head, her face barely an inch from mine. "I want to help people. I want to love fearlessly. I want my heart to be so full that it's near combustion before I go to bed every night. And I want to keep this feeling forever, this feeling of looking at you and knowing that I'm lo—" She bites her lip. "Knowing that I'm cared about."

I *love you.* The words are right there, on the tip of my tongue, but they're glued there.

She takes a deep breath and looks up again, to the sky. "I want the world," she says. "And I want the stars."

Her hand's resting right next to mine. I grab it. "Then make it happen."

Her smile grows. "What do you want?"

And now I look up again, at the billions of stars crowding the night sky. The world would be nice, but that'll take an awful lot of time. What matters is what we do with that time. "All I want is a life I'm proud of," is my answer.

She squeezes my hand. I turn my head right as she does, meeting her gaze. "Then make it happen," she whispers.

chapter twenty-seven

The locker room door screeches as I yank it open before practice on Monday afternoon. Coach called me out of my last class early, so the room's empty and quiet—too quiet—as I head to his office. It's weird, walking through here this close to the end of the season. The lockers are full now, but our final home game is in less than a week. After that? Empty. They'll be filled up again next year, but for the first time in four seasons, not with my things. There'll be a new pitcher, probably Eric, leading the Bulldogs. This won't be my turf. The Bulldogs won't be my team.

I stop in front of Coach's office door. He won't be my coach.

I knock on the door. When he calls out, "Yeah," I push it open. Dressed in his practice gear, he waves me in from behind his desk.

"You wanted to see me?" I ask, sliding into the leather chair in front of him.

He lifts the brim of his cap and shuffles the papers on his desk before setting them to the side. "Just real quick before the guys file in. Wanted some quiet time with you. Away from prying eyes. Nosy ears." He leans back in his chair, grinning as he swivels back and forth. "It's been a hell of a few years, Braxton."

That's the understatement of the century. "Yes, sir."

He chuckles, tossing his head back. "I remember when you were a snot-faced kid coming out for JV. You thought you were hot stuff because your Little League coach talked you up."

I grin. I remember that like it was yesterday. I was in the lineup of freshmen trying out for the JV team. Coach stared me up and down, shook my hand, and told me he was going to give me the most worthwhile ass-kicking of my life. "Well, you did switch over to coach varsity once I moved up. I must've been hot stuff."

He points at me. "Yeah, and you knew it. That was the problem."

"Yeah," I say, scratching the back of my head. "I was a punk then."

"Still are," he says with a smirk. "But you're growin' into a good man. I'm proud as hell of how you're turnin' out." He pauses and adds, "I know it's not necessarily what you want to hear, but your dad would be real proud of you, too."

Pursing my lips, I nod. So that explains this random pre-practice meeting. "Is that why you wanted to see me in here instead of the field?"

"So you wouldn't lose your cool in front of your team? You bet." He leans forward, resting his elbows on his desk. "We've had this talk before."

"It ended awfully bad last time," I remind him. My leg bounces as I hold his stare. "I'm not sure why you're trying again."

My sophomore season was rocky to say the least, considering Dad died right before tryouts. Coach brought me into his office then, laying into me about going to Dad's grave. Told me I needed to face my anger head-on. I called him an asshole and told him to shove the psychobabble BS up his ass.

He benched me for three weeks.

"I think that forgiveness goes a long way," he says. "I told you this last time we had this discussion, and I'll tell you again: forgiveness isn't for the other person. You forgive for yourself. For your own sanity. If anything, at least go to the man's grave. Say what you need to say."

He and Momma keep going on about this. It's like some tired-ass Ping-Pong game they've got going, and honestly, I'm getting sick of it. What Coach doesn't know is that I've crossed the forgiveness bridge. But going to Dad's grave? That's like asking me to jump off that bridge. Confrontation and I don't get along too well.

"What if I don't?" I ask. "Go to his grave?"

Blowing out a breath, he shrugs. "Then you get to carry his ghost around with you for a long, long time. He'll follow you to college. He'll follow you when you're drafted. He'll be in the back of your head when you're pitching. When you close your eyes. He'll always be there." He folds his hands. "I'm talking about closure here, Austin. Everyone deserves closure."

"Why do you even care?" I spit out. My throat tightens. I rub my sweat-streaked face and lean forward on my knees. "Why the hell do you care what I do? I'm off your hands after this year."

"Because you're like a son to me. Now watch your mouth." He points at me again. "I care because I know what it's like for guilt to eat at you. I care because I saw how much that man meant to you, and I still see it right this second. I know what his memory has done to you, to your life. If you leave town without making peace with this, you'll regret it for the rest of your damn life. You can quote me on that."

My jaw stiffens, and I blink quickly, hiding the stupid, stupid, *stupid* tears that are threatening to creep out. "Well," I say, clearing my throat. "If this is so important to you, will you excuse me from today's practice?"

He stares at me for a moment. "And why would I do that?"

I narrow my eyes. "I got some feelings that need sortin' out, right? Thought I'd take a drive to the cemetery. Do my sortin' there."

He nods to the door. "Only time I'm lettin' you slide. Make it count."

I'm already in the doorway when he calls my name. I whirl around. "What?"

He lifts an eyebrow, but lets that one slide. "Friday's game is Senior Night," he says. "I need your best memory of the team. Be thinking about it."

Right now, best memories aren't at the top of my list. Storming out of his office, I stride through the locker room, out of school, and to my truck. He wants me to go to Dad's grave? Fine. Let's give this shit a try.

I smack my steering wheel and yell. Yell. Yell until my throat's raw and my lungs are out of air. Yell until my heart stutters and my cheeks flame up. Once my throat can't take any more, I crank the engine and peel out of the parking lot. My pulse pounds in my ears as I speed down the back roads toward the cemetery. I navigate through the narrow paths of the graveyard until I come to the familiar spot. And for the first time in over two years, I get out of the truck.

Michael David Braxton
Beloved Husband, Father, and Friend
All Our Love, All Our Promises, All Our Swears

All our freakin' love. Promises. Swears.

When I was a kid, Dad patted me on the back after every game. Praised me up and down, whether I won or lost. At those moments, more than ever, I knew he loved me like crazy. And nearly every day, he swore he'd love me and Momma 'til the day he died. But the funny thing is, our love didn't keep him from leaving. It didn't keep him from dying. It wasn't enough for him.

We weren't enough for him.

"You—" My voice cracks. I bite my fist, gnawing on it, but my head goes blank as I glare at his headstone. There's no air out here. There's no air. I don't know how Momma ever breathes out here because there's no air.

And it's quiet. Too quiet. All you can hear are your own thoughts, mingled with the silence of death, which is louder than a bullhorn. My breathing returns with a vengeance, coming too fast, too quick, too much at once.

"You," I say again, struggling to keep my voice even. "You died over two years ago, but you're here every damn day. You won't leave me alone."

I take a step forward and try swallowing back the lump in my throat, but it's useless. Tears swim in my eyes, blurring his headstone, his name, the line between the year he was born and the year he died. That little line dictates our lives. How insane is that? Everything we do in our lifetime is encompassed in that one stupid line.

Momma and Coach say I need to forgive him for what he did. But what they don't understand is that I don't need to forgive him—not anymore. Somehow, in the slightest, most miniscule of ways, I get it. Because of Marisa. Because now I've seen firsthand how even the best of people can fight demons and almost lose. Because I've seen that bad shit happens to good people.

But Dad—Dad did lose. And I can't fix that. I wouldn't have been able to if I'd tried.

For the longest time, I hated him. I hated him for not telling someone what was bothering him. I hated him for not getting help. I hated him for being selfish enough to take his life when there were people behind who loved him more than their own lives.

Earlier this season, Coach told me to suck up my pride and that real men know when to ask for help. But that's not always true. Sometimes pride is debilitating, especially in a town where people put their heroes on pedestals.

"We wanted you here," I choke out. "You know that, right? We would've done anything to keep you here. All you had to do was ask."

Tears slip down my cheeks. No matter how tightly I squeeze my eyes, they just keep coming. I fall to my knees. The wet grass squishes against my skin as I stare at the marble headstone.

"For a long time, I hated you for leaving us. For how you left us. But now—" My voice cracks again. Now that I've seen the pain that leads up to that decision, the ache, the freakin' torture that goes through someone's head... "—I hate myself for hating you. And I'm sorry. I'm so damn sorry."

Wiping my nose with my arm, I stand. "Coach sent me to forgive you, Dad, but I just hope you can forgive me." I take a step back. And another, and another, until I hit my truck.

I climb into the Chevy, and I sit. I sit for a long, long time, staring at the grave-markers ahead, stretching across the cemetery. I stare at good people, bad people, okay people. People who lived their lives to the fullest and people who screwed their way through life without thinking. I'm sure I'm staring at other people who were like my dad, who had the world at their fingertips but were haunted by something.

And I think that's my biggest regret: not knowing what led him to the bridge. I don't know what was going through his head that night, what made him think death was the only way out. But if there's one thing I do know, it's that I hope every single person in my life knows how much I love them. And that I would really miss them if they were gone.

It's dark by the time I pull into Marisa's driveway. Raining, too. I'm not sure how I ended up here, to be honest. All I know is that she's the only person I want to see.

The truck door creaks as I push it open. My practice cleats, which never got used today, splash in a puddle when I step out onto the driveway. Their porch light is on, which means they're still awake. That's a good thing. Waking up your girlfriend's parents in the middle of the night is kind of a deal-breaker for said parents.

I push the doorbell, prepared for my usual wait, but the door swings open almost immediately. Marisa steps outside, her face all scrunched-up and confused as she says, "Oh, my God. Austin, you're soaked."

Am I? I look down. Yep. I am, in fact, soaked. Not entirely sure when that happened.

I gesture to the door. "How're your parents?"

She crosses her arms. "They're fine," she drawls. "Why? What's going on?"

I nod. "Good. That's good." I jerk my thumb over my shoulder. "I just got back from seeing my dad."

Her expression softens. She wraps her arms around my waist, pulling me against her. "Are you okay?"

I nod again. "Yeah. I think I am." And finally, I look at her, really look at her, and realize why I came here. Why she was the only person I wanted to see tonight. What I wanted to make sure she heard.

"I love you," I tell her.

Her eyes widen, but all I want to do is say it again, and again, and again. So, as I wrap my own arms around her, I do. "I love that your eyes crinkle when you smile.

I love that you laugh at anything and everything. I love that you love baseball and flowers, and now you love barbeque and fries. I just love you."

Her lips quirk. "I'm a mess sometimes."

Doesn't matter. "You're a beautiful mess."

"I can be hard to handle."

Doesn't matter. "So can I."

"I'm not perfect."

Really doesn't matter. "You're perfect for me."

And now she's crying, full-blown teardrops trailing down her cheeks, but she's also smiling, so I think it's a good cry. She inhales deeply and loops her arms around my neck, pulling me down and kissing me like her life depends on it. And when she murmurs, "I love you, too," against my lips, I'm falling. I'm drowning. I can't breathe. This is why I came here: to tell this girl that she's worth every tear, every meltdown, every smile, every laugh. That she's worth everything. I back away just enough to look into those gorgeous eyes, and I'm an absolute goner.

"What kind of look is that?" she asks, searching my face.

My lips are chapped, my eyes hurt like the devil, and my muscles suddenly feel like Jell-O. "It's a look that says you're the first thing on my mind when I wake up and the last before I fall asleep. That every word out of your mouth is coated in gold, even if it's the cheesiest thing I've ever heard. Even if I'm kind of the master of cheese in this relationship."

Tears spring to the corners of her eyes again. For a split second, I'm terrified. I'm scared as hell that I just crossed some invisible line into stalker territory, even if I am her boyfriend. But her lip stops trembling, and she smiles.

"How'd we get lucky enough to find each other?" she asks.

"Because the universe can be a jerk, but I think it knows when people need something amazing."

Her smile widens. "Now I really want to kiss you again."

"Then stop talking. Start doing." And once she reaches for me, there's no turning back. Not that I would want to.

She's not perfect. I'm not perfect. But together, we're imperfectly perfect for each other.

Talk about making an ol' boy fall hard.

chapter twenty-eight

$\mathcal{I}'ve$ nearly chomped off my entire thumbnail while sitting at my table, watching Mr. Matthews grade my Chem exam. Every test for the past few weeks has ended the same way, with me staying behind while he grades my answers with that red marker. The difference between the beginning of the semester and now is that his marker doesn't run out of ink by the time he's finished. My eligibility isn't even an issue anymore. My 3.0 is solid. I've got to hand it to the guy. He's actually interested in getting me even higher than what's required.

He's also a huge USC fan. I think it's safe to say that's more incentive on his part. But I'll take whatever the heck I can get.

He re-caps the Sharpie, flips the test over, and holds it out for me. I take a deep breath and make my way to the front of the room. This is the last exam before the final. I've always thought baseball season was do-or-die, but this class has made ball feel like child's play.

Taking the paper from his hands is like being the lucky bastard who snatches the Holy Grail. This can't be right. "A ninety-eight?" I ask.

He grins. "Just one wrong answer. You nailed that sucker."

I gape at him. No way. No freakin' way. "So what's my average look like now?"

He turns to his computer and hits a few keys. "This brings you up to a B-plus, Mr. Braxton. Not half-bad at all."

My lungs deflate like a hot air balloon as I stare at the paper in my hand. A *ninety-eight*. I don't think I've gotten a ninety-eight on anything science-related in my life.

"I know I shouldn't ask a magician the secret to his tricks," Mr. Matthews says, "but how'd you manage?"

Backing away toward the door, I smack the paper against my hands. "I have a freakin' genius of a girlfriend-slash-tutor, that's how."

He stands and stuffs his hands into his khakis. "Maybe there's a little genius in you, too. Don't let her take all the credit." He glances at the clock. "You should get out to the field. Can't have Senior Night without the star senior."

"Yes, sir. Thank you, sir." I toss up a wave and stride through the hallway, unable to tear my eyes away from the test. It's a miracle. A Christmas-in-April miracle.

I push through the double doors, the spring air washing over me as I head outside to the parking lot with a grin on my face. Today's game starts early, which means a certain pretty girl got off work even earlier. As soon as I see that girl waiting for me at my truck, my cheeks damn near hurt from smiling even bigger.

You see, crazy-love is pretty much the greatest thing to ever exist in this universe. It's not always easy, but it's a freakin' blast. It's the "can't eat, can't sleep, can barely breathe until I see her" kind of love. It's the "just one more kiss on her front porch" kind of love. The kind of crazy that no one else understands, except me and her. Love ain't right until you've lost your mind and that girl finds it and holds it for safe-keeping.

"Ninety-eight," I call out, waving my test for her to see.

She shrieks and jumps up, wrapping her arms around my neck as I hug her back. "That's amazing!" She scrunches her nose at me. "And three months ago, you were calling yourself an idiot. Idiots don't get ninety-eights, Austin."

I toss my backpack into the bed of my truck and grab my gear bag. "Well, someone had to help me get all smart and stuff. Remember?"

She rolls her eyes. "Your mom said she'll be here as soon as she can. She was about to close up the shop when I left."

Draping my arm across her shoulder, we start for the field. Tonight's Senior Night, which means us seniors are going to be on display after the game, along with our parents. That's all well and good, but part of me is depressed as hell. It's the last official home game. It's like one last nail in the high school baseball coffin. We've got playoffs and hopefully State, but after that, it's over. Done. I've played ball with most of these guys since Little League. After graduation, we'll be split across the country.

This day kind of sucks now.

Marisa wraps her arm around my waist. We've still got a couple hours before the post-game ceremony starts, but Brett and Eric's momma is already on the field, talking to Coach. Their dad hasn't been to any of our games since the wedding. Their momma hasn't missed a minute. I always knew I liked Mrs. Perry.

I stop once we reach the bleachers. Take a deep breath. Grin. This? This is my home field. It doesn't matter how ready I've been to leave, doesn't matter how often I've counted down the days until August. This may be a nowhere town, but it's my town. My home. And yeah, I'm gonna miss it.

Marisa heads on to the bleachers to wait for Momma. I hurry to the locker room to change, using its outside entrance. I swing the door open and the A/C hits me full-force, taking my breath away. Lockers stretch along the walls of the room, the open space in the middle empty except for the lone bench. It's quiet. Still. That'll change any minute now. The other guys will be here soon enough.

It shouldn't be this hard. My gut shouldn't feel like it's ripping in half. But it is. And it does. My throat tightens as I head for my locker. The number 3 is scribbled on masking tape that stretches along the top, tape that's worn and ragged and halfway falling off the metal. I claimed that number years ago. My dad claimed it before me. For today, the number's still mine.

The locker room door slams closed. Jay strolls in, with his bag slung over his shoulder, looking about as doom–and-gloom as I feel. Like his gut's shredding right along with mine. His jaw's stiff as he says, "Damn. Thought I'd catch you crying."

If he'd come in thirty seconds later, he might have.

He drops his bag onto the floor and sinks onto the bench, staring ahead at his locker. He shakes his head. "This sucks, dude. Does it feel like goodbye to you, too?"

Yep. I sit beside him and follow his gaze. Our lockers have always been side by side. In a few months, our lockers won't even be in the same state. The guy's been my right-hand man since we were zit-covered kids. I don't know what I'm going to do without him.

"How you feelin' about next year?" I ask. "New team. New coach. New pitcher."

He blows out a breath. "Scared as hell. You?"

"Scared as hell."

He leans forward, resting his elbows on his knees. "At least you'll have Marisa. I'm losing my best friend and my boyfriend at the same time."

"Does it suck as bad as I think it does?"

"Worse." He straightens, stretching his arms above his head. "Here I thought I'd find you crying, and you've got me about to break."

I slap his shoulder and stand, mostly so he won't see my face fall. My locker door squeaks as I swing it open. "There's no cryin' in baseball, Torres."

He steps to his own locker. Looks me straight in the eye. "I'm gonna miss your sorry ass, you know that?"

And I'm going to miss him more than my right arm. I hold up my hand. He high-fives me, holding on for a beat before letting go. "All-Star Duo forever, bro." Exhaling heavily, I pull my undershirt out of the locker. "Your parents comin' tonight?"

He snorts. "Dude, you'd think I was graduating already. My mom's got her camera charged and ready. Dad nearly cried when I asked where my cleats were this morning."

I laugh along with him. "Seriously?"

"Seriously. Y'all might as well get the umbrellas ready for graduation 'cause that man's going to flood the stadium."

My chest tightens. I look at the practice glove in my locker, the one Dad gave me so long ago. He won't be here tonight. He won't be at graduation. I may have screwed up a lot in the past couple of years, but I've done the best I could. If anything, I hope I've done him proud.

The locker room door slams closed. Jay and I both glance over as Brett walks in, his eyes downcast. But when he looks up and his gaze falls on Jay, his lips curve into a half-smile. He lifts his chin to me and heads to his locker, which is a few down from mine.

"How's it goin'?" I ask.

He pauses with his hand on his locker. "Momma just told me that Dad's comin' tonight." He says it casually, but relief floods his face as he pulls out his clothes. I silently thank sweet baby Jesus for progress. Ever since the wedding, Brett's been wrapped up in his own head. I think part of him honestly believed his dad wouldn't talk to him again.

Jay moves to my side, his arms crossed. "You all right?" he asks carefully.

Brett nods and tugs his shirt over his head. "I think so."

The door opens again, and the other guys file in, one by one. The volume in the room grows from silence to a low rumble, with lockers slamming and bags rustling.

After changing, I grab my game glove from my locker. That stupid lump returns to my throat. I've pitched every varsity game with this glove. I'll probably need a new one next season, but this old thing—it's done me a lot of good.

"Fellas," Eric says.

I turn. The other guys are grouped in the center of the room, geared up and ready to go. Eric stands at the front, arms crossed.

"Y'all are gonna be strolling memory lane during your ceremony," he continues, "but we want to hear your real favorites. The memories you don't want your mommas to hear."

Jay chuckles and leans back against the lockers. "Oh, boy," he says on an exhale. "Too many damn memories to pick a favorite, Junior." He slaps my arm. "Probably watching Braxton get chased out of Matthews's pond last summer."

Nice to know someone got a kick out of that. I shove him. "After you dared me to do it, asshole."

He snorts. "Then what's yours?"

I toss my glove. Catch it. Jay's right; there are too many memories to pick a favorite. "I'll go with sophomore year. Bus ride home from the Beaufort game. Pulling up alongside that group of girls and mooning them while Coach was asleep. The bus lurched and Jay fell onto Coach, with his pants down."

Jay bursts out laughing along with the others, the sound echoing through the room. "That got us a night full of laps from Coach. After getting our asses whooped by Beaufort."

Our laughter dies down as we all turn to Brett, who's leaning against the lockers, watching us instead of laughing. His mouth twists into a smirk as he stares down at his glove. "I'm gonna be the lame-ass who says you guys." He straightens, eyes me, Jay, and then the rest of the guys. The room falls silent, so quiet you could hear a fly buzz. "My dad's barely looked at me since the wedding. He's comin' tonight, and that's all well and good, but y'all, you're here. You've been here the whole time." He swallows audibly. "And you don't hate me."

Hell.

Coach's office door closes, its soft latch nearly booming in the silence. He steps into the room, his head down, his hands on his hips. He clears his throat. When he does look up, his gaze settles on Brett.

"We're family," he says. "And family sticks together." He nods toward the door. "Now let's go get warmed up."

───────────

My heart hammers against my chest as I stare down batter number seven. In the seventh inning. While the score is 7-3, our favor. Triple sevens are good luck, right?

These are the games I've always lived for: adrenaline pumping, crowd cheering, sweat soaking my hair and streaming down my cheeks. But as my gaze flickers to Jay, who's signaling curveball, my throat constricts along with every muscle in my body. We're not done yet, not by a longshot, but we're almost there. He won't be my man next year. There'll be some other guy calling the shots behind the plate, one who can't read my mind. It's gut-clenching.

I look to the stands, where the crowd's on their feet. Marisa's right up front, with her parents on either side. She's got sunglasses on, paired with my hat, and I don't think I've ever felt more head over heels than I do right now, with that girl cheering me on. I'm not sure why it thrills me just as much every time—she's been my cheerleader from the get-go—but it'll never get old.

Inhaling deeply, I focus on the batter again. *Tunnel vision.* This guy's been fouling off pitches for ages. It's time to sit him down and wrap this game up.

Wind up. Release. Swing. Nothing but air.

Mission complete. And that's the season.

Jay jumps up and charges toward me, leaping into my arms with a yell. "Braxtoooooon!" he shouts above the deafening roar of our team. "You did it!" He drops to the ground and claps my hand in a shake.

"Nah," I tell him. "We did it."

Eric and Matt run out of the dugout, each carrying a side of the Gatorade container. And that quick, Coach's bright white uniform is as blue as the sky, soaked with Glacier Freeze Gatorade. He grins, and the rest of the guys pour in, yellin' and slappin' and it's craziness. It's insane. And I love every damn second.

A tiny hand claps on my shoulder. I spin around. Marisa grins up at me, all sun-kissed and bright smile. Grabbing her by the thighs, I lift her up and whirl around, making her squeal. And when she kisses me, it's freakin' magic.

"What's next?" she asks, resting her forehead against mine.

"Hmm." I pretend to think. "Playoffs. State. A whole lot of you."

"You seem awfully sure of yourself."

"What can I say? I'm a confident guy."

She laughs and kisses me again, long and sweet and utterly, insanely perfect.

These are the moments that matter. These are the moments I'll remember for the rest of my life. With this girl, every day's the start of something amazing. And there are a lot more days to come. This is only the beginning.

"We'll see you fine folks at playoffs!" the announcer, Skip, shouts over the stadium's speakers. "Now stick around and help us congratulate our Bulldog seniors on another outstanding season as we honor them with a special ceremony."

Marisa hops out of my arms, still grinning while backing toward the fence. "It was an outstanding season, Floral Prince."

The other guys bump and shove into me, but my jaw drops as I watch Marisa dart off to the bleachers. I don't care how much I love that girl; I'll always hate that name.

After handshakes with the other team, they spill off the field, leaving only Jay, Brett, and me standing at home plate. The crowd's still on their feet, though they've quieted to a low rumble. A beaming Hannah Wallace moves in beside us, holding the bouquets that Marisa was in charge of putting together yesterday.

Hannah winks. "You guys are always going to be my favorites."

I scoff and cross my arms. "Please. You'll be in Florida for two days before you forget about us."

Her jaw drops. I was joking, but she looks seriously offended. "We've all known each other since kindergarten. Brett was my first crush. Jay was the first guy I chased down on the playground and kissed. And you were the first player who ever made me believe in the magic of baseball." She shakes her head. "There are some things, and some people, that you never forget, Austin. You're one of 'em."

Way to make me feel even more feelings.

"First up," Skip says, "we've got Javier Torres, better known to y'all as Jay." Jay jogs out to the mound, where his parents wait with Coach (whose poor uniform is tinged with blue). His momma snatches him in a huge hug, one so tight I'm surprised he's still breathing. Once she releases him, he passes her the bouquet as his dad pats him on the back. Skip continues, "Jay's played for Lewis Creek for four seasons. When asked about his greatest memory, he said it was watching Braxton follow through on every dare, no matter how stupid it was."

I shake my head. He grins like a fool and points at me. Seriously, dude?

"He's an idiot," Brett mutters.

"Yeah," I agree. "But I'm gonna miss that idiot."

He nods. "Me too, man."

Skip adds, "Jay also notes that winning last year's state championship was at the top of his list. He hopes to repeat that victory this year. His future plans include attending the University of Arizona in the fall."

The crowd claps as Jay and his parents move to the foul line. Brett's up next, and his momma heads to the mound, with Pastor Perry trailing behind her. I slap Brett on his sling-free shoulder. It's not some huge production, but it's something. You can work with something.

"You all right?" I ask.

He smiles. "Yeah. Better late than never."

"Next, we have Brett Perry," Skip announces. Brett hesitates before striding out to the mound, his head held high. And as the crowd bursts into applause for him, my pride for that guy nearly explodes. He shakes Coach's hand, and his momma beams as he hands her the bouquet. He nods to his dad, who brings him in for a hug. When Brett pulls away, there's a grin on his face.

Again, it's something. And I think that something's exactly what Brett needed.

"Brett's the best third baseman I've seen here in a long time, a giant who's quick as a whip," Skip continues. "He's wrapping up his fourth season with Lewis Creek and is on his way to Campbell University in the fall. His best memory is watching his brother turn into—quote—'one hell of a player.'"

The crowd cheers again while I step up to home plate. Momma makes her way to the mound, waiting for them to announce my name. She smiles, and God as my witness, that woman's the best person I've ever known in my life. I wouldn't be out here without her.

Hannah passes me the final bouquet, her perfume mingling with the roses. "And last, but certainly not least," Skip begins, "we have Austin Braxton. Let's hear it for one of the best pitchers in the history of Lewis Creek High."

I don't know about all that, but I'll take it.

The crowd roars as I walk out to the mound, grinning. Coach waits beside Momma, his hands clasped in front of him. His mouth twitches when I reach them. He grabs my hand in a shake.

He swallows. Nods. And when he says, "I am so damn proud of you," I swear I see a tear in his eye. "Now go take your place, son."

My throat tightens. I wouldn't be out here without him, either. "You're always going to be my coach."

I turn to Momma, whose smile is brighter than the stadium lights. I hand her the flowers and hug her tight as Skip adds, "Austin's been a shining star at Lewis Creek, both during his year on JV and his reign on the varsity team. He's heading to University of South Carolina in the fall to play for the Gamecocks. His best memory is meeting the friends who became family and the coach who stood by him every step of the way." He clears his throat and says, "And I must say, it was a privilege to watch this player grow."

Momma squeezes me and pulls away, her eyes shining with tears. "The privilege," she says, "was all mine."

Damn it, no. I'm not about to cry. I'm NOT.

I look out to the bleachers, where every single fan is still on his or her feet. Where the kids are covered in crimson-and-black Bulldog face paint, and wearing baseball jerseys, and holding their own ball gloves. Where the girls are still cheering like we just won the World Series. Where Marisa's watching me like I'm the only person on this field. I always complained about the guys who were in this for the glory, but I've got to say, the glory's pretty amazing sometimes.

The team's lined up in front of the dugout, all of them decked out in dirt-stained uniforms, clapping and whistling and cheering right along with the crowd. I'm proud to call those guys my brothers. I'm proud to say I love that girl in the stands. And I'm so damn proud to call this place my home.

Life throws some crazy curveballs, but I've got a secret: My swing is golden.

acknowledgments

I promised myself I wouldn't cry while writing this section. I've already broken that promise. There are so many amazing people in my life, people that I've known for years and people that I've met since *Play On* began its journey toward becoming what it is today. These people have pushed me, they've cheered for me, and they've made my heart so very full.

First and foremost, I must thank my editor, Danielle Ellison. You saw this book not only for what it was, but for what it could be. Thank you for loving Austin and Marisa, for giving them a voice, and for constantly encouraging me to dig deeper. Thank you for your passion, for your guidance, and for your unwavering support.

Traci Inzitari, thank you for making me answer the tough questions. And thank you for reading this story over, and over, and over again. And then again, for good measure.

To everyone at Spencer Hill, thank you for letting me be part of your family. Dahlia Adler and Rebecca Weston, thank you for your fabulous copy editing skills. Meredith Maresco, thank you for all your hard work on the publicity side. Jenny Zemanek, thank you for my gorgeous cover. There's a 99.9% chance that I'm staring at a poster of it now. (Actually, let's just round up to 100%.)

To my agent, Lana Popovic: there are absolutely no words to convey how lucky I am to be on your team. You're the best hand-holder/cheerleader/support system that a girl could ask for. Thank you from the bottom of my crazy writer heart.

And huge thanks go out to the following:

To the early readers of *Play On*: Linnea Thor, KK Hendin, Cristina dos Santos, Steve Knapp, Veronica Bartles, and Nykki Mills. Thank you so much for all your time, your comments, and your enthusiasm.

To Megan Whitmer, Dahlia Adler, and Kelsey Macke. I'm convinced that all of you are made of sunshine. I wouldn't be writing these acknowledgements at this exact moment without your guidance. Thank you for encouraging me to trust my gut. Thank you for letting me camp out in your inboxes. And thank you for being you.

To Becca Kofonow. There just aren't words, sweet lady. You make my heart happy.

To Cheryl Ham, Marlana Antifit, Diane Bohannan, and Rina Heisel. You're the most amazing CPs. I have no idea what I'd do without you.

To my church family. Your love for God and for others is absolutely contagious. I'm so very thankful for your open arms and warm hearts.

To those on Twitter who keep me laughing and smiling and sane throughout the day. You're the absolute best.

To my parents. You've shown me what it means to keep going, even when life throws a curveball. Thank you for never letting me give up.

To Brandon. You've always, always had my back. Every day, I wake up grateful that I get to walk through this crazy, beautiful life with you.

To Tristan. You laugh freely and love wholeheartedly and dance without a care in the world. You are so brave, my sweet boy, and you inspire me daily.

To God. Thank you for putting these amazing people in my life. And thank you for keeping me here.

About the Author

Michelle Smith was born and raised in North Carolina, where she developed a healthy appreciation for college football, sweet tea, front porches, and a well-placed "y'all." She's a lover of all things happy, laughs way too much, and fully believes that a little bit of kindness goes a long way.

She now lives near the Carolina coast with her family. You can visit her online at msmithbooks.com.